V-Clan Series
Blood Sector
Night Sector
Eclipse Sector

X-Clan Series
X-Clan: The Origin
Andorra Sector
X-Clan: The Experiment
Winter's Arrow
Bariloche Sector

Exiled Sector World
Venom Island (Enrique's Story) by Lexi C. Foss
Outcast Island by Jennifer Thorn
Nightmare Island by Mila Young

NIGHT SECTOR

V-CLAN SERIES

USA TODAY BESTSELLING AUTHOR
LEXI C. FOSS

This is a work of fiction. Names, characters, places, and incidents are either the product of the author's imagination or are used fictitiously, and any resemblance to actual persons, living or dead, business establishments, events, or locales is entirely coincidental.

Night Sector

Copyright © 2023 Lexi C. Foss

All rights reserved.

No part of this book may be reproduced in any form or by any electronic or mechanical means, including information storage and retrieval systems, without written permission from the author, except for the use of brief quotations in a book review. This book may not be redistributed to others for commercial or noncommercial purposes.

Editing by: Outthink Editing, LLC

Proofreading by: Katie Schmahl & Jean Bachen

Cover Design: Manuela Serra

Cover Photography: CJC Photography

Cover Models: Marcel Pospiech & Jenna Pospiech

Published by: Ninja Newt Publishing, LLC

Print Edition

eBook ISBN: 978-1-68530-138-5

Paperback ISBN: 978-1-68530-253-5

Hardback ISBN: 978-1-68530-254-2

NIGHT SECTOR

V-Clan Series

NIGHT SECTOR

I never wanted a mate.
Especially not *her*—the notorious assassin known for killing Alphas.
But as fate would have it, she became mine.

Fortunately, we have an agreement. One where I rarely have to see her and she pretends I don't exist.

Everything's fine.
Until she's kidnapped by a sadistic Vampire Alpha hell-bent on turning her into his own personal Omega blood bag.

Now I'm the only one who can hear her screams.
And I'm really f-cking pissed off.

I might not want her as a mate. But she's mine.

Mine to protect.
Mine to avenge.
Mine to *hunt*.

Don't worry, little killer.
I'm coming for you.
And when I find you,
I'll hand you the silver blade,
And watch you slay.

A NOTE FROM LEXI

Night Sector is a standalone in the V-Clan universe. No other books need to be read prior to this one to follow the storyline.

This is a shifter romance with strong Omegaverse themes. There are Alpha/Omega dynamics, nesting, purring, estrous cycles, and, of course, *knotting*. If you're unfamiliar with these terms, don't worry—they're explained throughout the book. ;)

Those of you familiar with my X-Clan series will notice these similarities.

However, you'll also likely notice that Lorcan is a bit different from the Alphas of the X-Clan world. He's an Alpha male who understands the importance of respect and consent.

Alas, the nemesis of this story isn't as kind. He's an Alpha who believes in taking what he wants because he can. **As such, there are darker undertones and themes of non-consent that may make the reader uncomfortable.**

That said, Kyra is a survivor. And Lorcan is all about supporting his Omega with her recovery and with her plans for revenge.

This is a tale filled with passion, healing, and vengeance. Lorcan and Kyra may start as a mating of convenience, but they're going to grow into so much more…

Enjoy! <3

INTRODUCTION

Nearly a century ago, a zombielike virus spread across the globe, destroying over ninety percent of the human race. Many of the supernatural species of the world were immune to the plague. Others were not.

Those who have survived—both human and supernatural alike—now rule their own territories, otherwise known as sectors.

You're about to enter the V-Clan world, a breed of shifter wolves with vampiric traits. These beings prefer the night. They thrive on magic. And perhaps most importantly of all, the Alphas of this kind cherish their Omega mates.

KYRA

Fucking Alphas and their damn knots.

The grumbling thought tumbled through my mind as I tucked a knife into my boot. I *really* wanted to kill whatever supernatural entity had decided it would be a good idea to make Omegas reliant on their Alphas during our heat cycles.

Alas, I couldn't exactly annihilate the unknown creator above, so I'd have to settle for some V-Clan Alphas instead.

Specifically, the Alpha Prince of Blood Sector. Also known as my best friend's intended mate. And the male she'd been screaming for all morning.

"Whatever you're thinking of doing, don't." Fritz's deep voice floated through the air from the entrance to my room.

I arched a brow as I glanced over my shoulder at the male Omega. He cocked an eyebrow right back at me as he leaned against the door frame and crossed his thick arms over his sculpted chest. His dark sweater stretched deliciously in response, revealing even more of his athletic form.

If I were an Alpha female, I might have been tempted to hop right on that. But the only thing *Alpha* about me was my spirit.

Physically, I was all Omega.

Five foot one.

Petite.

Outwardly fragile in appearance.

However, looks could be deceiving. And I very much enjoyed when others underestimated me based on their misinterpretation of my small stature.

Fritz, however, never underestimated me. He knew better.

As he proved now by saying, "Kyra." My name on his tongue echoed with warning. "You're about to shadow into Blood Sector. You can't do that while covered in weapons."

"Pretty sure I can, Fritz," I countered as I refocused on my closet of violent toys. "After all, I have many times before."

"Yeah, while stealing blood from their supply," he pointed out. "That made sense for defensive purposes in case you were caught. This time, you're intending to be caught by an Alpha Prince. And he's not going to be all that willing to talk if you show up covered in knives."

"Or…" I pinched my lips to the side, my eyes narrowing at one of my favorite blades. "Hmm."

"You can't kill him."

"I mean, I could," I mused conversationally. "It would be kind of fun."

Of course, Quinn wouldn't be all that thrilled about it. And I really didn't want to piss off my best friend. Even if I did think she was crazy for selecting *Kieran O'Callaghan* as a mate.

"You can't," Fritz corrected, his tone matching my own. Then it took on a serious quality as he added, "Quinn tried to bring him here. You felt it as well as I did. That means she's officially chosen him."

"Unless he found a way to coax her into it somehow." That had been my primary concern since Quinn's unexpected arrival the other day—had she tried to shadow him to the Sanctuary willingly? Or had he somehow manipulated her into doing it?

"I'm sure there's been a lot of coaxing," Fritz drawled from behind me. "Alphas are good at that. But the only way Prince Kieran could have even known about this place is if Quinn finally told him the truth."

Yes, I'd come to the same conclusion. Plus, Quinn had told me that she wanted him here. Except she didn't know how to get him through the magical shield surrounding this island, and now she was too debilitated by her impending heat to shadow back to him.

There was also something strange going on with the barrier spell that hid this place from the rest of the world. I couldn't be sure, but it seemed to be weakening Quinn, too. Which was strange, given it was her bloodline that fueled and maintained the protective enchantment.

Regardless, it seemed I had no choice but to shadow over to Blood Sector and have a word with the Alpha Prince.

It just felt severely wrong to do so while only armed with a small blade tucked into my boot.

Pinching my lips to the side again, I evaluated my sweater and jeans, wondering if I could get away with hiding some sharp objects in my pockets.

Maybe a few throwing stars or—

"Perhaps you should try calling first," Fritz suggested, interrupting my thought. "Request a meeting to discuss Quinn and present him with the vial."

I glanced at the *vial* in question, my nose twitching as my vampiric half scented the familiar blood inside. *Quinn's blood.* She'd given it to me in hopes that it would provide Kieran with the protection he needed to step through the magical barrier.

The spell only allowed Omegas to enter the island. It didn't matter the type—X-Clan wolves, V-Clan wolves, vampires, Shadow wolves, W-Clan wolves, Z-Clan wolves, and several other rare species—any and all Omegas could pass through the enchantment.

But no Alphas or Betas.

Unless...

Unless the Alpha is a mate to an Omega inhabitant.

Quinn had already bitten Kieran, thus marking him as her intended. All he had to do was bite her back, but he hadn't done so yet. Which meant the mating was only partially complete.

However, imbibing blood was the key component to the mating ritual. So, hopefully, giving Kieran a vial of Quinn's essence would be enough to trick the protective enchantment into letting him pass.

If not, I wasn't sure what we would do.

Because the whole plan hinged on me bringing Quinn's gift to the Alpha Prince and convincing him to do what was needed to help her.

Most Omegas could survive a heat without their Alpha. But something about Quinn's estrus felt... different. *Life-threateningly* different.

I chewed my lower lip. Whatever was happening to my best friend wasn't normal. That much I'd deduced from her pale and shaking state this morning.

Hence the reason I'd volunteered to venture into Blood Sector to face one of the most lethal V-Clan Alphas in existence.

It certainly did not help matters that he was always flanked by two other renowned Alpha Princes—Lorcan and Cillian. Also known as Kieran's infamous *Elites*.

"All right." I faced Fritz fully. He'd said something about calling to request an appointment. But I wasn't going to do that. We were short on time. I also didn't see a point. If Kieran truly loved Quinn the way he should, he wouldn't care about my unexpected arrival. "I'll go in with just the blade."

I already knew my way around Blood Sector, thanks to my stealth visits. There were weapons vaults all over Kieran's headquarters. I could easily shadow into one of those rooms if I needed to.

Or I could just shadow right back here.

It wasn't like the Alphas could follow me. Not just because of the magic protecting the island, but because the coordinates of the Sanctuary were unknown to everyone outside of the barrier.

I pulled my blue-black hair up into a ponytail and considered my leather jacket on the wall.

So many places to hide knives in there, I thought with a mental sigh. *Alas, Fritz is right.* I needed to approach Kieran with at least a hint of diplomacy.

Maybe all of this would be for naught.

But for Quinn, I had to at least try.

I pocketed the vial and nodded once at Fritz. "The Sanctuary is in your capable hands and all that jazz. I'll be back soon." I engaged my shadowing ability before he could reply, the drill one we both knew well.

Strictly speaking, Quinn was our queen and therefore in charge. But she hadn't been around for over a century, leaving me as the Sanctuary's primary leader. I couldn't say when that designation had fallen to me; it just sort of naturally had. So I'd chosen Fritz as my second-in-command, making him the overseer whenever I left.

And while Quinn was technically within our borders right now, she was lost to her heat.

Thus, Fritz had to maintain control.

The familiar Icelandic landscape appeared around me as I illegally entered Blood Sector. I always shadowed into the same woodsy area near a waterfall renowned for its black rock formations.

My fingertips touched the icy earth below while I engaged my enhanced hearing.

As a hybrid, I'd inherited the best traits from both my parents. Shadowing, magic, and my wolf from my V-Clan mother. Inhuman speed, sharp eyesight, stealth abilities, and hunting instincts from my vampire father.

The only downside to my unique genetic makeup—I craved blood. A lot of it.

Hence the reason I often illegally ventured into Blood Sector to tap into their product supply.

V-Clan wolves only needed blood every few weeks, the essence the fuel for our magical elements. Or that was my understanding, anyway.

However, as a Vampire Omega, I needed blood much more often. Primarily because I didn't have an Alpha to sustain my needs.

Well, technically, that was a lie. I used to have an Alpha. But I'd killed him.

And now he haunts my nightmares. The thought sent an unwelcome shiver down my spine. *Definitely not the time or place to think about* him.

Swallowing, I slowly stood and listened for any signs of an approaching wolf or a mortal.

Both were equally as likely in this sector, as Iceland had saved most of its humans from becoming Infected.

It was one of Kieran O'Callaghan's redeeming qualities— his ability to protect *everyone* in his territory, not just his wolves.

What did he ask for in return for his protection? A blood tax.

Fucking brilliant, I thought begrudgingly.

Not that I'd ever admit it to his face. I'd sooner carve that handsome face up with a blade than praise him.

Sighing, I began my routine trek across the island, shadowing into various hiding spots I'd established over the years and listening for any signs of being detected or followed.

As usual, I went unnoticed.

Unfortunately, that wouldn't last for long.

My lips twisted as I teleported to a familiar street corner in Reykjavík, only two blocks from Kieran's estate.

Technically, that residence belonged to Quinn. Hell, the entire sector was hers as the only MacNamara left in existence. She was royalty. A true princess. *The future Queen.*

But Kieran had maintained Alpha Prince status in her absence after she had tricked him into a betrothal and run.

I supposed his sticking around to lead should also count in his favor.

Except what Alpha wouldn't jump at the chance to take over Blood Sector, the unequivocal capital for all of V-Clan kind?

There was so much power and affluence here; he would have been an idiot to turn down the opportunity.

Right. No more stalling, I told myself as I started down the sidewalk. *I'm going to walk in there and demand a meeting.*

I paused.

Actually, no. I'm just going to shadow inside and surprise him.

The fewer people who knew I was here, the better.

A quick in and out. Just like the blood runs.

Except this would be a bit more complicated than stealing a few liters of human blood.

Stop stalling, Kyra, I told myself. *Just do it.*

I visualized Kieran's suite—a room I'd only been in once before while snooping around his palace—and appeared in his living area.

A quick glance around told me he hadn't decorated much since my last visit. Still all masculine tones and woodsy accents.

But no male Alpha.

"Of course you're not here," I muttered, checking his bedroom and the bath area. "Why would you be easily found? It's not like your intended mate needs you or anything."

Unless he'd chased her off.

I still wasn't entirely convinced Quinn had chosen him, even with all the obvious evidence.

Because what Omega in her right mind would take an Alpha? All they ever wanted was a vessel to knot.

"And breed," I grumbled aloud.

Although, Alpha Fare had never wanted that from me. He'd just desired a toy he could share with all his friends.

I swallowed, my mind instinctively shoving memories of *him* into a mentally fortified box—one that seemed to constantly open at the most inopportune times.

Like right now while pacing an Alpha Prince's quarters.

Over a century had passed since I'd killed Alpha Fare, and yet he still managed to torture me. "Asshole," I hissed.

"Hello to you, too," a deep voice drawled in response, causing me to spin toward the entryway of Kieran's suite.

A muscular male leaned against the door frame, his head only a few inches shy of the top. Definitely an Alpha. Stealthy, too. With a hint of a lethal aura.

But this isn't Kieran.

No. I'm Cillian, the male replied, his masculine tone easily entering my mind as he arched one perfectly sculpted brow. *And you are?*

I narrowed my gaze. "Get out of my head." The words left me on a low growl, my fingers flexing with an intrinsic reach for my blade.

I'd never met a V-Clan wolf with telepathic abilities, but I knew several vampires who could enter the minds of others. *Alphas like Fare.*

"That's a rather long name," Cillian murmured as he pushed away from the door to step inside. "Care to provide a nickname?"

My jaw ticked. I'd spent the last century working hard to avoid Kieran and his two *Elites*. All three Alpha Princes were notoriously lethal. They were also known for their lack of mercy, something Cillian's impatient expression only seemed to accentuate now.

"I'll provide my name to Prince Kieran," I informed him flatly. "Where is he?"

Cillian paused midstep, his dark irises running over me and lingering on my boot long enough to suggest he knew I had a weapon hiding there. Then he met my gaze once more. "Prince Kieran is currently indisposed. But I'll happily show you to a holding cell where you can wait for his return, if you'd like."

My lips curled. "I think I'll wait here."

"I don't believe I offered that as an option."

"I don't believe I requested options," I countered. "Just an audience with your pack leader."

His lips twitched. "I'm not sure the future Blood Sector King would appreciate being referred to as the *pack leader*."

"Then what do you call him? Sire? Sir? Master?"

"Cousin," a new voice inserted from right behind me.

I spun around in response, only to find my hip caught in a firm grip as an Alpha with impossibly black eyes stared down at me from a severely high height. His dark hair fell over his tanned forehead, the unkempt length tickling his ears as he canted his head ever so slightly to the side.

"Hmm," he hummed, his gaze assessing.

I waited for him to say something else, but he didn't. Instead, he merely observed me in silence, his aura leaving me uncomfortable in a way I couldn't define.

It wasn't oppressive or suffocating, and yet, I felt trapped. Ensnared. Incapable of movement.

I attempted to take a step backward but found my feet glued to the ground, almost as though I'd been encased in cement.

Alpha power, I realized, my eyes slitting into a glare. "What are you doing to me?"

"Why are you here?" the male demanded, ignoring my question.

"To see Prince Kieran."

His grip tightened, just enough to allude to his perceived dominance of this situation. "Regarding?"

"None of your business."

"On the contrary, it's very much *our* business," he replied, his voice holding a raspy quality to it, almost as though he didn't often speak. "If you want access to Kieran, you need to go through us. Now tell us who you are and why you're really here."

LORCAN

Omega.
Hybrid.
Dangerous.

My mind lingered on that final descriptor as I slowly coiled my power around the female before me.

Cillian's intruder warning had sent me straight here, my instinct to protect Kieran and Blood Sector an immediate reaction. However, I hadn't anticipated our intruder being a petite vampire-wolf with blue-black hair and green catlike eyes.

Gorgeous didn't even begin to encompass her stunning appearance. And she smelled divine, too. Like blood oranges sprinkled with cinnamon.

An alluring little trap with an ancient aura.

Which was how I'd deduced in a split second that this woman was a threat. She might be small—most Omegas were—but this one possessed a unique genetic makeup that had my wolf growling inside.

Danger. Danger. Danger.

And she'd somehow shadowed right into my cousin's suite.

Her jaw clenched, giving me another descriptor for my list—*stubborn*.

Fine. If she wanted to play it this way, we could. "Don't think for a second that your Omega status will protect you. We don't take kindly to intruders here."

I'm not sure what fascinates me more—your ability to lie or the fact you've strung together more sentences in the last few minutes than you have over the last six months.

Cillian's sardonic tones were an unwelcome invasion in my mind, but I'd long grown accustomed to his telepathic tendencies.

I'm taking her to my den, I told him, my shadowing power already wrapping around me and the Omega.

Her pupils dilated half a second before the room dissolved around us. Then her nostrils flared as my personal quarters came into view.

"Release me," she demanded as she tried to move out of my invisible grip.

"No." I moved even closer to her, causing her chin to bump into my chest before I wove my telekinetic gift through her hair to gently tug her head back.

Her plump lips parted in surprise, her expression confirming that she was beginning to understand the full extent of my power. I didn't often use it in this way, but something told me this little Omega was a flight risk. And I wasn't going to let her disappear until she answered a few questions.

"Give me your name," I growled down at her as Cillian appeared behind her.

I suddenly find myself uncertain of what to do. Usually, you play the silent, deadly role while I lead the interrogation.

I ignored his unhelpful commentary and focused on holding the Omega's glare instead.

"I'm not here to cause any trouble. I just want to talk to Kieran."

My eyebrow inched upward. "Illegally entering Blood Sector and sneaking into Kieran's quarters are both actions that suggest otherwise. Perhaps you should try arranging a meeting through normal channels next time."

Her green eyes flicked upward in a motion of irritation.

"Fucking Fritz."

I arched my brow higher, her statement not making sense.

When she refused to say more, I started a mental sweep of her body for weapons and other items. My telekinetic abilities were exceptionally useful in situations like this.

She has a knife in her boot, I told Cillian.

I'm aware.

Of course he was. We both could smell the metal on her. Just as we both could smell the *blood* in her pocket. *Quinnlynnn's blood?* I asked, recognizing the scent.

So it would seem. Cillian circled the female to step up to my side. *Perhaps that's how she managed to shadow into our lands without detection?*

I responded with a mental grunt, my outward appearance otherwise bored as I kept my focus on the dangerous Omega.

"Why do you have Princess Quinnlynn's blood?" Cillian asked her.

She glanced at Cillian, her expression giving nothing away. "I'll only explain myself to Kieran."

"Then I suggest you give us a name for us to relay to him," Cillian murmured, his tone deceptively charming.

I said nothing, simply observed as the female seemed to consider his words. A muscle ticked in her jaw, the only tell she was losing her patience with this situation. I tightened my telekinetic hold around her, aware that she might try to disappear at any moment.

But that would be impossible with my power securing her before me.

"Kyra." The name came out on a low growl, her annoyance palpable. "Tell him Kyra is here to see him about

Quinn. The blood is for him. And inform him that my offer to talk has a time limit."

Kyra, I repeated to Cillian, very familiar with the name.

The Alpha killer, he surmised, his mental voice flat. *Half vampire, half V-Clan wolf. Gives no fucks about illegally crossing our boundaries. Doesn't appear to be afraid of us. All seems to add up to her reputation.*

Hmm, I hummed in response. I'd already decided this female was dangerous. Now I considered her a true threat. She could easily be here to kill Kieran. I'd suggest we bind her with chains, but I doubted they would hold her.

Although, now I wasn't entirely sure my telekinesis would secure her long-term either.

This Omega had taken down a millennia-old Vampire Alpha. Her *mate*. As well as a few other unidentified Alphas. She was the black widow of her kind, the one Alphas feared because she could so easily be underestimated.

A pretty little deadly package.

I'll reach out to Kieran, Cillian said. *See how he wants to proceed.*

I nearly grunted. Given Kieran's current mood, he'd probably want to proceed by killing the Omega. He'd just been betrayed in the worst way by his intended mate, making him borderline unpredictable.

If Kyra wanted to survive his wrath, she'd need to appear as defenseless as possible. Her size certainly helped that along, but her eyes revealed the power within.

Ancient. Angry. Antagonistic.

I released her hip. "Follow me." I pulled back just enough of my magic to allow her to walk as I started down the hall toward my office.

"I'd listen to him," Cillian advised conversationally. "He's Kieran's cousin. If anyone is going to be able to convince Blood Sector's future King to talk to you, it's him."

A snort built inside me, Cillian's words positively ludicrous. *He listens to you more than me.*

Only because I actually talk to him.

This time I did snort. Because he wasn't wrong.

"If your *future King* takes too long to agree, then I'll make sure he never sees Quinn again," Kyra retorted, causing me to pause midstep.

"Are you threatening Quinnlynn MacNamara?" Cillian asked, his tone holding a lethal edge to it that rivaled the heated response thrumming through my veins.

Kyra scoffed. "As if I'd ever harm my best friend. But I will protect her against an unfit Alpha, which is exactly how I'll interpret Kieran's disinterest if he continues to let his Elites speak for him."

"So you know where she is?" Cillian pressed.

"Obviously," she deadpanned.

Cillian cocked a brow. "And you're willing to tell Kieran?"

She folded her slender arms, her stance defiant. "That depends on his punctual response to my *meeting request*." Those last two words were underlined with irritation—an irritation I didn't quite understand. "But if he makes me wait much longer, then I'll leave and make damn sure he never finds her again."

Well, that wasn't true. With my power leashed around her being, she wouldn't be going anywhere easily. But I didn't bother correcting her assumption.

Instead, I studied her profile, curious about her supposed friendship with Quinnlynn. She certainly sounded protective of her. However, that didn't guarantee that any of her claims were true.

Ask Kieran if he knows about Kyra, I told Cillian. *And tell him about the blood.*

"You can wait for Kieran in my office," I added aloud, my words for Kyra.

I didn't wait for her to comply, nor did I anticipate a response from Cillian.

Rather, I entered my study and moved toward my empty

desk. There were weapons hidden all over my office, making this an ideal place to hold Kyra. Mainly because I would be able to defend myself.

Of course, that would change if she found any of my concealed toys. But that was a risk I was willing to take.

A few seconds passed, my inner wolf expectant. This female seemed to interest him and not just because she was an Omega.

His intrigue heightened as her citrusy scent invaded my den, her catlike gaze taking in every inch of my personal space as she entered my office.

I pulled out my desk chair—the only available seat in the room—as a silent offer for temporary peace.

Kyra considered it for a moment, then shrugged and settled into the chair as though it were her own personal throne.

The hairs along the back of my neck danced as her hand went to her pocket, my power reigniting in preparation of taking hold of her wrist. But all she did was pull out a vial of blood—*Quinn's blood*—and set it on my desk like some sort of offering.

I glanced at it before meeting her gaze once more.

She said nothing.

I also remained silent.

After several minutes, she canted her head, a question lingering in her gaze.

I didn't bother asking what she wanted to know. I likely wouldn't answer her. I also doubted it would be anything I wanted to know.

Her irises flickered with concealed magic, her aura seeming to pulse with ancient energy.

Alluring, I mused, taking her measure once more.

If those deadly vibes were present in any other Omega, I might be tempted to play. I always did fancy a bit of a fight.

But this particular Omega might be a little too much for me to handle.

I could practically hear her plotting my death, which would explain that slight twitch of her lips.

This female enjoyed inflicting pain.

While that might be intriguing on some levels, I hadn't stayed alive this long just to be seduced by the prospect of a sensual death.

He's coming, Cillian informed me as he joined us in the office.

Kieran's scent tickled my nose in the next instant, the source of it coming from my bedroom. Given that we were the same size and stature, I assumed that meant my cousin had shadowed in there to borrow a pair of pants. He'd probably been out for a run with his wolf, likely to help expel some of his aggression.

I started toward my office door, suddenly feeling the need to assess my cousin's emotional state. It wouldn't do any of us any good if he aggressively approached the Omega in my study. She was an unknown threat. An ancient Omega with untold powers.

An Alpha killer.

And I really didn't want to set her off in my den. Not when I wasn't sure how well I could keep her contained.

Kieran met me at the entryway to my study, his dark eyes meeting and holding mine.

Most wolves would cower in response, the urge to submit inherent in his presence. But my age and power rivaled his, just like Cillian's did, making it nearly impossible to look away.

Cillian and I followed Kieran because we wanted to, not because we had to.

My cousin gave me a searching look while I quickly evaluated his mood. He didn't ask any questions or demand that I move; he simply stared at me with a hint of curiosity in his expression.

Good enough for me, I decided, moving out of his way and revealing the Omega sitting at my desk.

He sauntered into the room with a fluidlike grace that suggested his wolf was still very much near the surface. His attention went to the vial first, his nostrils flaring before he scanned Kyra from head to toe.

"Where is she?" he demanded, not bothering with any pleasantries.

Fortunately, Kyra seemed to share his impatience. "At the Sanctuary," she replied without hesitation.

I moved closer to Kieran, my focus entirely on the lethal Omega seated before us. Her mention of *the Sanctuary* suggested she was telling the truth about her friendship with Quinnlynn, as Quinnlynn had also previously mentioned the term to Kieran.

And he'd shared the details with me and Cillian.

That was the location Quinnlynn had promised to take Kieran to earlier this week. Alas, she'd betrayed him and escaped instead.

"Tell me where that is. Right now." Kieran's tone brooked no argument, his Alpha status clear.

"I can't. You need to drink that first." She pointed a sharpened nail at the vial on the desk. "But I'll warn you—I'm not sure it'll work."

Kieran frowned. "Work for what?"

"Work for breaking through the barrier spell on the island. It requires you to be fully mated, but I'm hoping we can trick it by having her blood in your system." She pushed away from the desk and stood. "So drink up. Then I'll take you to her."

Oh, fuck that. I stepped forward, my hand going to Kieran's shoulder. Because no. That was absolutely not going to happen.

"Why would I go anywhere with you?" he demanded. "I know all about your penchant for killing Alphas, Kyra. And I'm not about to become your next victim."

I assume that means he confirmed that Quinnlynn knows her? I guessed, my words for Cillian.

He wasn't surprised by her presence, so I interpreted it as a known familiarity.

Hmm.

Kyra's lips curled into a feline-like grin that matched her eyes. "I only kill Alphas who deserve it, Kieran. Have you done something to earn my wrath?"

"I don't know," Kieran replied. "Have I?"

"You're starting to." She prowled toward him, her movements sleek and alluring, underlining her reputation as a seductive little killer. "Your intended mate is injured and going into heat. If you continue to choose not to help her, then yeah, you're going to earn my wrath."

Kieran merely stared her down, but I knew he wouldn't underestimate her. The three of us had survived too long in this world to allow our egos to overshadow clear and obvious logic.

"She's my best friend, Kieran," Kyra continued. "And I left her screaming in her nest. So if you're not going to work with me, say it now. Because someone needs to comfort her, and even though it's you she wants, I can't just leave her to suffer alone."

Kieran's dark eyes narrowed. "She rejected me rather spectacularly. So forgive me for not believing anything you just said about her *wanting* me."

"Did he lose his hearing when the barrier shoved his soul back here?" she asked casually, her gaze going to me and then to Cillian. "Because I swear I've already explained this."

"How about you try again?" Cillian suggested, his tone lacking emotion.

She rolled her eyes and looked at Kieran again. "The *barrier* rejected you. Not Quinnlynn. And that spell damn near killed her as well."

"The spell she used to shadow without me?"

Her irises slit into a glower. "No, jackass. The barrier spell that protects the island."

I growled at her tone and the insulting nickname she'd chosen for my cousin. He was the future Blood Sector King. That required some respect.

But Kyra ignored me entirely and went on to say, "It knocked her out on her way in and caused her to crash into an ice block, which sent her rolling into the nearby water. Then she woke up and went into heat not too long after. And now I'm here because she needs you."

"What is this barrier spell protecting?"

"The Sanctuary."

No shit, I thought.

"What is the Sanctuary?" Kieran asked, impatience underlining his tone and thickening his Irish accent. "Tell me what it is, and I'll consider going with you."

"Kieran." His name left me on a growl, his potential acquiescence not acceptable.

He held up his hand in a gesture to pause, making me bristle inside. *He can't possibly be considering this,* I thought at Cillian. *He knows what Kyra is capable of.*

He's blinded by his need to find his mate.

Then we need to wake him up.

Indeed, Cillian agreed.

"Quinnlynn said she had to show me for me to understand," Kieran continued, his tone slightly less severe than before yet equally as stern. "I don't trust her or you to do that, given everything that's happened. So tell me what it is instead."

"She never told you?" A hint of unease had crept into Kyra's features and tone, her eyes roaming over Kieran with wary regard.

"Obviously not."

"But she... she said she wants to mate you," Kyra said

slowly, her expression morphing into confusion. "I... I'm here to help her. I thought. Unless... maybe it's the heat?"

Kyra took an unsteady step backward, her shadowing ability flickering to life against my telekinetic bindings. I instinctively shadowed to her back, my hand going to her hip to enforce my magical hold over her being.

She shivered in response, her heart skipping a beat.

Her power ignited once more, causing my own to flare in response.

Not so fast, little killer, I thought at her, aware that she couldn't actually hear me. But I conveyed the words by subtly tightening my grasp. *You snuck into our sector and demanded a meeting with our future King. Now you're going to stay right here until he says you can leave.*

Kieran's dark irises met mine, his gaze knowing. *You've tethered her,* he seemed to be saying.

I have, I confirmed as Kyra tried to flee for a third time.

Her pulse escalated when her ability failed her, the Omega showing the first signs of uncertainty in her situation.

So you can be subdued, I mused. *Now can you cooperate? Or will I be forced to introduce you to some of my deadlier traits?*

Kieran could be patient. But he would do whatever it took to find his intended mate. Just as I would do whatever he asked of me to aid in his quest.

Including interrogating the little killer in front of me.

Start talking, I tried to tell her with my touch. *Or I'll be forced to make you talk.*

KYRA

K<small>IERAN DOESN'T KNOW</small> what the Sanctuary is…
Did I…?
I should've brought more knives…
What if…?

The thoughts circled in my head, making me dizzy. The words seemed to jumble together.

Pull yourself together, Kyra, I told myself. *You can't afford to let your guard down now.*

Especially with *Lorcan* controlling my ability to shadow. He might not have given me his name, but I'd deduced it through our interaction. There was one only one other Alpha in Iceland who could possess this much power, and as I'd already met Cillian, it left Lorcan as the obvious culprit.

I nearly growled in frustration, my wolf pacing inside with growing agitation. In all my preparations, I hadn't anticipated an Alpha's ability to ground me. This was certainly new and not at all appreciated.

"Tell us about the Sanctuary," Kieran demanded.

I swallowed. "I… I thought you knew… She… she was trying to take you there. Why would she…?"

Did I read all of this wrong? Was Quinn trying to escape him again?

"It's been so many years since I last saw her," I added aloud, my voice a whisper. "Maybe I misunderstood?"

Which meant I'd put myself in significant danger by coming here and making my presence known.

Because now I was surrounded by three lethal Alphas. One of whom had somehow thwarted my ability to shadow at will.

This isn't going to—

"She told me it was a place I needed to see." Kieran's Irish lilt interrupted my thoughts, his tone flat. "Then she said only she could shadow us there, which was when I decided to trust her and she betrayed me with her rejection spell."

"Why would she try to take him there if she wasn't planning to tell him the truth?" Cillian interjected as he moved to stand beside Kieran.

"Or it was all a ruse," the Alpha behind me muttered, his grip tightening once more on my hip. He seemed to be trying to tell me something with his touch, but I had no idea what it could be.

A warning, perhaps? A way to remind me that he's grounded my power?

Or is it a subtle request for me to comment? To defend my friend?

"It wasn't a ruse," I replied, my words for Lorcan more than the others. "I felt her try to bring Kieran with her. Then Fritz found her floating along the icy shore. He helped me bring her inside."

"Fritz?" Kieran repeated. "Who the fuck is Fritz?"

Shit. I shouldn't have said that.

But I couldn't seem to stop myself from replying. It was as though Lorcan's touch commanded my truths, even the ones I wanted to hide deep within.

"A Protector." The admission left me on a whisper. "The Sanctuary..." I trailed off, my attention returning to Kieran. "It's a Sanctuary for Omegas. The MacNamara magic protects the island. And that magic serves as a barrier. Only Omegas can pass through. Or their mates."

His eyebrows lifted. "An island of V-Clan Omegas?"

I shook my head. "Omegas of all kinds." And I'd just betrayed them all in the worst way.

Unless Quinn truly wanted Kieran to know. Why else would she have tried to bring him through the barrier?

He hadn't shown any signs of trying to coerce her into doing it. Actually, his story made it sound like she'd wanted to show him the truth as a gimmick to achieve her own freedom.

But Quinn would never have even mentioned the Sanctuary to him in that situation. She would have found another way to escape him.

So she meant for him to know.

It was the only explanation for why she'd tried to take him through the barrier. And I was here now to help her. To bring her mate to her. To ensure my best friend survived.

Yet here he is, allowing his Elite to manhandle me.

A jolt of annoyance helped ground me in the moment, reminding me of my strength. My purpose. My *existence*.

I wasn't an Omega who allowed Alphas to push her around. I slaughtered them for even trying.

Something about this trio had made me forget my place. Perhaps it was their combined power—they were three of the strongest V-Clan Alphas in existence.

And they didn't appear to be underestimating me in the way most Alphas would, I realized, my brow threatening to furrow. *They're treating me like they would an equal by binding my powers and forcing me to talk.*

Not violently, just… assertively.

"That's why an Alpha murdered her parents," Kieran murmured, his words drawing me from my thoughts. "But how did murdering them provide answers? Because it weakened the barrier magic?"

My brow furrowed. "No. The magic held because of Quinnlynn."

"Then what did their murders accomplish?"

"He didn't exactly murder them," I said slowly, thinking through my response before elaborating.

However, Quinn had obviously told Kieran our suspicions about an Alpha Prince killing her parents because everyone else believed the jet had just malfunctioned and exploded. Only a select few knew the truth.

And that select few now included Kieran and his Elites.

So it wouldn't hurt to provide a deeper explanation.

"He put a tracking enchantment on their jet, and the only way to thwart it was to land elsewhere," I told them. "Except there was no safe place to land... not where they were. Not without revealing too much. So they... chose to die at sea."

"That's what Quinnlynn meant," Kieran replied. "She said the culprit bespelled the plane and they had to crash it. But she didn't elaborate on why." He paused for a moment before adding, "That's why she stayed in Bariloche Sector. Why she needed my healing powers. Why she ran."

"She couldn't trust anyone," I admitted aloud. "Especially not an Alpha Prince."

He nodded, his expression one of understanding, and underlined with a hint of remorse.

Good. You should feel bad for doubting her, I thought before saying aloud, "But she tried to take you to the Sanctuary. And now she needs you more than ever. Not only has she gone into heat, but her healing is also slower than it should be, probably because all of her excess energy is used to power the shield."

He continued to study me, his remorse seeming to deepen.

Which meant I needed to take the plunge and tell him everything. Make him understand. Make him *agree*.

Because Quinn didn't have much time left before she fell into the full throes of her heat, and I wasn't sure what would happen to her and to the Sanctuary when she did.

"I don't know if drinking her blood will get you through the barrier, but we need to try," I informed him, my tone holding a note of urgency. "The Sanctuary needs her. Fuck, the Sanctuary needs her Alpha, too. I've never seen her so weak. It's like she's using all her life energy to keep the magic thriving."

Kieran studied me for a long moment, his expression giving nothing away.

Now was the moment where he'd either live up to my expectations or he'd prove my prejudices wrong.

What's it going to be, Alpha? Do you really care about my friend? Or are you just like all the others?

"We're not letting Kieran go anywhere alone with you," Cillian said, causing me to blink. I'd almost forgotten about his presence despite him standing beside the other male.

Lorcan took that moment to remind me of his existence as well with a subtle twitch of his fingers against my hip.

How had I forgotten he was there? And why haven't I tried to fight him yet?

I *hated* being touched by Alphas. Mostly because my inner wolf seemed to crave it. Even now, she was curled into a content ball and purring in response to his nearness, which was precisely the wrong reaction to have to such a deadly male.

Fortunately, my inner vampire was made of logic.

Because if these two Elites weren't going to let Kieran go to the Sanctuary with me... "Then you can't help me."

Which meant I'd wasted precious minutes here and it was time to go.

I tried to sidestep my way out of Lorcan's grip, but he just tightened his hold once more and pressed his mouth to my ear. "He's not saying Kieran can't go," he told me in a low voice underlined with a warning that matched his touch. "He's saying we won't let him go *alone* with you."

Kieran gaped at his cousin, an expression I would have shared if Lorcan had allowed me to turn and face him.

"One of us is coming with you," he added against my ear.

Cillian nodded in agreement. "Yes. One of us will join you for Kieran's protection."

These two can't be serious. "Have none of you been listening to me?" I demanded. "The barrier only allows Omegas and their mates."

"And you're unmated," Cillian replied, not missing a beat. "Since you killed your vampire mate."

I did, I nearly asserted aloud.

But then... then his words started to translate in my head. Or rather, the *implication* underlining his statements.

He can't possibly mean...

"Mate one of us so we can cross over with you," he stated flatly, validating the trajectory of my thoughts. "That way, if Kieran still can't pass through, one of us can bring Quinnlynn back to him."

"You think I didn't try to bring her here? Because trust me, I did." I'd tried last night, as uniting Quinn with Kieran had been my first instinct. "But the barrier reacted, and Quinnlynn screamed so loud that she woke up the entire Sanctuary."

"Trust you?" Cillian asked. "I believe—"

"You haven't given us a single damn reason to trust you," Lorcan interrupted. "We found you lurking in Kieran's quarters with a knife."

I rolled my eyes. I hadn't even produced the knife, as it was still in my damn boot. *Besides, it was...* "For my protection," I gritted out through my teeth. "I'm not here to hurt anyone. I'm trying to help Quinn."

"And other than provide a few fancy explanations—that may or may not be true—you haven't given us any real reason to trust you," Lorcan countered, his Irish accent far more subdued than Kieran's and Cillian's.

Not that I gave a fuck about that right now. Not with these assholes questioning my every word.

"So you're giving me an ultimatum," I translated, my words punctuated by my mounting irritation.

"No, we're giving you an opportunity to prove your loyalty," Cillian countered.

"By forcing me to mate one of you." I huffed a humorless laugh. "How chivalrous."

"You think we want to take a mate? Let alone one known for killing her last Alpha partner?" Cillian asked.

I narrowed my gaze. He knew nothing about Alpha Fare or why I'd killed him, yet he made it sound like *I* was the bad guy. *Dick.*

Unfortunately, he wasn't done talking.

"We're both well over a thousand years old, Omega. If we wanted a mate, we would have taken one by now. Our duty is to Kieran and Kieran alone. If it means taking an errant brat for a mate so we can guarantee his safety, so be it."

"That's true loyalty," Lorcan added. "We would die for him. Would you do the same for your supposed best friend?"

I couldn't suppress the growl growing inside me. Because fuck *this* and fuck *them*. "You both know nothing about me." Or what I'd been through. Or what I would do to help Quinn.

"We know enough not to trust you, little killer," Lorcan returned, his tone and nearness and words making my blood boil.

I'm done playing along with this bullshit.

I grabbed Lorcan's wrist and sank my nails into his skin. He hissed in response, momentarily releasing me and allowing me to spin toward him. "You don't trust me, yet you want to mate me?"

"I don't want to mate you at all," he countered. "But it's the best way to protect Kieran. And it forces you to prove your intentions."

"I shouldn't have to prove anything at all. Quinn needs her intended mate. Either he wants to go to her or he doesn't. End of discussion."

"The question isn't whether or not Kieran wants to go to her. The question is whether or not you'll do whatever it takes to help your friend." He arched an arrogant brow. "We'd do anything for Kieran, including mating a renowned Alpha killer. How far will you go to protect Quinnlynn, Kyra? Or are you all talk?"

Cillian murmured something behind me, but I couldn't hear him over the rushing of blood in my ears.

These Alphas had the audacity to question my loyalty to Quinn after I'd risked my life to come here for Kieran's help.

"I don't fucking have time for this," I snapped. "But you'd better believe that I will be handing you your arse when I return, *Alpha*." The slip of my English accent—one I'd grown out of centuries ago—just further confirmed how pissed off I was at this situation and these arrogant Alphas.

Fuck this and fuck you, I thought as I engaged my shadowing ability.

Only for it to fizzle out. *Again.*

Lorcan's expression was cold and calculating as he asked, "Problem, *Omega?*"

I snarled at him. "Fine. You want a display of loyalty? I'll show you loyalty." I grabbed a fistful of his long hair and yanked him toward me.

Then I sank my fangs into his neck.

"Fuck!" Kieran shouted from behind me.

Fuck *is right*, I thought, intent on ripping Lorcan's damn throat out.

But then the asshole *growled.*

A warning sound.

A low vibration of power.

A whisper of intent from his wolf to mine.

My legs instantly went weak, my insides melting from that sound alone. He caught me as my knees buckled, his sturdy arms lifting me into the air as his mouth closed around my throat.

Shit. Shit. Shit.

His teeth punctured my skin, drawing a whimper from deep within.

My wolf side purred.

My vampire side cringed.

And I... I just... went limp.

"Have you lost your fucking mind?" Kieran snapped.

"We're your Elites," Cillian replied. "Your life is ours to protect."

"Not at the expense of your own," the future Blood Sector King retorted.

"It's done," Lorcan replied, his voice deep and hypnotic to my senses. It made my head spin. One minute, I wanted to kill him, and now...

Now I want... I want something else entirely.

Never going to fucking happen, little killer, he said into my mind as he released me.

I blinked. *What?* My eyelashes fluttered, his stern features coming in and out of focus before me. Then I felt his presence in my head. In my heart. *In my soul.*

Just like him.

Just like Alpha Fare.

My heart stopped beating, my breath stilling in my chest.

We're mates.

Lorcan and I are mates.

That's what happens when an Omega bites an Alpha and he bites her back. Lorcan's deadpan statement echoed through my thoughts as he played inside my head.

Stop, I demanded.

But he didn't.

He was searching for something, exploring the depths of

my mind while leaving his equally open for me to return the favor.

So I did.

If he wanted to rummage through my thoughts, I'd frolic through his.

Except the first one I found gave me pause. Because it immediately confirmed that he hadn't been lying about not wanting a mate. The very notion of tying his soul to another was abhorrent to him. However, he did it anyway.

For Kieran.

His cousin.

They were as close as brothers, having survived over a millennium together. Lorcan had pledged his loyalty to Kieran forever ago, and he would do literally anything to guarantee the other man's safety.

Including mating me.

Something he deeply regretted having to do but would live with the consequences as required.

I gaped up at him, shocked by the truth. Not because it upset me or even hurt my feelings, but because it seemed so abnormal.

Most Alphas took mates to satisfy their need to rut and procreate.

Not Lorcan. He had no desire to do such a thing.

Oh, he wasn't innocent by any means. I could see glimpses of history in his mind, of previous Omegas he'd taken to bed. But none of them had meant anything to him. Not in the *mating* sense, anyway. He'd slept with Omegas out of obligation, to help them through their heat.

While always taking a form of birth control that would prevent offspring from occurring.

How... different, I mused. *An Alpha who doesn't want a progeny.*

Lorcan snorted in response in my head. Then he looked over my shoulder at Kieran and said, "She's telling the truth."

"No shit," I muttered as I prodded the bite mark on my

throat and glanced back at Cillian. "At least I know your friend meant it when he said you didn't want mates."

"We need to go," Lorcan said, ignoring me. "Drink the blood. If it doesn't work, I'll bring Quinnlynn back here."

Kieran's near-black eyes flashed with obsidian fire as he glowered at my *new mate*. "We're not fucking done with this discussion." He shadowed over the desk to grab the vial, his movements holding a lethal edge to them.

"You can thank me later," Lorcan deadpanned.

Kieran's gaze further narrowed, but this time he glanced from Lorcan to me, his jaw clenching. "You'd better not be tricking us, Omega," he warned as he unscrewed the cap from the vial.

After all this and he still doesn't believe me?

Well, fuck him. Fuck this. Fuck everything.

Besides, I wasn't afraid of him. What else could he do to me, even if I was tricking them?

"Pretty sure there isn't a worse punishment you could give me right now, Alpha," I told him through my teeth.

I'd been mated against my will once before. While I might have instigated the mating with Lorcan today, it'd certainly not been my *choice*.

Lorcan glanced down at me, his eyes flashing. *Mating me wasn't meant to be a punishment, Omega. Nor did I make you mate me. You bit me first.*

You may not have made me mate you, but you did force me to take a mate today, I returned. *It was that or let my friend suffer. Hence, there wasn't a choice. And by definition, that implies force.*

If he felt bad, he didn't show it. Nor did he bother replying. Instead, he watched Kieran drink the vial of Quinn's blood, his expression and mind giving nothing away.

Because why would he feel bad? He was an Alpha, and Alphas took what they wanted. Always.

"Take me to Quinnlynn," Kieran commanded when he finished.

"Us," Lorcan interjected, holding out his hand toward me. "Take *us* to Quinnlynn."

"Sure," I muttered under my breath. "At least I'll have more knives there." I grabbed his palm, then reached for Kieran before loudly adding, "I hope this fucking hurts. *A lot.*"

LORCAN

My wolf paced inside me, eager to taste his new mate.

He didn't care at all that she wasn't really ours. That none of this had been by design or choice so much as *need*. He simply wanted her. His Omega. The fiery little Alpha killer with angry eyes and alluring curves.

I pushed away his desire, focusing instead on the icy landscape appearing around me. Kyra's thoughts were loud in my mind, her fury over this situation palpable.

Fucking Alphas, she kept thinking. *Arrogant assholes.*

She wasn't wrong. We *were* arrogant. Usually.

But when I heard her thoughts about not having a choice, about being *forced* into this mating, I'd had a moment of pause.

I'd seen this as a dutiful decision, one meant to protect my cousin and best friend. I'd expected her to feel the same. However, mere seconds inside her complex mind had told me her choices in life were far more complicated than my own.

She was loyal to Quinnlynn; that much I knew for certain.

But Kyra had a dark past, one I was trying very hard not to explore. Because it wasn't my business or my problem. This arrangement between us was strictly professional. An arranged mating with mutual rewards. I helped my best friend and she helped hers. Nothing more and nothing less.

"Kyra?" a deep voice echoed from the icy mist.

"It's fine," she replied from beside me. "He's here for Quinn."

"And the other?" the male pressed, his presence cloaked behind some sort of magic curtain. Because all I could see around us were frigid waters and ice caps.

"Is someone I'll handle on my own," she stated dryly.

I glanced at her, my eyebrow arched. *And how do you intend to handle me, little killer?* I mused. *With that knife in your boot?*

She grunted in response, saying nothing else. However, her mind showcased a myriad of ways she would like to *handle* me, and none of them were pleasant.

Which only caused my wolf to purr with expectation because the animal inside me enjoyed a good fight. Especially when the opponent resembled a gorgeous Omega with a penchant for violence.

She's not ours, I informed my inner beast. *Stop salivating.*

"Does she often fall unconscious when she visits?" Kieran asked, his gaze taking in our surroundings and the enchanted veil before us.

"No, but it's been a very long time since her last visit," Kyra answered, her tone wary. "She came here after your betrothal. Then she left to pursue a lead and never really returned."

Kieran nodded. "The island is requiring her to make up for lost time. Take me to her."

Kyra swallowed and took a step forward, her focus on that shimmering curtain.

Is that the barrier? I asked her.

The entire island is a barrier, she returned, her mind elaborating where her words did not.

It seemed we'd already passed through the initial dome hovering over these bespelled lands, leaving only the icy cloud before us. However, that cloud wasn't really a shield. It was actually a spell created by the male who'd asked about my presence.

Fritz, I realized, the name loud in Kyra's thoughts. *The Protector she'd mentioned to Kieran.*

Only, he was an Omega, not an Alpha.

A *V-Clan* Omega.

And he stood just inside the mist as we passed through, his muscular stature surprisingly robust for an Omega. He was no match for me or Kieran, but I could see how his size had earned him the Protector title on the island.

"We need to walk," Kyra said, her focus on Kieran as we moved toward the mist. "I'm worried the shield will react to you shadowing."

Kieran nodded in response, following with ease along beside her while I kept pace behind them, my gaze searching the landscape for any potential threats.

Will the barrier let him remain on the island so long as he doesn't shadow? I wondered at Kyra. *Or could it still reject him?*

She ignored me, but her mind provided the response I needed—she didn't really know. And she was conflicted on how she felt about that. Part of her wanted this to work, while a darker part of her would enjoy watching the spell rip him apart.

You'd better hope it's not the latter, I told her.

Not a fan of bloody ice? she returned, her catlike gaze glittering beneath the moonlight as she glanced over her slender shoulder at me.

"This enchantment is unlike anything I've ever felt. How old is it?" Kieran asked.

When Kyra didn't readily reply, I pulled the response from her thoughts. "Older than us."

She fired another glare my way. "Stop poking around in my head."

"No. Not until I'm sure we're safe here."

"You're not safe here," she countered.

"Exactly," I replied.

She clenched her jaw and turned on her heel, her steps beautifully deft despite the frigid land beneath her boots.

"I told you it's fine, Fritz," she said as she started toward the shimmering wall. "Open the door."

Magic glinted ahead of us, revealing the "door" she'd just mentioned. Except it wasn't really a *door* so much as a grand entryway made of fire.

Impressive, I mused, admiring the way the fire glimmered against the snow around it. None of it was melting, just glittering from the fiery light.

Kyra skipped through the flames, her blue-black hair waving us onward in her wake.

I shadowed in front of Kieran, my silent way of telling him I would be stepping through those flames first. Kyra's mind didn't indicate any potential threats, but that didn't mean I trusted her.

Because if anyone could hide dangerous thoughts from a mate, it was Kyra.

A crystallized courtyard appeared as I stepped through the inflamed entryway, the image reminding me of parts of Iceland in the heart of winter.

Given how far north we were, I suspected it stayed this way year-round. This place wouldn't be inhabitable at all for humans. Hell, it was only livable for supernaturals because of the magical elements in the air.

"It's safe," I called back to Kieran as I eyed the various sentries throughout the land. *Safe* might not be the right word, but I had a good idea of what we were facing now. Partly because of my access to Kyra's mind, but also because of what my wolf could see and smell.

The biggest threats were the archers hiding in ice towers around the yard. All of their weapons were currently trained on me.

Not a problem.

I simply grabbed hold of their arrows with my telekinetic strands, ensuring they couldn't be released.

The archers wouldn't know until they tried to shoot me, and by then, it would be too late for them to react. Because I'd shadow into their towers and dismantle their bows with my hands.

There were more archers behind me on the wall I'd just stepped through. No flames, though. That ornate decoration was apparently just for the front entrance.

Kieran joined me just as a trio of Omegas stepped into the courtyard ahead, their expressions wary.

"It's fine," Kyra repeated. "I'm not being coerced. And that's the future King of Blood Sector that you have in your sights, Jas!" She yelled the words at one of the sentries on the ice wall. I assumed it was for the one who had an arrow pointed right at Kieran's head.

I didn't bother telling Kyra that I already had it handled. If she was as in tune with my thoughts as I was with hers, then she already knew.

"How far away is Quinnlynn?" Kieran asked.

Kyra pointed at a glittering ice palace on the other side of the courtyard. "She's secured in her rooms there. Maybe a fifteen-minute walk from here."

"And if we run?" he asked her.

My lips flattened. Given what I'd read from Kyra's mind... "I don't recommend it," I told him. "The Omegas have an army, and it seems we're breaking their usual guest protocols. Which is why we have so many weapons pointed at us right now."

Of course, I had them all wrapped up in invisible strands that I controlled, but it would be best not to test the strength of my telekinetic powers at the moment. Not when the limits of the enchantment barrier were so unknown.

"Thank you for stealing information from my mind, *mate*," Kyra said in a sarcastically sweet tone.

You're welcome, little killer, I thought at her.

She shot me yet another glare, the expression one she seemed to favor.

"Let's walk quickly," Kieran suggested, ignoring our commentary. Likely because his focus was on finding his mate.

Kyra moved alongside Kieran while I took up the rear once more, my attention on both Kyra's thoughts and our surroundings.

Army might have been a generous term. *Militia* seemed more appropriate. They were trained to use their natural gifts against intruders. An intelligent tactic, especially when applied to a group of significant numbers.

However, at the end of the day, they were all Omegas.

An Alpha of my caliber could wipe out a quarter of their population, perhaps more, if desired. Fortunately for the Sanctuary, not many Alphas in existence measured up to my abilities. But that didn't mean the Omegas here were wholly safe.

I caressed the bows and arrows with my power before moving on to the other weapons positioned around the courtyard. Most of them were antiquated, not new. Perhaps because the majority of the Omegas here seemed to be wolves and we often fought with our teeth and claws, not guns or other tech.

But when facing a stronger enemy—such as Alphas intent on pillaging and taking Omegas against their wills—upgraded weaponry would be advised.

I continued to scan the courtyard grounds as we maneuvered past ice sculptures resembling frozen fountains and other glittering decor. It truly was a beautiful landscape, the delicate nature of it appropriate for its inhabitants.

Two petite sentries met us at the gates as we approached, their scents depicting them as shifters, but not V-Clan wolves.

W-Clan, I picked up from Kyra's mind.

They bowed their heads ever so slightly her way, indicating they saw her as a leader among them. I confirmed the title within her thoughts. Apparently, she was their queen during Quinn's absence. But now that Quinn and Kieran were here, Kyra would be the second-in-command, similar to the role Cillian and I shared in Blood Sector.

Although, with Quinn in heat, I supposed that meant Kyra was still very much in charge.

She glanced at me as we moved through the gates, her gaze still narrowed in disdain. Probably because she could hear me analyzing everything about the Sanctuary, including her role here.

I wouldn't apologize. She'd admitted that Kieran and I weren't safe here, something her thoughts continued to confirm as she mused about the various ways she'd like to kill me.

I only agreed to take a mate, not to keep one, she told herself. *Till death do us part and all that jazz.*

My lips twitched when she turned away to focus on Kieran. Her promises of death intrigued my wolf more than frightened him. I didn't doubt her ability to carry out her mission—she'd killed Alphas before, after all. But I fully intended to fight back.

Most Alphas doted on Omegas and treated them like fragile little dolls.

Unfortunately for Kyra, I wasn't most Alphas.

I respected Omegas, protected them, even cherished a few of them in the past, but I knew better than to underestimate their intentions.

Kieran took over the lead, his steps long and purposeful as he headed into the palace and up a flight of stairs without Kyra's guidance. My nose told me why—*Quinnlynn's scent.* Her sweet Omega perfume filled the air, begging her Alpha to find her, to knot her, to help her through her estrus.

I slowed my pace to give Kieran a wide berth, aware that if I followed too closely, I risked being attacked. Alphas became notoriously aggressive around Omegas in heat, especially when the Omega was a desired mate. The last thing I wanted to do was set him off.

With each step, I hung back a little more. I remained close enough to protect him should the need arise, while staying far enough away so as not to trigger his hunting wolf.

I had no desire to knot Quinnlynn. She was very much his. But in the throes of an oncoming rut, his wolf might forget our millennium of friendship and feel differently.

At the top of the grand staircase, we started down a corridor adorned in crystal glass along the walls and ceiling. It was elaborately done, the etchings artistic in nature and matching the delicacy of the courtyard outside.

The patterns shifted and changed as we moved, the corridor stretching on for minutes rather than seconds.

This part of the palace was far less populated than the outside and initial interior, helping my wolf ease back even more. These were clearly Quinnlynn's private quarters, which meant I wouldn't be welcome here for long.

Kieran pushed through a set of thick doors, the movement causing Quinnlynn's scent to slam into my senses. *She's close. Very close.*

Kyra glanced at me with a *No shit* expression on her face.

I ignored her, my focus on Kieran's quickening movements. He seemed to be aware of himself enough not to hurry too much, but he was definitely moving faster now.

Another flight of stairs loomed before us, the steps ones Kieran took two at a time.

I waited until he reached the top before I slowly ascended in his wake. The glass disappeared, revealing only doors that I imagined opened to bedrooms.

Kieran headed straight for the one at the end, Kyra hot on his tail, while I lingered in the hall near the top of the stairs.

His purr echoed back to me as he disappeared into the room at the end of the hall, Quinnlynn's responding mewl soon following.

Energy hummed through the air as Kyra paused at the threshold, her spine rigid as she observed Kieran and Quinnlynn in the room. I didn't dare come any closer, aware that one wrong step could set off my cousin.

"What are you doing?" Kyra demanded.

He's giving her what she needs, I told her.

By doing what? Looming over her and forcing power upon her?

He's healing her, Kyra.

"Kieran," Quinnlynn whimpered. "I'm sorry."

"Shh," he hushed her. "I'm here, little one."

"You hate me," she replied, her voice small and sad. "This is a fever dream."

"Not a dream." His purr deepened with the words, his healing aura intensifying. I recognized it because I possessed a similar ability, just not as robust as Kieran's. "And I could never hate you, Princess."

We should leave them now, I informed Kyra. *They need to be alone.*

Kyra didn't budge, her muscles seeming to lock up as Quinnlynn began to sob.

I promise he's not hurting her. I punctuated the words by brushing her spine with a hint of my healing essence, just so she could feel it. *He's empowering her.*

Kyra flinched, those catlike eyes slitting toward me. *Don't touch me.*

I simply held her stare from over twenty feet away and arched a brow. Because obviously I wasn't touching her. I was trying to make a point. *Look in my mind for the truth.*

I already have.

Then why are we still standing up here? I asked.

When she didn't respond or move, I shook my head and started back down the stairs. I needed to find a room to stay in while Kieran and Quinnlynn mated. Because I definitely wasn't leaving them alone in this foreign land during such a vulnerable state.

However, I couldn't stay too close either. I needed to find guest quarters near enough to guard them without bothering Kieran's wolf.

Staying in the family quarters would be ideal for protection, but the proximity wouldn't work.

I searched Kyra's mind for an understanding of who lived where within the palace and learned that her rooms were in this wing but were accessed via a different staircase that existed a little farther down on the second floor.

I headed that way, only for the female in question to shadow in front of me with her arms folded over her chest. "Absolutely fucking not. You escorted him here. You see that I meant every word I said. Now you can go back to Blood Sector and wait for his call."

My eyebrow inched upward again. Apparently, this was the look I intended to always give Kyra, just as she perpetually glared at me. "I am not leaving Kieran and Quinnlynn here unguarded."

"They're perfectly safe here."

"Are they?" I countered. "Because of the magical barrier or because of your Omega army?"

There's that glare again, I mused as her green eyes flared with unveiled fury. "What exactly do you think is going to happen to them here, Alpha?"

"I don't know," I admitted. "Which is precisely the problem. This island is full of unknowns. And you've said yourself that it isn't safe for Alphas."

"If he mates Quinn, he'll be fine."

"And I'm supposed to take your word for it?"

"I don't care if you trust me or not. But you're not staying here."

My lips threatened to curl, her confidence both alluring

and infuriating at the same time. "I'm not asking for permission, Omega," I informed her softly. "You can either be accommodating and accept my presence here, or I can make myself at home. Because I don't care if you want me here or not. I am staying here."

Daggers practically formed in her eyes as I threw her own words back at her.

But then the expression melted with a blink, her mind taking on a new train of thought. One involving my impending demise.

I didn't bother to comment on that deadly little track. If she thought my staying here would make it easier to kill me, then she was in for a rude awakening.

"Fine," she said, her voice sickly sweet. "Follow me."

KYRA

He wants a room? Okay. I'll give him a room. In the fucking dungeon.

I started forward, only to find my feet suddenly rooted to the floor as Lorcan's power wrapped around me in invisible ropes.

Telekinesis. I'd figured that out shortly after arriving in the Sanctuary when he'd rendered all our defenses useless.

His ability was vast. Unpredictable. *Threatening.*

And now he'd made me the subject of his power, holding me hostage in my own home.

He slowly moved around to stand before me, his expression giving nothing away. However, I could hear the amusement in his thoughts.

You can try to lock me up, little killer. But I promise it won't hold me. His mental grip squeezed my midsection, ensuring I could feel every inch of his power over me. *The same can't be said for you, though, can it?*

I gritted my teeth. *You don't want to play this game here, Alpha. One word from me and an army of Omegas will be breathing down your neck.*

That requires you to be able to speak, he replied, that damn eyebrow of his arching upward.

My lips tingled, causing my heart to skip a beat. Because that sensation was from him, not from me. I opened my mouth to speak, except... except I couldn't. I couldn't move my jaw at all. *Lorcan...*

Kyra, he returned, canting his head. *Care to show me to an appropriate guest room, or should I continue this lesson?*

A growl taunted my chest, yet the air between us remained silent. No vibrations. No sounds. Not a single fucking twitch.

Because he was controlling me entirely.

Just like Alpha Fare.

Ice drizzled through my veins at the realization, dozens of memories slamming into me with enough force to steal the air from my lungs.

Alpha Fare's fangs in my neck.

His friends taking turns with their knots.

His taunting remarks.

His compulsion.

"You'll like it, I promise. Now spread those pretty thighs and—"

"*Kyra.*" The deep voice reverberated through my mind, confusing my senses. Because it didn't sound right. "Look at me."

I blinked. *What? That's not how we—*

"*Now,*" the male demanded.

My wolf whimpered in response. But my vampire half... hissed.

This doesn't make any sense.

I blinked again, startled by the sudden glitter of lights all around me. *Windows. The moon above. Ice.*

Not a black cave. No scent of fresh blood. *Not in heat.*

My core clenched in response, not out of want but out of fear. And I sighed when I felt nothing wrong. No pain. No residual burn. No agonized sensations.

Because it was all in the past.

It'd happened over a century ago. In the Pre-Infected Era. Right before the outbreak.

I shivered. *Fuck. What triggered that?* My throat resembled sandpaper, my insides frigid from being momentarily paralyzed by my nightmares.

Except, no... no, that wasn't what paralyzed me.

My eyes widened as I finally followed the command to *look...*

Lorcan.

His name tumbled through my mind on a growl as I yanked my gaze away from his chest and up to his face. I'd momentarily lost my sight, too consumed by the past to see the present.

He stared down at me with those unfathomably black eyes, his expression still unreadable. But I caught a hint of regret in his mind.

"Don't pity me," I snapped at him, my voice a rasp of sound.

"I don't."

Now it was my turn to lift a brow at him because I heard the lie in his mind. "Don't ever do that to me again."

"I don't make false promises," he returned. "But I won't hurt you without cause."

I snorted. "Without cause." Typical Alpha. "And let me guess—turning down your knot would be justified cause, yes?"

"What makes you think I'd ever offer you my knot?" he countered.

"We're mated. Isn't that your right now, *Alpha*?"

He cocked his head to the side. "This is a mating of convenience, Kyra. We both did what we had to do to protect our best friends."

A mating of convenience, I repeated to myself with a mental snort. *Is that even a thing?*

Although, I supposed most Alphas would find it rather *convenient* to have constant access to an Omega for knotting purposes.

He made a sound that suggested he'd overheard my analysis. But that didn't make it any less true.

I knew Alphas. I understood their desires. It didn't matter what species they were; they all had one goal in mind—to procreate.

That was why they took Omega mates.

And while our circumstances might have been different today, Lorcan would eventually cave to his wolfish instincts. It wasn't a matter of *if* he would but *when* he would.

"Look, Kyra, all I want is a room I can stay in while I protect Kieran and Quinnlynn during this vulnerable time," he told me, his voice sounding more tired than before. "And, if you're feeling amenable, I wouldn't mind a tour of the Sanctuary so I can better understand the security limitations."

I waited for him to say more, but he didn't. He simply stared at me while his thoughts confirmed that his only intention for staying here was to safeguard his cousin and Quinn.

However, underneath it all, I sensed his hungry wolf. He might be tamed at the moment, but I doubted he would stay that way for long.

Which meant I needed to prepare for the inevitable. Although, I couldn't do that with Lorcan breathing down my neck.

I guess I have no choice but to behave. For now.

Lorcan sighed and ran his fingers through his hair. "We don't know each other, Kyra. Assumptions could be made on either side. Rather than make those assumptions, let's figure out how to move forward. Cordially, preferably."

I shrugged. "Fine." It wasn't fine at all. But I couldn't just stand here and dwell on it. "There are no rooms available near my nest. So you'll have to sleep on Fritz's floor if you want to remain in this wing." Fritz was the only one who had a few empty beds nearby, mostly because he preferred his space.

Technically, Quinn had a few beds near her quarters as well, but I already knew from Lorcan's thoughts that those rooms wouldn't work for him.

As much as I'd enjoy watching Kieran and Lorcan try to rip each other apart, I wouldn't enjoy observing it *here*—in a place where there were too many vulnerable innocents that could be hurt by brawling Alphas.

I turned on my heel and started down the hallway, past the staircase that led to my nest and to the next one on the left. Lorcan followed silently behind me, his steps impossible to hear. But I *felt* him there, prowling in my wake like a dangerous predator waiting to pounce.

Except his mind conflicted with that sensation. He was too busy cataloging every detail of the palace to focus on me.

Fritz stood near the stop of the stairs when we arrived, his expression wary.

"Lorcan needs a room to stay in," I told him by way of greeting. "Which one do you recommend?"

His jaw clenched, his blue eyes saying, *None of them.*

I understood his hesitation. All the security consoles were on this floor. But Lorcan would have found this area with or without my help. Because he was rummaging through my thoughts as freely as I was his, thus allowing him to know every secret this island possessed, much to my chagrin.

Alas, there wasn't a damn thing I could do about that right now.

"He also wants a tour of the Sanctuary," I continued. "One that details our security practices."

I could practically hear Fritz's teeth grinding together.

"It's my understanding that the MacNamara magic is what holds this island together," Lorcan said as he leaned against the hallway wall. "My cousin is currently healing that magic, and he's about to become Quinnlynn's official mate. As his Elite, I'm entitled to understand the security of the territory he's about to inherit."

"Inherit," Fritz repeated. "That word alone tells me you don't understand the Sanctuary at all. An Alpha can't *inherit* this land. It's owned by Omegas."

"And protected by the Blood Sector King and Queen," Lorcan countered before I could comment.

Not that I had much else to say. Fritz had summed it up quite nicely.

"As Kieran's Elite, I will be part of this island's protection detail," Lorcan continued. "Therefore, I want to be briefed on the Sanctuary's security so that I can have a better understanding of any potential weaknesses that may need to be fortified in the future."

Fritz and I snorted at the same time.

"Of course you would assume we have weaknesses," I muttered.

"Typical Alpha," Fritz added under his breath.

Lorcan remained silent, his presence growing more and more imposing by the second. Mostly because I could hear the irritation in his thoughts. He didn't appreciate our disrespecting his position and power, yet he miraculously managed to hold back his desire to teach us both a lesson.

It almost made me admire his self-control. *Almost.* But I knew too much about his kind to trust that display of restraint.

A door opened to our left, causing my brows to furrow. Only Fritz had keys to the rooms on this level, and I knew from experience that he left them all locked.

Lorcan took a step forward, only for Fritz to intercept him. "Not that room," the Omega said through his teeth. "That's *my* nest."

The Alpha merely shrugged. Then another door swung open.

Understanding hit me in the chest, causing my heart to skip several beats. Lorcan was using his telekinesis to not only open the doors but *unlock* them, too. It served as a quiet statement about his power. Or perhaps I should have translated it as a threat.

We wouldn't be able to hide anything from him here.

The only defense we had against him was the barrier, but because of our mating, he would have endless access to every inch of our island.

Either we worked with him, or he worked against us. And right now, he was choosing to work against us because we'd refused his offers to collaborate.

I cursed under my breath, hating him for his existence, and hating even more that I'd translated his actions because of my link to his mind.

It made me feel trapped. Tied down. *Mated.*

Ugh.

I could still sense the lingering ties to the first Alpha I'd mated, and he was dead. I in no way wanted to experience that all over again.

Hopefully, killing Lorcan swiftly would limit the residual impact of our bond. Fare had been tied to me for centuries, which was why his presence seemed to linger.

Well, that and the nightmares.

Lorcan disappeared, causing Fritz and me to jump into action. But then I heard his thoughts from the other room. *This will do,* I heard him saying.

Rolling my eyes, I pointed to the open door to indicate where he'd shadowed to.

Fritz gave me another look, one that probably rivaled my own annoyed expression, and moved to the entryway. "Don't expect me to bring you any sheets or towels," he grumbled at the Alpha.

"I don't expect anything from either of you," Lorcan replied flatly. His mind told me he meant that in more ways than one.

I almost snorted at the lie, but then I overheard what he planned to do next.

"Hold on," I interjected quickly, intent on stopping him from vanishing again. "I'll show you around so you don't spook the Omegas." Because I could only imagine how they would feel if they found his hulking form wandering the perimeter.

While word of his presence here—and Kieran's, too—had most certainly already spread to all the Omegas on the island by now, I didn't want to risk anyone being uncomfortable.

Or anyone attacking him and suddenly becoming the subject of his telekinetic restraints.

Lorcan stepped through the threshold into the hallway, that fucking eyebrow of his already cocked.

Whatever, I thought, turning yet again on my heel. "Follow me."

I didn't bother to wait for his reply or for him to acquiesce. He might be used to issuing orders back home, but this was *my* territory. If he wanted something, he'd have to play by my rules.

Lorcan stepped up beside me as we reached the floor below, his hands tucked casually behind his back as he moved with a predatory grace.

My inner wolf purred at the sight of such a strong male, his confidence a drug she longed to take a hit from.

Fortunately, I was only half wolf. My vampire side kept me grounded, reminding me of what happened when an Alpha got inside my head.

Just focus on the tour, I told myself.

"All the Omegas nest in the palace," I explained, my tone sounding forced. Being polite in the presence of an Alpha didn't come naturally to me. Not anymore, anyway.

Once upon a time, I'd bowed at their feet. Kissed the ground they'd walked on. Bent over every time they'd demanded it. Taken their knots in whatever way they'd required. Drunk from their veins. Allowed them to bite me in return. Handed them my fucking soul on a bloody platter.

I shuddered, the memories potent and unwelcome. And entirely Lorcan's fault.

Fucking forced mating.

Was it for our friends? Yes. Would I do it again to save Quinn? Also yes. But that didn't mean I had to be happy about any of this.

Particularly as it was permanent.

My teeth ground together as I started listing details about the palace to Lorcan in my thoughts, the words easier to form there than out loud. He was already plowing through my mind; might as well give him something to listen to.

All of those lead to Omega nests, I told him, gesturing to the various staircases along the second floor while we walked. *Please don't disturb them.*

I cringed at how pitiful that plea sounded, but it had to be said. This was our literal sanctuary. Our safe space. Alphas didn't belong in an Omega's nest unless invited in.

I won't disturb them or yours, Kyra.

My responding snort couldn't be helped. I knew better than to believe that. Especially since I could scent his wolf's interest.

Alphas couldn't help themselves.

They were programmed to crave Omegas, just as we were programmed to crave them. The moment my first heat came about, he'd be there ready and willing. And I'd accept him because my body wouldn't be able to say no.

Dining hall is on the first level, I gritted out, needing a distraction. *Just hang a right at the bottom of the grand staircase and follow your nose. Meals are served all night. Day snacks are limited.*

He said nothing, just listened.

Probably because this wasn't what he wanted to know, but it seemed appropriate to give him the full tour on our way back outside.

There's a gym, indoor pool heated by magic, and several other amenities on the first floor of the palace. There are also numerous courtyards, some of which are more temperate—again, because of magic.

I started detailing the greenhouses we had as well, the variety of foods we grew there, and how it was all possible through a myriad of enchantments.

Every Omega in the Sanctuary has a job or a role. Protection, agriculture, food preparation and cooking, cleaning, midwives for our heat cycles, and many other trades. A lot of us achieve our tasks by using our supernatural traits, but there are those who do things the old-fashioned way.

Not all Omegas had special abilities. X-Clan Omegas, for example, didn't have access to magic. As Lorcan would already know all that, I didn't elaborate.

Instead, I led him outside and passed a group of gawking Omegas.

He ignored them, dutifully following me as I explained the sentry positions that he'd noticed upon our arrival.

Then I took him to the perimeter to show him the boundaries of the barrier spell.

Neither of us spoke aloud, all the details streaming from my mind to his while he listened and analyzed everything around him.

It was almost unnerving to hear him picking apart every layer of our security, yet part of it proved to be enlightening as well. Every item he mentally noted as a potential weakness, I filed away to discuss with Fritz later.

We needed to remain a step ahead of Lorcan. Because I didn't trust him.

His mind might imply that he wanted to protect the Sanctuary, not harm it, but I'd learned long ago that thoughts could be deceiving.

Especially when those thoughts belonged to a powerful Alpha.

Lorcan paused and looked at me, his expression darkening.

"I think I've seen and heard enough," he told me. "I'll be back."

With those ominous words, he vanished once more, leaving me gaping at the vacant spot on the ice. *Where the fuck did you go?* I demanded, looking around.

He didn't reply, forcing me to dig into his thoughts for the answer.

Blood Sector, I realized, my eyebrows lifting. *Does that mean you're not staying?*

Silence.

But his thoughts seemed to echo his last words at me—*I'll be back.*

Perhaps as a taunt.

I shook my head and muttered, "Fine."

"It's very much *not* fine," Fritz retorted as he shadowed into view. He must have been watching us on the security feeds, thus witnessing Lorcan's disappearing act. "He's going to be a problem, Kyra."

"No shit," I grumbled. "But it's my problem. I'll take care of it."

Or rather, I'd take care of *him*.

I'd agreed to mate him and bring him here. I hadn't agreed to stay mated to him.

Till death do us part, I mused.

If Lorcan heard me, he didn't reply.

Maybe that meant he'd taken a break from my thoughts.

Good. I'll use that to my advantage.

"Time to go play with some knives," I told Fritz.

His wary expression melted into a grin. "That's my girl. I'll help you sharpen them."

"It's a date," I murmured, shadowing back to my nest to select my favorite toys. "Time for another episode of *How to Kill an Alpha*."

Fritz appeared beside me with a chuckle. "Your favorite show."

"Damn straight," I replied. "Now let's go craft a decent script."

LORCAN

A Few Days Later

Has *the bratty little Omega tried to kill you yet?*

I glared down at Cillian's text and replied with a flat *No*.

His telepathic abilities couldn't stretch across the globe, thus requiring us to use technology to communicate. I'd rather hoped the same limitation would apply to my connection with Kyra, but I'd quickly discovered the other day that distance did absolutely nothing to quiet the link between our minds.

Which meant I'd heard every damn word of her deadly plans for me.

Along with all her ingrained prejudices about Alphas.

I hadn't delved too much into her memories, but the few I'd overheard had provided a pretty good foundation for her bias against Alphas.

However, I wasn't a Vampire Alpha.

I also wasn't anything like *Fare*.

Her poor expectations of me had grated on my nerves, chasing me away back to Blood Sector for a much-needed break from her mental castigations. Yet they'd followed me all the way home, punching at my spirit with every wrongly conceived notion.

And those heinous thoughts had been there when I'd shadowed back to the island as well. If anything, my return had inspired even more hateful commentary because Kyra had realized I could come and go at will now that I had a mental lock on the Sanctuary's location.

Thus, I'd spent the better part of the last few days avoiding her and instead focusing on protecting the Sanctuary.

The Omegas might not see me as their protector, but that was exactly what I'd become the moment Kieran had agreed to mate Quinn. I just hadn't realized the task existed until recently. And now that I did, I was making up for lost time.

My routine mostly consisted of prowling the perimeter, eating, checking in with Cillian, and sleeping. Although, I hadn't done much of that final activity. Not because I feared what Kyra might do while I slept, but because her nightmares kept waking me up.

They were so damn real, telling me they stemmed from her memories.

Each one made me wish Fare wasn't already dead so I could fucking kill him myself.

I ran a hand over my face and stared up at the moon above. I'd already been out here for several hours, surveying the boundary lines and ensuring there were no lingering threats.

The barrier was designed to keep intruders out, the spell clearly powerful. But my wolf remained uneasy. Or perhaps the better word was *distrusting*.

Something just... didn't feel right.

Maybe it was the foreign energy that stirred the hairs along my neck. However, I hadn't survived this long by simply *accepting* plausible explanations.

Until I felt confident in the perimeter spell, I wouldn't be able to have faith in it.

I stared out at the icy beach, watching a few napping seals along the frigid shores.

Animals thrived in this new world, the lack of human interference allowing much of their habitats to slowly begin to turn back to normal. They still had a long way to go, the destruction to the global environment catastrophic, thanks to general carelessness.

Several of the Post-Infected Era sectors had programs in place to help it along.

Others were too poor to even try.

I supposed we truly did live in a dystopian world now. But the seals seemed quite pleased with it.

A scream echoed through my mind, making me wince and curse out loud. *Kyra*, I thought, my shadowing ability igniting in an instant.

Only for my rational senses to yank me right back to the beach.

Just another nightmare, I told myself with a grimace. *Fuck.*

My innate response to run to her was really starting to fuck with my head. I wasn't used to this overwhelming drive to protect a *mate*.

Guarding Kieran came naturally to me after over a thousand years of serving by his side. Helping to care for a sector full of wolves and humans also came naturally to me because it was my duty as a high-ranking Alpha.

But this... this *need* to ensure Kyra was safe...

"Fucking hell," I muttered, running my hand over my face again and palming the back of my neck.

My wrist buzzed right then, indicating a new text. I grumbled another curse before looking at it, fully aware that it would be a response from Cillian.

Seems like she's into delayed gratification. Might be your soul mate after all.

I grunted at his idiocy but decided two could play this game. *Speaking of soul mates, how's Ivana?* I typed back.

His response returned to me in a handful of seconds. *Fuck you, Lor.*

My lips curled as I dismissed the message. Ivana was an Omega hell-bent on mating Cillian, but he rejected her at every turn. His loyalty, like mine, was to Kieran. Neither of us had the time or the desire to take a mate.

Something I really wished Kyra would fucking understand.

She seemed to think I intended to force my knot on her.

Like I would ever fuck an unwilling woman. Hell, I wasn't even sure I could trust Kyra around my knot. She'd probably try to cut it off with one of her fancy blades.

An image of her dancing around me with knives populated my thoughts, giving me momentary pause. Mostly because I'd pictured her doing it while wearing nothing but a pair of sheaths on her thighs.

Yeah, that would be fun.

Too bad it was never going to happen.

Blowing out a breath, I started my trek back toward the palace. Cillian's message had reminded me that it was nearly time to eat.

I typically indulged in midnight breakfast, then did another security check before popping over to Blood Sector to deliver my daily report. Cillian was acting as the Sector Alpha in Kieran's absence, a role that actually suited him quite nicely.

Next time Cillian taunted me about Kyra, I'd be sure to mention his profound leadership skills. He'd hate that almost as much as me commenting on his compatibility with Ivana.

She really wasn't a bad choice for a mate, though. I'd told him that more than once.

Ivana was a beautiful Omega with long, white-blonde hair, ice-blue eyes, and a confidence that put others to shame. That confidence was well earned, too. Kieran often relied on her for important sector-related tasks, much to Cillian's annoyance.

Or maybe it was because of Cillian's annoyance that Kieran gave her those projects. Probably some combination of both reasons—her competence and the fact that it irritated Cillian.

I wandered along the stone path in the frozen courtyard, through the gates, and into the palace. A few Omegas had stopped to stare at me along the way, but most of the sentries on the towers and walls didn't bother to lift their weapons this time.

I considered that a win.

My first two days here, the Sanctuary's Protectors had aimed their arrows and other instruments at me every time they'd seen me.

The third day, some of them had lowered their guard.

Yesterday, more of them had simply watched me move.

And today, only two members of the patrol had me in their sights. One of whom was Jas, an Omega who seemed to hate Alphas as much as Kyra did.

My wolf growled inside at the scent of breakfast, all my prowling around the boundaries this evening having spiked my hunger.

I slid into the mess hall, only to pause near the threshold at the sight of all the Omegas bustling around the large dining room. It seemed like every single one of them who resided in the Sanctuary was down here tonight, making me frown.

I'd eaten midnight breakfast at the same hour every day since my arrival, thus establishing a bit of a routine. And it seemed the cafeteria grew more crowded each time I visited, almost as though all the Omegas were purposely trying to align their schedules with my own.

The very notion of it sounded conceited in my head. However, I wasn't sure how else to explain their obvious change in routines.

Unless something unique is happening today, I pondered as I started toward the food line. *Is there some sort of event on the schedule, perhaps?*

I turned to ask one of the Omegas openly observing me from a nearby table. But the moment I attempted to make eye contact, the group of females all bowed their heads and blushed furiously.

Sighing, I refocused on the buffet and grabbed a plate.

Omegas were notoriously submissive, which was partly what made Kyra so alluring. She wasn't the type to bow easily. Hell, she'd absolutely force my wolf to chase her. He'd fucking love it, too.

Never going to happen, I reminded myself as I piled a bunch of food on my plate. It was mostly vegetables, grains, and seafood, which made sense given our Arctic location.

By my estimation, we were somewhere between Svalbard and Greenland, on an island that had never been documented on any map. Livestock wasn't a thing because the animals would never survive, yet the greenhouses allowed the Omegas to harvest grains, fruits, and vegetables.

However, they'd had pork the other night, which told me they had a source for it somewhere.

I grabbed a cup of coffee to go with my food and settled into my usual table in the corner, my seat giving me an open view of the whole cafeteria.

Seriously, pretty much every Omega in the Sanctuary is here right now except my *Omega,* I thought, scanning all the faces. *Even Fritz is here.*

His blue irises burned as he stared at me from across the room, his dislike palpable. Despite sharing a floor, we hadn't really spoken. He was trying to hide the security consoles from me, but I'd already snuck in and reviewed his impressive setup. He clearly knew what he was doing.

If only I could identify the nagging sense of wrongness that kept scraping at my instincts. Everything seemed secure here, but *something* irked my wolf. Something I really needed to define.

It wasn't Kyra's constant mental threats about wanting to kill me, or the abundance of weapons I'd felt pointed at my back since arriving. It wasn't even the very obvious hatred some of the Omegas cast my way, either.

Just... something dark. A niggling presence of some kind.

Whatever it was, I'd figure it out. I just had to keep searching for the source.

My wrist buzzed with another message from Cillian, this one all business. *I gathered all of Kieran's bedding and worn clothes. They're in a basket in his suite.*

Thanks, I shot back at him. *I'll be by in an hour to pick it up.*

Most of Kieran's and Quinn's needs had been seen to already, the Omega midwives having provided them with food, water, and other essentials. However, Quinn would be itching to fortify her nest with Kieran's belongings. All Omegas did that during their heats, especially newly mated ones.

I would have picked the items up earlier for them if I could have, but I hadn't wanted to risk interrupting Kieran's mating instincts. However, now that he'd officially bitten Quinn, he'd hopefully be calm enough to let me drop the items off outside their door.

That said, I wouldn't be sticking around for long. Mated or not, he'd still probably try to kill me if I got too close.

"Um," a soft voice mumbled from beside me, drawing my attention to a petite, light-haired Omega with big blue eyes.

Rather than continue speaking, she set her tray down on the table and took a chair beside me.

My nose twitched, my wolf taking in her unique scent.

Z-Clan Omega, I realized with a start. *How... rare.*

Most of her kind were extinct, thanks to the carelessness and general brutality of their pack leaders. The Z-Clan Alphas treated their Omegas like chew toys, not treasures.

"Your spirit is… complicated," she murmured after several silent beats. "I'm struggling to read your intentions. But your nature is to protect, not to harm."

Ah, that explains why this little Arctic wolf is still alive, I thought. Z-Clan shifters were notoriously intuitive, their abilities to read auras a renowned trait. And it seemed this one had learned how to harness that ability for survival purposes.

I took a sip of my coffee while I considered how to reply to her. But I eventually decided the truth would suffice. "I don't wish to harm anyone here," I confided. "This is a safe space."

She dipped her elfin chin a little, her expression shifting into one of confidence. "Yes. I believe you."

Hmm, if only Kyra was so easily convinced, I mused.

I swore I heard a mental snort in reply, but when I reached into Kyra's mind, I found her busy showering and immediately retreated. That was *not* what I needed to think about right now in a room full of Omegas.

"Many of the others think they could take you down if you decided to attack, but I keep telling them that you won't hurt us," the Arctic wolf informed me. "Although, I suspect that if you did, there wouldn't be much we could do to stop you."

"That's true. You wouldn't be able to stop me," I agreed. *Not easily, anyway.* "But I'll share a secret with you."

Her blue eyes gleamed as she leaned forward a little, eagerness written all over her innocent features.

"Those with superior strength are supposed to nurture and protect those who need it. Weaker Alphas don't understand that. But I'm not weak. Neither is Alpha Kieran. We understand our duty to the Sanctuary. We understand our duty to *you*." I kept my voice soft, hoping she would understand what I was trying to tell her—*your Alphas failed you, but that doesn't mean I will be like them.*

She considered me for a long moment, then dipped her chin once more. "You're telling the truth."

"I am." The two words weren't necessary, her intuitive ability clearly allowing her to decipher truth from fiction. But I felt the need to confirm her assessment, mostly for those eavesdropping around us.

Or perhaps for the Omega listening to my thoughts right now, I added for Kyra's benefit.

She didn't reply or acknowledge me, maintaining the status quo from the last several days.

The Arctic wolf smiled. "I think I'll like you just fine," she decided aloud before popping a piece of fruit into her mouth. "You should help with our training."

My eyebrow slid upward. "Training?"

She nodded, but it was another voice that said, "Defensive training." A tray landed on the table as another Omega took over the seat on my opposite side.

This one appeared to be an X-Clan shifter.

"Kyra's been teaching us how to defend ourselves against Alphas," the new Omega explained. "She's a good teacher, but she's small. We need a real Alpha to practice with."

"I doubt he'll be up for that," a third Omega commented as she joined the table. This one appeared to be a vampire. "And Kyra might not like him learning our secrets."

"But he's here to protect us," the Arctic wolf argued. "Teaching us how to fight is a good way to help."

There is no fighting when it comes to an Alpha and an Omega, I thought, frowning at their conversation. "The best way to defend yourselves is with a weapon," I said out loud. Omegas would never physically win in hand-to-hand combat with an Alpha.

"Yes, we have swords and knives," the Arctic wolf told me.

"I'm referring to long-range weapons. Like guns."

All three of them blinked at me.

"Guns… are human toys," the X-Clan Omega whispered slowly. "Why…?"

"If you're going up against an Alpha, you need all the help

you can get," I told her sternly. "Knives and swords won't cut it."

"They work for Kyra," the Arctic wolf hedged, her brow furrowing.

"Yes, because the Alphas I killed assumed my size made me weak," Kyra replied as she shadowed into a seat across from me, her expression thunderous.

The X-Clan Omega and vampire bowed their heads and apologized before leaving the table in a rush, their cheeks flushed with color.

But the Arctic wolf didn't leave as quickly. Instead, she looked at Kyra and said, "I want to know why he suggests we use guns instead of knives."

"Because he doesn't believe an Omega can take down an Alpha without cheating," Kyra stated flatly.

My lips twitched. *Guns aren't cheating, little killer.*

"Knives are efficient and easier to conceal than a gun," she went on. "We also use our size to our advantage, Ashlyn. Alphas always underestimate Omegas, which is the cause for their demise every time. Trust me."

Those last two sentences were uttered while Kyra held my gaze, the words obviously meant for me more than *Ashlyn*.

"Hmm," the Arctic wolf hummed, causing Kyra to glance at her.

"You don't believe me?" Kyra demanded.

"It's not what I believe that matters here, Kyra," Ashlyn murmured thoughtfully as she gathered her tray. "But I stand by what I said. I think it could be beneficial to have an Alpha help with our training."

Kyra's nostrils flared at the words, clearly agitated by the notion.

But Ashlyn merely smiled in response before looking at me and saying, "It was nice chatting with you, Alpha Lorcan. I hope you'll consider what I've said." Then she bowed her head in subtle reverence and stepped away from the table to find a seat elsewhere in the cafeteria, thus leaving me alone with Kyra.

I picked up my fork to take a bite of my food—which was mostly cold now—and waited for whatever Kyra might have to say.

Because I could hear her mind firing with all sorts of phrases. Most of them resembling death threats.

"Shopping for an Omega?" she asked through her teeth, her chosen accusation not the one I'd expected her to voice at all. While I'd heard that sliver of annoyance running through her mind, I'd expected her to squash it. Because why the fuck would she care if I was *shopping for an Omega?*

Still, it seemed prudent to answer her honestly.

"Having one unwanted mate is more than enough, Kyra. I have no desire to take on another."

Her responding snort matched the one I'd heard in my thoughts earlier. She seemed to favor that sound. It expressed her disbelief, something I was becoming quite accustomed to. Similar to the lingering death threats pulsating through her consciousness.

She *really* wanted to stab me, even more so now that I'd insulted her weapon of choice.

I nearly sighed aloud, exhausted by her mental gymnastics.

This Omega was going to need a lesson in futility soon.

Her eyes narrowed, suggesting she was very much listening to my mind right now.

Make that very soon, I thought, hoping she took that for the warning it was meant to be.

I finished my food while she glared daggers my way, then picked up my coffee to enjoy the last few sips. Neither of us spoke, our minds simply dancing in tandem via our connection.

Hatred poured out of her.

I accepted it, mostly because I understood that, deep

down, I wasn't the actual source of her anger. Another Alpha had that mantle. I was just the one she felt the need to take it out on now.

Because she saw our mating as forced. Cillian and I hadn't given her a choice. Not really. But perhaps one day she'd realize that she wasn't the only one who would suffer eternally due to this permanent link between us.

I'd never wanted a mate. I still didn't want a mate. But I accepted our fate because it was for the best of V-Clan kind.

It would also be for the best of the Sanctuary, too.

Because now these Omegas had another Protector. One who could actually defend them against other Alphas.

Kyra's jaw ticked, clearly insulted by my mental trajectory.

Too bad. It was the truth. If she couldn't stomach that, then perhaps she wasn't truly fit for her position.

"Have a good evening, *mate*," I told her as I stood to do another security loop. Once I finished, I'd pop over to Blood Sector for Kieran's belongings. Then I'd come back here and figure out how to handle my murderous little Omega.

Because Ashlyn was right.

These Omegas needed more-efficient training.

And who better to teach them about self-defense against an Alpha than one of the most powerful Alphas of V-Clan kind?

KYRA

A Week Later

"You need to see this."

I lifted my gaze to find Fritz in my doorway, his words holding an ominous thread to them that I really didn't want to tug on. Primarily because I fully expected Lorcan to be at the other end of that thread.

Ugh.

I'd spent the last week avoiding him. Hell, longer than a week. More like ten or twelve days. Since he'd arrived. Since our mating. Since *everything*.

To add insult to injury, I couldn't quite figure out how to kill him. Every concept I manufactured was quickly shot down by a single glimpse into his thoughts.

The bastard seemed to be perpetually ready for me, making me hate this bond between us that much more.

"Earth to Kyra," Fritz drawled. "Did you hear me?"

"Unfortunately," I muttered, my feet begrudgingly moving toward the floor. I stood and stretched, my joints popping in protest from my early evening workout.

Apparently, I'd pushed myself a little too hard on my run today, but I'd needed it after my most recent nightmare.

Ignoring the pangs shooting up my legs, I pulled on a pair of jeans and my favorite boots and grabbed a sweater to cover my tank top. After a cursory glance in the mirror—*I look presentable enough*—I faced the male Omega filling up my doorway.

"Where am I going?" The words sounded petulant to my ears, making me wince.

Since when am I this moody, woe-is-me type? I wondered.

Since Lorcan, that whiny part of me replied.

I nearly rolled my eyes at myself. This was getting out of hand. I didn't do *angst*. I just murdered the problem.

Except this *problem* was proving difficult to kill.

Something that became increasingly clear as Fritz grabbed my hand to shadow us to the situation he'd said I'd needed to see.

And yep, that ominous thread led right to Lorcan.

In the middle of a makeshift sparring ring.

With three Omegas.

One of whom was a determined Ashlyn.

My eyes narrowed as the three Omegas circled Lorcan, all of them attacking at once.

"He's teaching them about strength in numbers," Fritz growled. "The entire purpose of today's lesson is to demonstrate how attacking as a group helps even the odds."

I glanced at the crowd gathering around the demonstration, noting the avid interest coming from all the Omegas. Less than two weeks ago, they'd all hated Lorcan on sight. Yet now they were gazing at him with what could only be described as growing affection.

Fucking Alpha pheromones.

Or maybe it was just the protective vibes.

Well, okay, it could also be Lorcan's genuinely good looks

and all that sinewy muscle on display that had everyone so captivated.

Because he was shirtless.

Shirtless.

Why the fuck does he need to be shirtless?

And did he have to be so damn *gentle*, too?

He was absolutely holding back. *What the hell is the point of teaching Omegas to defend themselves if you're just going to provide false hope?* I demanded.

Of course, he didn't answer. He probably wasn't even hearing me over all that Omega attention.

Ashlyn jumped on his back, her arms going around his neck as the other two tried to stab him with wooden knives.

I rolled my eyes. This was ridiculous. He just wanted an excuse to play.

This wasn't a *lesson* but an *audition*.

And I hated it. I hated him. I hated *this*.

A group attack wasn't always feasible. Sometimes an Omega only had herself to rely on, not a pack. All he was doing was teaching the Omegas how to flirt.

Case in point, Ashlyn laughed when Lorcan shadowed out from beneath her, causing her to fall to the mat on her rump.

This shouldn't be *funny*. It should be *serious*. What if he actually tried to attack them? Would they just climb on top of him in response?

I gritted my teeth. *No. Fuck this. Fuck him. Fuck everyone.*

I shadowed to the training weapons and picked up two real blades. Sharp ones. The kind I used when sparring with Fritz.

And shadowed into Lorcan's path before the three Omegas could jump on him again.

"If you want to give them a demonstration on self-defense, then let's do it properly," I snapped at him.

That damn eyebrow of his arched upward, like it always

did in my presence. Then he canted his head to the side and fell into a fighting stance. *Show me what you can do, little killer.*

I growled, *hating* how that endearment seemed to caress my inner wolf. She liked that he saw her as a killer. She assumed that meant he respected us.

He didn't.

Hence his adjective of *little* before *killer*.

I'll show you little, I thought at him, the daggers twirling in my fingers. *Unless you cheat and use your telekinesis, anyway.*

It's not cheating to use your abilities, he drawled as we began to circle one another.

Oh? Is that why you were holding back with the Omegas, then?

We were having a preliminary lesson on how to defend themselves as a team. I can see now that their leader required that lesson more than they did.

"Are you saying I don't know how to be a team player?" I demanded, switching to my external voice. "Because I'm pretty sure everyone here would disagree with you."

Especially considering I'd stepped up to lead in Quinn's absence.

Not because I'd wanted to, but because I'd had to. To protect the Omegas of this island. To ensure our infrastructure didn't collapse. To continue moving us *forward* when the entire world had collapsed due to the Infection.

For him to suggest otherwise just showed how little he understood and knew about me.

"I'm not doubting your ability to lead and collaborate, Kyra. And I already know that your primary defenses here stem from fighting as a group. Which is why I don't understand your self-defense mindset. Why fight alone when you don't have to? Why not apply the same mindset to taking down an Alpha in combat?"

"Because you never know when you'll need to face an Alpha on your own," I gritted out.

He considered that for a moment. "A fair point. But you

should also be learning how to coordinate your attacks as a group."

"What do you think our sentries are doing?" I demanded.

"That's a different type of coordinated effort," he returned. "Some of the Omegas showed interest in sparring with an Alpha. I suggested they learn how to take me down as a team first. Then we can move on to advanced studies."

"You mean one-on-one training," I deadpanned. "How fun for you."

It was a known fact that Alphas could take more than one Omega mate. However, Omegas could rarely have more than one Alpha, mostly because the arrogant bastards were too possessive to share.

Alphas only ever thought about themselves. Lorcan was certainly proving to be no different, especially since he was openly shopping for Omegas right in front of me.

He made a noise in the back of his throat that sounded a lot like impatience. *I already told you that I had no interest in taking a mate, let alone two of them,* he muttered into my mind.

"You just said that you wanted everyone to know how to defend themselves when faced with an Alpha alone, Kyra," he added out loud, returning us to the more important conversation at hand.

Because he was right. I had just said that. Yet the notion of him training anyone alone infuriated my inner wolf, causing me to speak without thinking.

How did we even get into this debate? I wondered, dizzy from the circular logic swirling in my mind. *And must there be so many people watching us right now?*

Some leader I was shaping up to be.

Shit.

"My suggestion would be to run and use your small size to your advantage by hiding somewhere an Alpha can't access," Lorcan added, glancing at the crowd before looking at me again. "But if *you* feel everyone should be able to fight an

Alpha head-on, then..." He spread out his hands and mentally whispered, *Your move, sweetheart.*

My inner vampire snarled while my wolf practically danced around in anticipation. The conflict of interest didn't help my already dizzy state.

This Alpha is going to make me lose my mind.

No, not just him. This mating bond.

However, he'd just given me permission to attack him. With knives. And given how easy he'd just gone on the others, he'd probably do the same with me.

I could use that to my advantage.

Create a weak spot.

Plunge the dagger into his neck or heart and incapacitate him long enough to kill him.

Yes, yes, my vampire hissed.

Even though I was sure Lorcan could hear my thoughts, he appeared bored. Like he didn't believe I was capable of actually hurting him.

Good. Let him think that.

I shadowed behind him and swiped my blade toward the back of his nape, but he disappeared in a breath, his arm banding around my middle in the next second as he easily lifted me off the ground.

The Omegas around us gasped.

But I simply growled and shadowed out of his grip, my knack for stealth kicking in as I flounced around him in various false strikes, all of them meant to confuse his senses.

Each time I thrust my blade forward, I vanished before it could make a mark. I wanted to put him on high alert, overwhelm his instincts, make—

My back hit the ground, knocking the air out of my lungs as Lorcan settled over me, his telekinetic bonds throttling my attempt to shadow out from beneath him.

Fuck! I shouted in my mind. *Cheater.*

You engaged your abilities, so I engaged mine, he replied flatly. *And if you think for a second that I'm going to underestimate you, then you haven't been poking around enough in my mind.*

Why would I want to poke around in there?

Because you're hell-bent on killing me, he returned. *However, you've yet to even consider the one advantage you have over me—your direct access into my thoughts.*

He pushed off of me to deftly move to his feet.

It's making me wonder if you really want to kill me or if you're just flirting with me, he added, that damn eyebrow inching upward to its usual position. *Maybe all these threats are foreplay.*

You wish that were the case. I shadowed into a standing position, relieved that he'd already released me from his powers.

"Most Alphas don't have magical abilities. They take Omegas by brute force. Maybe it would be more prudent for this demonstration to focus on natural combat rather than rare supernatural strength."

He considered me for a moment. "By that logic, most Omegas also do not possess unique talents."

I shook my head. "Many of us here do. But it's not usually V-Clan Alphas that we have to fear. Unless you think there is a reason to feel otherwise?"

Hmm, he hummed. *Well played, little killer.*

I didn't acknowledge the compliment and instead waited for him to respond out loud.

"Vampire Alphas are prone to supernatural abilities, and they're not known for their kindness," he replied, a dangerous gleam in his eyes.

Low blow, Alpha.

Perhaps, but it's still a valid point, Omega.

I disagree. "Only V-Clan Omegas and Vampire Omegas need to worry about them. Other Omegas don't appeal to them."

"So for the intents and purposes of this demonstration,

you want me to use brute force and nothing else, while you can call upon all your talents."

"Yes. If you're brave enough," I taunted him.

His lips twitched. "Bravery isn't the question, Kyra. Adequate training is my primary concern."

"So then you think we need to learn to protect ourselves against Alphas like you—V-Clan Alphas?" I pressed, aware that I was putting him in an unfair position. But I wanted to make him squirm.

And I *needed* an advantage other than being able to read his mind.

"There are very few Alphas in existence who rival me in power. One of those Alphas is Kieran, Quinnlynn MacNamara's *chosen* mate." His gaze searched the crowd while he spoke, addressing our audience instead of me. "Kieran would never use his talents to harm an Omega, and neither would I."

He held out his hands then, his focus returning to me.

"I'll hold back my magic, Kyra. But I won't attack first. Your move."

LORCAN

How the hell did I end up here? In the middle of a sparring ring surrounded by Omegas while my mate foreshadowed my untimely demise with her eyes.

Oh, right. The petite Z-Clan Omega had interrupted my perimeter sweep and asked me to show her and her friends some self-defense moves.

Which had led to Kyra showing up and throwing a mountain of resentment at my feet.

Resentment I didn't deserve.

But it was resentment I'd accept if it helped heal her wounded soul.

Fuck, Cillian is never going to let me live this down, I thought as Kyra began to prowl around me. *If he were in my shoes right now, he'd just lock this fiery Omega up in a cage for eternity. Yet here I am, indulging in this silly game.*

She didn't want me to use my powers because she thought it would even the playing field between us.

It wouldn't.

My powers aided my Alpha status; they didn't define it.

Kyra shadowed to my back, her stealth powers igniting.

From what her mind told me, that talent was supposed to diminish her scent and make her hard to track.

But my wolf could still smell her just fine.

Spiced blood oranges.

It was an aroma that had started to infiltrate my dreams. We were linked now, for better or for worse. And that made me incredibly in tune with her movements.

She'd told me not to use my powers. She hadn't said anything about not tapping into our connection. Of course, I couldn't turn that off any better than she could.

Pain lanced across my back as her blade struck my bare skin, the superficial wound making my wolf purr inside. He'd liked that little bit of foreplay far too much.

"Oh, sorry," Kyra said, shadowing in front of me. "Did you also want a weapon?"

I stared down at her impassively. "You wanted a realistic demonstration. So no, I don't want a weapon. Alphas attack Omegas because they want to conquer and rut them, not maim or accidentally kill them."

"Say that to the nearly extinct Z-Clan Omegas," Kyra muttered.

"Z-Clan Alphas are feral maniacs who pride themselves on ripping apart anyone beneath them in power," I retorted. "And they do so with their *claws*, Kyra. Not weapons."

Ashlyn winced out of the corner of my eye, making me instantly apologetic for my crass summary of her former pack.

I didn't know her history, but I suspected it was gruesome.

And I'd just summarized it without a hint of remorse.

Fuck. This was why I avoided Omegas. I didn't have the tenderness to handle situations like this. I also didn't have the desire.

I led through means of protection, not by offering emotional support.

Swallowing, I faced Ashlyn, an apology forming on my lips.

Only to have a dagger suddenly lodged in my side.

I spun around, my hand going to the hilt to yank it out as I moved.

My healing ability ignited, the burning sensation ripping through my veins immediately cooling. I wasn't nearly as powerful as Kieran when it came to this familial talent, but I was powerful enough to cure myself without much thought.

Gasps flooded the air in response to both my speed and my instantly healed wound, but that didn't stop my spitfire of a mate from trying to stab me with her other blade.

Right in the fucking heart.

I grabbed the weapon by the sharp end and threw it at the ground. The sharpened point dug into the ice, eliciting more gasps from the crowd. It wasn't every day someone was strong enough to break ice with a knife, but it was a perfect display of my Alpha power.

I didn't need telekinesis or miraculous healing to bring an Omega to her knees. I just had to exist.

Yet my mate refused to bow.

She'd somehow grabbed a third knife and was now hell-bent on slicing it across my throat.

I grabbed her wrist before she could follow through with her deadly plan and yanked her back into my chest. "That's enough," I growled into her ear.

This wasn't about teaching the Omegas how to fight. This was about Kyra wanting to kill me. And while I'd known that was her intention from the beginning, I'd hoped to turn this into a useful lesson.

However, there was no reasoning with Kyra in this state.

She shadowed behind me, her knife whispering along my skin.

I whirled with her, grabbed her by the hips and shadowed us both to her nest.

This dispute required privacy, and I was done allowing her to disrespect me in front of the other Omegas.

She might hate Alphas, but that didn't mean she could take her prejudices out on me publicly. Especially since Kieran was about to inherit this territory, making him the Sector Alpha and me his Elite.

I pinned her to the bed, my legs holding hers down as my palms pressed her hands into the mattress.

She snarled like a little wildcat beneath me, fury dancing in those feline irises.

"*Enough,*" I repeated.

But it was like she couldn't hear me.

Murderous intent echoed through her mind as she shadowed out from beneath me to grab one of her hidden weapons.

I latched onto every sharp item in the room and secured them in place. She'd asked me not to use my power during the demonstration, but we were done with that now. My telekinetic abilities were officially fair game.

However, I refrained from restraining her. I didn't want to risk triggering her again.

Instead, I simply stood and growled again. This time deeper. More potent. An Alpha demanding submission.

Her knees locked, the stubborn Omega fighting the need to kneel.

Chaos erupted in her thoughts, memories clashing with the present as she likened my growl to that of another.

Which led to her whimpering like a broken pup.

Then snarling once more as she attempted to grab one of her throwing stars.

When the metal wouldn't budge, she jumped to another hiding place, only to be faced with the same issue.

"Stop!" she demanded, spinning toward me.

"*No.*" I underlined that word with power, my growl so deep that her knees buckled in the next breath.

I caught her before she hit the ground and set her

quivering form on the bed. Fear and anger seemed to be battling for purpose inside her.

I'm weak, she whispered to herself. *No. No, fuck that. I'm not weak. I'm... He... This... Ugh!*

"Kyra." I stood beside the bed, careful not to touch her. Because I heard the trajectory of her thoughts, the ominous expectation for what would come next.

She expected me to punish her, and she had several creative methods in mind. Most of them were sexually violent.

I might enjoy sparring as foreplay, but I certainly didn't enjoy any of the twisted scenes sprouting in her thoughts. I assumed her former mate was the inspiration for many of those savage concepts.

"Kyra," I tried again. Only for her to launch herself at me with renewed vigor.

This time, I had no choice but to pin her to the mattress again. I followed the move with a growl meant to force supplication.

Her wolf whined in response, then Kyra completely shut down beneath me.

I sighed, hating this.

"Look. If you keep fantasizing about killing me, I'm going to have no choice but to lock you in a cage," I told her.

I wasn't sure if I really meant that, but thinking about how Cillian would handle this situation inspired my commentary.

She must not have heard that part in my mind, just the words from my mouth, because she blinked as though waking up. And then she hissed.

Or maybe she considered that little hissing rumble a growl.

Regardless, my wolf answered in kind.

This was fucking ridiculous.

I pushed away from her, needing space. Especially since I was in the middle of her damn nest—a fact my inner wolf was far too pleased about. He didn't care that she'd tried to kill me in the most spectacularly stupid way possible. He just saw it as a seduction tactic.

And now that we were in the heart of her territory, he wanted to intimately introduce himself to his Omega.

But that wasn't happening. *Ever.*

"I have no desire to consummate our mating bond," I informed both Kyra and my inner beast.

This female didn't want me. That much was very fucking clear. And I would *not* take her or any other female by force.

Just because an Alpha could do something didn't mean he should do it or that he was entitled to it.

"I haven't remained here to kindle a relationship with you or to find another potential mate. I'm here for Kieran and Quinnlynn. And I'm here because this island is officially under Blood Sector protection. That's it."

She stared up at me from her nest of sheets, her petite form appearing that much smaller while engulfed in her fragrant blankets.

My wolf purred at the welcoming sight.

I ignored both him and the alluring scent of spiced blood oranges.

"Once Quinnlynn and Kieran are ready to return to Blood Sector, I will go with them," I added flatly. "Our interactions going forward will be minimal."

She gaped at me, a note of surprise fluttering through her mind. I didn't really understand why. I'd made my intentions clear from the beginning—I didn't want a mate, and I only wanted to stay for Kieran.

"What about my heat cycle?" she asked, the question one I hadn't anticipated.

My eyebrow inched upward. "What about it?"

"You're not going to offer to see me through it?"

"Would you like me to offer to see you through it?" I countered, fairly certain of the answer.

"No."

"Then no, I'm not going to offer my assistance. Besides, it would require me to leave Blood Sector for an extended period, which is not something I wish to do."

She slowly sat up, her blue-black hair ruffled and falling out of her ponytail. But she didn't seem to notice or care. Her focus was entirely on me. "You actually mean that."

"Yes." I didn't feel the need to elaborate. I'd been saying this to her from the beginning, but it just now seemed to be resonating with her.

"Oh." Her nose scrunched. "I..." She frowned. "But we're linked."

I lifted a shoulder. "It might be useful in some respects. You'll be able to alert me quickly if anything were to go wrong in the Sanctuary." I gave her a cursory glance as I added, "Or on one of your inventory hunts."

Because yes, I'd searched her mind for information on how she'd managed to sneak into Blood Sector without detection.

I'd since informed Cillian of her penchant for stealing resources from our quarterly blood tax collection. He was already in the process of reallocating our supply to allow for a monthly shipment to the Sanctuary.

"I fully intend to offer you my support," I told her softly. "Cillian does as well."

"For what price?" she asked warily.

"There is no price, Kyra. The Sanctuary falls under our jurisdiction, and we protect our own."

She shook her head. "We're not joining Blood Sector."

"It's not about Blood Sector. It's about Kieran. His healing magic is all over the Sanctuary right now, his power marrying Quinnlynn's to reinforce the barrier. That means this place is under his protection, which therefore makes it under mine."

"Because your loyalty is to Kieran."

"Always."

She nodded slowly. "I'm beginning to understand that."

"Good." I took a step back from her bed. "Then we have an agreement. We will stay out of each other's way, and you'll cease all this murderous plotting."

She didn't immediately reply, but I heard her thinking it all through. She was finally hearing me, which was a fucking relief.

"All right," she murmured. "I won't promise not to fantasize about your death. But I'll… I'll back off for now."

Her thoughts told me that was the best answer I was going to get from her tonight. So it would just have to do. "Brilliant. Have a good evening, Kyra."

I disappeared before she could reply, mostly because her scent was starting to drug my senses. And I really didn't want to alarm her with my hungry wolf.

He'd calm down eventually.

Maybe.

Alas, it didn't matter. Nothing would happen with Kyra. And in a few short weeks, I'd be gone anyway.

KYRA

Hmm...

The hum in my head sent a chill down my spine. It was one I knew well. One I feared. One a morbid part of me still craved.

I sense... a change... the deep voice whispered. *Another Alpha, my love? Is that what I hear you dreaming about?*

My heart skipped a beat, the question so real, so *timely*, that I could almost be convinced that this was actually happening. But I knew better. This was just another dream. A nightmare. A new way for Fare's ghost to haunt me.

Who is he? he asked softly, his words a brush against my mind. I could almost envision him sweeping those long fingers through my hair while he spoke to me in his placating tone.

It was all a lie, though.

Fare had only pretended to care. He would purr and coo and offer me tender words, just to lull me into a false sense of security. Then he would shatter my world, destroy my nest, and laugh while his friends ripped me apart in front of him.

All that blood and destruction, my safe haven demolished.

You're my toy, he would say. *My precious, pretty little toy. And I adore breaking my toys.*

My stomach churned, his voice a permanent fixture in my thoughts.

Tell me who he is, hmm? he continued now. *Tell me who has you all tied up in knots.*

I shivered, his silky tones worming their way through my subconscious and plucking at the strings of my sanity.

My nightmares had intensified over the last few weeks.

Because of Lorcan. Our bond. The *mating of convenience* I'd been forced to accept.

"Tell me what I want to know," he said against my ear, his palm wrapping around my throat. "Or do you want me to fuck it out of you?"

His bare skin felt cold against my back. Wrong. *Real.*

A chill traversed my spine as ice slithered through my veins. I could feel his knot pressing against my rump, the threat of violence lingering against the surface.

He would force me to take him. Make me enjoy it. Flood my insides with his venomous essence.

But a rebellious part of me refused to give him the name. Refused to talk about Lorcan. Because that was my secret. *My true reality.*

This is a dream.

Fare's not really here.

He's dead. I killed him.

His chuckle against my throat certainly felt real, though. It felt ominous. Like a lethal promise. *A taunt.*

"I love it when you fight me, pet," he whispered against my pulse, his words spoken aloud rather than in my head. "It makes this so much sweeter."

His fangs bit into my tender skin, shooting pain through every ounce of my being and drawing a scream from my throat.

I jolted.

And flew upward in bed, my hand against my neck.

No blood. No puncture wounds. No rose-like scents.

I shuddered as my nest came into view. My safe haven. Intact. Smelling like me.

No. Not just me. *Lorcan, too.*

It'd been that way for over a week, since we'd last spoken. Primarily because I hadn't changed my sheets. I... I liked how he'd made them smell.

Like evergreens.

I swallowed, my eyes squeezing shut as my nightmare mingled with my reality.

Fare's dead. Lorcan's my mate.

I gripped my sheets and brought them to my nose. My wolf sighed as I inhaled, the lingering Alpha scent one that comforted her more than I cared to admit.

Lorcan hadn't so much as glanced my way in the last ten days. He'd kept to himself, only occasionally offering some self-defense tips to Ashlyn and the others.

Fritz wasn't a fan.

I wasn't either, but for entirely different reasons.

My wolf didn't want to share Lorcan. It didn't matter that he wasn't really ours; she didn't understand the concept of *convenience.* She saw him as her mate.

Meanwhile, I saw him as... well, I didn't know. He wasn't my enemy. Not really, anyway. He... he was different.

Our conversation after the sparring incident played through my mind, as it often had over this last week and a half.

I still couldn't believe that he didn't intend to knot me.

What kind of Alpha doesn't take advantage of his mate's heat? I wondered.

A good Alpha, I decided.

It was an oxymoron that I hadn't known existed. *Good Alphas.* Who knew that was a thing?

Sighing, I stretched out my arms and legs and considered my surroundings again. The familiarity of my nest helped calm me to an extent, but it didn't feel like enough right now.

I need to go for a run, I determined. An afternoon with my wolf always helped chase away Fare's residual touch. Probably because he'd really only appealed to my vampire side.

My inner animal had provided the strength I'd needed to survive him. Without her... well, he'd probably still be alive today. And I would forever have remained a slave in his den.

At least until one of his friends took the game too far. I'd always been the unbreakable one, my hybrid genetics making me hard to kill.

They'd enjoyed taking me to the brink of death just to watch me heal.

Swallowing, I shoved the thoughts of the past back into their beat-up box and slid out of my nest.

I was already naked, mostly because I liked lounging in my Lorcan-scented sheets.

Because my wolf was obsessed with *her Alpha.*

I released a huff and shadowed into my favorite ice cave on the island, then lowered myself to the ground to shift.

It'd been a few weeks since my last run, which explained why my wolf practically burst out of me. She shook out her coat, then collapsed onto the ice to begin rolling around.

While I could control her movements, I chose not to. It was more fun to give her free rein.

She flopped onto her side with a content pant, then pushed to her feet and fluffed out her coat again.

Ready to run? I asked her.

She snorted in reply and darted out of the cave to begin our usual trek around the perimeter.

Except... she veered a little off course as a familiar scent tickled our senses.

My eyes widened. *Wait...*

But it was too late. The moment Lorcan's evergreen aroma settled into her snout, she took off toward him at a sprint.

Shit.

What's wrong? Lorcan immediately asked.

His asking that suggested he hadn't been actively listening to my thoughts.

Thank fuck for that. The last thing I wanted or needed was for him to be aware of my worsening nightmares. Or the fact that my animal side seemed to fancy him.

My wolf is tracking you, I muttered. *Sorry.*

He didn't reply, but I sensed his surprise.

Then he appeared in the distance in all his wolfish glory. Or I assumed it was him, as none of the other V-Clan shifters on the island were that size.

Well, except maybe Kieran.

But he was still busy with Quinn.

Giant didn't even begin to describe Lorcan's wolf form. If there'd ever been any doubt of his Alpha status, this would clear that right up.

He stood on top of an ice block, his black coat glittering in the glow provided by the setting sun.

It was the middle of the afternoon, but we barely saw any sunlight here during this time of year. So I'd rather expected my wolf to want to bask in the setting rays. But no. She was far more interested in the majestic creature standing before us.

He turned toward us as we approached, his silky coat soft and smooth. I'd seen other Alphas in wolf form while visiting Blood Sector throughout the decades, but I'd never paused to admire one. That would have been a good way to be caught trespassing.

Lorcan tilted his head to the side. *You're up early. Another bad dream?*

So much for him not knowing about my nightmares. But given how in tune he seemed to be with my mind, that didn't surprise me. At least he didn't seem to want to talk about them.

My wolf needed a run, I replied. Not that he deserved an

explanation of any kind. *Why are you up?* The question left me in an almost awkward way.

Because I already knew the answer, which meant I was making an attempt at small talk, something I did not typically do. It was a waste of time, and I didn't enjoy wasting time.

I'm checking the perimeter.

Why? I asked, voicing the question I'd pondered for weeks now. *Why do you check the perimeter? It's a protected barrier. No one can enter unless they're an Omega or an Omega's mate. I've explained this.*

I didn't mean to sound so snippy with him. It just sort of came out naturally.

Rather than reply, he trotted toward me and met my eager wolf on an ice block a little closer to sea level. She immediately butted up against him, making me cringe inside.

Sorry. I attempted to pull her back, but she growled in my head. *I usually let my wolf lead.*

He remained silent but lowered his head for my wolf and let her nuzzle his snout.

Seriously, stop, I chastised my animal.

But she was having none of that. She'd been craving this Alpha for weeks and fully intended to take advantage of this situation.

I groaned internally as she rubbed up against his side to scent off his sleek fur.

An apology formed in my mind, only to freeze as Lorcan released a low purr. My wolf practically melted in response, her snout pressing into his chest as she reveled in that hypnotic rumble.

Ugh. If I were in human form, I'd be bright red right now. Fortunately, my black coat couldn't blush.

But inside, I was pretty much on fire. For a lot of reasons. Reasons I didn't want to evaluate at all.

Do you want to join me on a perimeter sweep? Lorcan asked, his mental voice flat despite that alluring purr vibrating in his chest.

I wondered if maybe his wolf was doing it more than him. That would make me feel a little better about how my animal was now trying to firmly attach herself to his much larger form.

A perimeter sweep sounds great, I thought back at him, even though it wasn't needed at all. But it would at least give my wolf something productive to do.

Except she had other intentions.

Because she'd just flopped down to expose her tummy to the big Alpha male.

Could you be any more embarrassing? I demanded of her.

She yipped in response.

No. She yipped at *Lorcan*.

But it confirmed that, yes, she could indeed be more embarrassing.

Gods, I groaned as she wagged her tail.

Lorcan made a noise that sounded a lot like a chuckle in his mind. But it was kind of rusty in nature. So maybe it was supposed to be a snort? Or his version of a groan?

Meanwhile, his wolf purred even more and leaned down to nip at my wolf's throat.

A gesture of dominance, one I should be fighting. Yet my animal positively preened, innately trusting his beast not to hurt her.

This is pathetic, I muttered at her. *You're so much better than this.*

Lorcan licked my wolf's snout and straightened. *Let's run, little killer.*

He started off at a trot, making me narrow my gaze inside as my wolf readily followed him.

Maybe he was more in charge of his animal than I'd realized.

To answer your earlier question, I'm doing these perimeter checks because something doesn't feel right to my wolf, and I have yet to figure out what's irking him, Lorcan said as he led us toward the shore. *So*

I've started checking at different times to see if I can determine the cause of the disturbance.

My wolf caught up to his side and bumped him playfully. He bumped her right back, causing my animal to trill happily.

I just can't with you, I thought at her.

She replied with a pleading little yip and picked up the pace, wanting to really run.

Lorcan joined her easily, his powerful legs marking him as stronger. But I suspected I might be able to beat him in a sprint. I was fast. Smaller, too. Which meant I had less mass to carry, thus making me quicker.

However, my wolf didn't crave a race. She just wanted to run, not trot.

I considered his words as we reached the icy shore, my mind searching his for what *disturbance* he sensed. But he couldn't seem to define it. Just an instinct that something wasn't quite right.

Maybe it's the foreign magic? I suggested.

Perhaps, he replied. *But I can feel my cousin's energy joining Quinnlynn's. And yet, something is nagging at my wolf. Some sort of intrusion I can't seem to define.*

Frustration echoed within his mind, his annoyance palpable. He couldn't determine the cause, and it was irritating the hell out of him.

I tried to sense whatever he was picking up on as we trailed the perimeter, my wolf finally focusing on a relevant task rather than the Alpha by her side. But nothing felt off to me as we moved.

Well, nothing except that it felt different to be running along the ice with someone else in wolf form. I usually used these outings to spend some quality time alone with my wolf. But she seemed rather content with this change.

A little *too* content, actually.

Fortunately, he would be leaving soon. *Quinn's heat should break in a little over a week,* I told him. *Assuming it functions like a normal cycle, anyway.*

Most V-Clan Omegas didn't go into heat until the summer months, which was partly why our kind tended to hibernate during that time of year.

That, and we weren't big fans of sunlight. Similar to vampires, but wolfish in nature. The sun didn't really hurt either species; it was just a nuisance we tended to avoid.

It seems to be a normal cycle, Lorcan replied. *Quinnlynn's pregnant.*

I know. I'd picked up on the familiar scent a few days ago.

I've already started making arrangements with Cillian, as we're going to need a stealth jet. His wolf started to slow to a trot as we reached the area we'd started from.

Cillian won't be able to fly here. And if I had to explain why one more time, I would—

I'll be the pilot, he interjected. *But I'll need someone to give me directions. Shadowing into the Sanctuary is one thing. Navigating an aircraft here is entirely another.*

Are you asking me to help? I wondered.

Yes. He paused near the place my wolf had rubbed up against him a mere hour ago. The island wasn't that big, making it easy to circle when on four paws. *Will you accompany me to Blood Sector and back? For Quinnlynn?*

Maybe we should wait to see if she wants to go back? I suggested.

But I already knew she would. She was pregnant now, which meant she couldn't shadow, and she was exceptionally vulnerable to attack. Kieran would want her in the heart of their kingdom for protection.

With Cillian and Lorcan right by their sides, too.

Never mind, I replied, suddenly feeling very tired. *That's where she'll want to be.* And there was no point in considering an alternative.

Unfortunately, that meant I would be remaining here as the Sanctuary leader. Not that I had anywhere else to be. But it felt like I'd been in this temporary position for an eternity, lingering right on the cusp of being the island leader without actually being the queen.

That role was reserved for Quinn.

However, she'd need to take on that mantle from Blood Sector, leaving me as the primary lieutenant in her absence.

I'll go with you, I told him as my wolf leaned back into a stretch, her legs stiffening from the long run. She yawned then, showing off our collective exhaustion. It felt like forever since I'd indulged in a decent night's rest.

Just let me know when we're going, I added as my wolf turned toward our favorite cave. *I'm going to go have a nap.*

It was one of my indulgences after a run—curling up in a ball on the ice. Something about it soothed me. Perhaps because it was quiet. Secure. *Reminiscent of my old cell.*

Sometimes relics from the past could be healing. Mostly because it gave me a semblance of control to remain in the cave for as long or as little as I wanted to.

I'm free.

That was the heart of it all, a reminder of what I'd fought for and won.

It wasn't until I reached the mouth of the cave that I realized Lorcan had followed me, his wolf a silent force behind me. I hadn't really been paying attention, though. However, my wolf didn't seem all that surprised. Actually, she seemed... *welcoming.*

She didn't turn to growl at him or tell him to fuck off with her tail.

Instead, she moved into the cave to our usual spot and lay down to face the entrance.

When Lorcan entered, she shut her eyes, making me frown inside. *What are you doing?* I asked her. *This is our place, not his.*

But then his purr filled the air, right as the warmth of his larger body settled beside mine. *Just relax, Omega,* Lorcan murmured. *Try to sleep.*

With you here? No.
Tell that to your wolf, he replied softly, his purr intensifying.

Another blast of exhaustion left me momentarily speechless, my mind a little foggy as I tried to pick up the threads of our conversation. But my animal seemed to already be lulling us both to sleep.

Because of that damn purr.

Still, it was kind of nice.

Much better than... *than my nightmares.*

My wolf yawned again, then settled even more into Lorcan's side. *One nap,* I told her. *You get one nap with the Alpha. That's it, okay?*

She didn't reply.

But somehow I knew she wouldn't obey me. She never did.

Fortunately, he would be leaving soon. Then things would go back to normal. *I hope.*

LORCAN

Kyra slept soundly beside me, her mind beautifully quiet.

She would never admit it, but she needed this. A nightmare-less sleep. A moment of true peace.

Kyra had woken me up with a mental scream on multiple occasions over the last few weeks, each time dragging me into her mind where I'd silently observed her past.

The first few occurrences, I'd tried to leave, not wanting to intrude. But her terror had kept yanking me back to her, my instinct to protect flaring to the surface.

For the last week, I'd tried purring—a sound I rarely made, as it was typically only meant for mates—to help soothe her mind. It'd been subtle, but it had seemed to help a little.

Given the reception I'd received from her wolf today, I'd wager that her inner animal was fully aware of my trying to help them rest at night.

It was self-serving, too, though. Because I needed more sleep. Which was impossible to do with Kyra's fear echoing through our bond every time she fell asleep.

Her wolf stretched along mine, her adorable little muzzle digging into my fur for a deep inhale. My animal rumbled in response, content with her intruding on his space.

It was odd, as my beast usually preferred to be alone. But he seemed more than happy to indulge the little Omega.

Because he saw her as his.

It was a complication of the bond that I hadn't anticipated. Which was naïve on my part, as of course my animal would feel proprietary over the female.

My wolf didn't understand the strategy of mating her for convenience. He saw her as his. And something told me that even without the link in place, he'd still be very interested in her.

She was strong. A survivor. A leader. Beautiful. Cunning. Maybe a little troublesome. Definitely a rebel. And loyal.

So many alluring traits.

Even her stubbornness was desirable. To an extent, anyway. It gave me a challenge and I liked challenges.

Not that I was thinking about accepting this one.

Still, I couldn't resist purring for her wolf now. She'd been wronged before, and some part of me wanted to fix her broken pieces.

It was a strange reaction, one I didn't quite understand. But I stayed with her in the ice cave, soothing her the only way I knew how.

Hours passed, the moon high in the sky before she began to stir.

I shifted back into human form and lifted her into my arms, then shadowed us to her quarters to gently lay her in her nest before leaving for my own room.

A few minutes later, I heard her whisper, *Thank you.*

You're welcome, I whispered back. *Let me know if you'd like to run again tomorrow.*

I didn't expect her to reply, but a soft *Okay* hummed through her mind.

Okay, I echoed, my lips lifting into a smile. Then I shadowed to Blood Sector to give Cillian another update.

There was still something bothering me about the patrol. We needed to make plans on how to fortify the boundary.

Because while Kyra might be my mate in name only, she was still mine to protect. And protect her, I would.

KYRA

Over A Week Later

My wolf paced beneath my skin, irritated by today's change in routine.

Or perhaps she was pissed because she knew what all of this really meant—an end to our afternoon runs with Lorcan.

Because after today, he would no longer be in the Sanctuary.

The jet rumbled around us as we flew across the Greenland Sea. Or that was what it used to be called when humans ran the world. Now it didn't really have a name, as these parts were supposedly uninhabitable.

Lorcan sat silently beside me, his focus on the numerous controls and panels before him.

I'd given him the coordinates once we were in the air, trusting him not to share them with anyone other than Cillian and Kieran.

It was strange providing such sensitive information to an Alpha, but if I hadn't done it, Quinn would have. She trusted Kieran entirely, and as a result, she trusted his Elites, too.

We hadn't had much of a chance to talk since she'd come

out of her heat, mostly because she'd just begun to surface from it a few days ago.

However, she seemed happy. In love, even. So different from the Quinn I knew a century ago.

I would never have thought she'd pick Kieran O'Callaghan as a mate, but at least she'd chosen a powerful Alpha. The magic at the Sanctuary was thriving, thanks to their mating, and I'd never seen Quinn in such good health.

Because Kieran has a healing power, I thought. *As does Lorcan.*

I didn't know much about it, just the snippets I'd overheard in Lorcan's mind. He could feel Kieran's energy bolstering the barrier, something he often thought about during our afternoon runs.

And I somewhat suspected he might be using that healing energy on my nightmares, as they'd weakened over the last ten days.

Or maybe that was from our post-run naps in the cave.

Because yeah, I hadn't been able to stop those from happening.

My wolf felt different around Lorcan. *Secure.* And sleeping by him somehow miraculously cleared my head.

I hadn't slept this well in over a hundred years.

It scared me and made me that much more relieved that he would no longer be in the Sanctuary after tonight.

Because I could not afford to rely on him. He didn't want a mate and neither did I. Whatever kinship we'd developed over the last few weeks was temporary at best. We'd work together going forward, but only as required.

Such as now, on this jet.

Except there wasn't much for us to do. From what I'd gathered, this thing pretty much flew itself.

I drummed my fingers against my jean-clad thigh and stared out at the clouds. It'd been a long time since I flew on a plane. Shadowing sort of made it irrelevant. I could go anywhere I wanted in the world.

Within reason, of course.

There were a lot of sectors I would never want to visit.

Like the various vampire sectors in Greenland.

I'd grown up with V-Clan wolves for a reason. Vampires were a whole different breed of nope.

Lorcan reached for something out of the corner of my eye, causing me to glance at the flashing light that'd seized his attention.

"Yes?" he asked, breaking the silence.

I frowned, not understanding what he meant until Cillian's voice came through the speakers. "I need you to do a sweep."

Lorcan's brow furrowed. "We already did that."

"I know. I need you to do another one."

Lorcan didn't say anything, just stared at the button he'd pressed with an expectant expression.

"Kieran called. He believes one of the Blood Sector Alphas is to blame for the death of Quinnlynn's parents," Cillian added after a beat. "I've locked down the sector, but I need you to do another security check, just to be sure that it's safe to land in the Sanctuary."

Lorcan's jaw tightened, yet somehow he managed to reply, "Will do," in a flat tone.

He ended the call and looked at me for a long second.

A Blood Sector Alpha may be the one who assassinated Quinn's parents? I thought, more to myself than to Lorcan. *That's...*

I wasn't sure how to finish that sentence. I'd always assumed one of the V-Clan Alpha Princes was to blame. Because whoever had killed the MacNamaras had to be powerful. And while all Alphas maintained a certain level of strength, it was the Alpha Princes who usually possessed intense magic.

Shit.

Lorcan flipped some sort of switch—one his mind told me engaged the autopilot feature.

Without a word, we both stood and started searching the

jet. Magic had a distinct scent to it, something our wolf senses would be able to detect.

But if the culprit had used technology, then that could become a bit trickier. Lorcan seemed to know what to search for, though, so he took over that task while I used my supernatural nose to hunt for enchantments.

We worked in silence, our minds communicating our lack of findings to each other.

The jet had been thoroughly inspected before we left—both outside and inside. We could only really check the cabin now, at least physically. But I tried to expand my magic search through the walls to the exterior.

An enchantment could be anywhere, could resemble anything, which made it decidedly difficult to find.

I moved closer to the jet door, wanting to find a better way to check the ext—

Power ripped through the air, causing the world to spin violently. A curse left my lips, the jarring sensation sending me toward the ground, only for a pair of sturdy arms to catch me in midair.

I tucked my head into Lorcan's chest as the dark energy rippled through us, the potency familiar in a way I couldn't define.

What is that? I asked, shivering against him.

I don't know, he admitted, holding me closer. *Do you still feel it?*

I nodded, the hairs along my arms standing on end. *It... it feels like a hum of power against my skin.*

Lorcan didn't say anything, but I heard the conflict in his mind. He'd only felt the initial burst of power, nothing else.

Yet that creepy energy seemed to be crawling all over me, sticking to my senses and coating me in some sort of invisible essence.

Except it disappeared in a flash, making me blink. *What in the world...?* Had it all been in my mind? A weird reaction to feeling so unstable?

My brow crinkled as I leaned back to stare up at Lorcan. He still had me cradled against him, his expression emotionless as he held my gaze.

That was weird, I told him. An understatement, but I wasn't sure what else to say.

I should call Cillian, he replied, but rather than walk toward the cockpit, he brought me over to one of the couches in the belly of the jet. There were a few executive chairs there for takeoff and landing, too. As well as a bedroom at the back.

He set me on the couch and squatted to make us eye level. "Are you okay?" he asked, his voice a rasp of sound from barely speaking aloud today.

I swallowed and nodded. "I think that strange energy explosion just knocked me off-kilter for a moment." I frowned. "What was it from?"

"Something linked to V-Clan magic, I believe," he replied. "It wasn't from the jet, but from something else. Which is why I need to call Cillian and check on Blood Sector." He tucked a stray strand of hair behind my ear. "I'll put him on speaker again."

He pushed away, leaving me staring at his muscular back. I suddenly found myself wishing he was shirtless like that day I'd found him sparring.

Why did I want him in clothes, again? So I could take them off myself?

An image danced in my mind.

Then I remembered that he could hear me.

And I quickly shoved it all out of my head.

But not before I heard the lingering amusement in his own thoughts.

Ugh, it's a good thing he's leaving.

Lorcan disappeared from view while I tried to find my sense of self-worth and sanity.

Cillian isn't answering, Lorcan informed me, his stoic tone failing to reveal the concern I heard echoing in his mind.

I forced myself to get up, irritated that I'd even allowed myself to be coddled in the first place. It was just some residual energy. I was fine. I didn't need to go fainting into the big Alpha's arms.

Lorcan met me at the threshold to the cockpit, his dark eyes oddly hypnotic.

It's okay to let someone else care about you every now and then, he whispered, his palm finding my cheek. *That doesn't make you weak, Kyra. It makes you strong enough to know your limits.*

I rolled my eyes. "It was a minor explosion. I've been through a lot worse."

"I know." His thumb brushed my jaw as he took his touch away. "I meant what I said as a general statement—it's okay to ask for help, no matter how big or small. I hope you remember that after I leave."

I... I didn't know what to say to that.

It was dangerous to put my faith in Lorcan, but a tiny part of me wanted to try. And that made me want to shadow myself back to my nest and dig a hole in my blankets.

He turned away from me as a light flashed on the console again. His movements seemed a little brittle as he flicked the button.

"What's happening?" he demanded, his Alpha tone sending a shiver down my spine.

"One of the Blood Sector Alphas just tried to kill Quinnlynn with the same spell used to take out her mother." Cillian's voice held an edge to it that twisted my stomach. And the words he said didn't make it that much better.

"Is she okay?" I asked, ready to shadow to the Sanctuary to find her.

"She's a little shaken up, but she's fine," Cillian replied, his tone slightly less harsh. "Her jewelry exploded when taken through the barrier."

My eyes widened. "The MacNamara family diamonds?"

"Yes. What do you know about them?" Cillian's tone sounded inquisitive more than accusatory. Which made sense. Obviously, I wouldn't try to hurt my best friend. And even if he thought I would, Lorcan could take one peek into my mind to determine my loyalty to Quinn and the MacNamara family.

"Her mom always wore them. There are earrings and a crescent necklace. I can't remember if Quinn had them when she arrived or not. I think she did?"

"She did," Cillian confirmed. "Kieran thinks that was part of what was draining her energy before he arrived."

"That's why it seemed like the barrier was weakening her," I breathed, remembering that inkling I'd picked up on before heading to Blood Sector last month. "I'd thought it might be because she hadn't been back in a while, or that it was related to her heat, but she'd seemed weaker than usual."

"Why didn't you mention that?" Lorcan demanded, a hint of annoyance weaving through his thoughts.

"Because she's been fine since Kieran mated her," I replied, my brow furrowing. "I didn't think it was important."

That damn eyebrow inched upward, the look one I hadn't seen from him much in the last two weeks. Maybe because he'd been in wolf form more than human form, but still, I wasn't all that keen on seeing it again now.

"Not even after I told you my concerns about the barrier?" he pressed.

"I honestly didn't think about it. I was too busy trying to figure out what you were sensing." I couldn't help the exasperated note in my voice.

It wasn't like I'd withheld the information on purpose.

What did he think, that I wanted Quinn to get hurt?

Is he blaming me for not mentioning what I thought was a trivial suspicion? An inkling I'd completely forgotten about because my life had been essentially turned upside down over the last month through a coerced mating bond?

He growled low in his chest, clearly having heard that question.

Cillian cleared his throat. "Kieran suspects there was a locator charm on the diamonds, something that could provide coordinates to the Alpha who'd cast the enchantment. There were several Alphas who tried to shadow right after the explosion; I'm going to detain them all for questioning."

"Good," Lorcan replied, his growl underlining that single word.

"Does that mean the spell worked?" I asked, suddenly feeling an urge to shadow into the Sanctuary to check the barrier for myself.

"Assuming we're right, then maybe. Our other working theory is that the jewelry was meant to kill Quinn and take down the barrier with her death," Cillian said. "Maybe a combination of all of the above. But Kieran triggered the explosion by throwing it away from the Sanctuary and toward the sea. So the island is secure."

I swallowed, unsure if I believed that.

"We need to finish sweeping the jet," I muttered. "Make absolutely sure everything is fine before we land."

Lorcan's nod was clipped. "We'll call you if we find anything, Cillian."

"Likewise," he returned.

The call ended and Lorcan glanced at me, then moved around me to resume his search. Only this time, our silence didn't feel as comfortable as it had before.

We spent an hour sniffing around and searching but found nothing.

All the while, I wondered if the MacNamara diamonds were somehow linked to the deaths of Quinn's parents. Had they sensed the enchantment on the necklace or earrings? Quinn's father would have been able to shadow them out of the jet, but he wouldn't have been able to shadow back into the jet. And her mother wasn't a pilot.

Is that how they died? I wondered. *Then why did they enchant the necklace to find Quinn?*

The crescent moon had arrived in Quinn's rooms before the news of her parents' deaths actually reached her.

The necklace had contained a hidden message from her mom telling her that their deaths weren't an accident but an assassination. She'd told Quinn to find their murderer and to not trust any of the Alpha Princes. Quinn had been searching for the culprit ever since.

If they knew the necklace was tainted, why would they use that to send Quinn a message?

Something about this wasn't adding up.

"The jet is secure." Lorcan's words were not for me but for Cillian.

"I'll let Kieran know" was the reply.

I hadn't realized Lorcan had even made an outbound call, too lost in my thoughts to overhear his.

Rather than comment, I took my seat next to him in the cockpit and stared out the window as he resumed piloting the jet.

We landed thirty minutes later, the stealth jet hovering over the ice in an amazing display of futuristic technology. V-Clan wolves were known for their advanced tech. This beauty only drove that point home even more.

A set of stairs appeared at the door, allowing us to descend onto the shore outside of the barrier. Fritz met us in a fashion similar to the one upon our arrival a month ago, his expression equally as wary.

"Where's Quinn?" I asked.

"In the palace," he replied.

I nodded, then shadowed to the hallway outside of her suite and knocked on the door.

Kieran opened it, his gaze searching. "Is Lorcan with the jet?"

"Yes."

His chin dipped. "I'll give you two a moment." He disappeared in a blink, leaving me with my best friend.

She took one look at my face and threw her arms around my neck. "I'm okay," she promised. "I'm okay because of you."

"Tell that to Lorcan," I muttered before filling her in on our jet ride here. "So yeah, he thinks I withheld information. After everything we've been through, why the hell would I do that?"

Quinn twisted her lips to the side. "He's just being protective. It's what Kieran's Elites do."

"I really don't envy you," I told her.

Her smile was a little sad. "You're really not going to try to make this work with him, are you?"

"Neither of us wants a mate, Quinn. As Lorcan has said, this is just a mating of convenience." I shrugged. "Maybe it'll be useful later on."

That was what he'd implied, anyway.

If the Sanctuary needed something, I would be able to notify him quickly, which could be a good thing if anything ever went wrong.

"I once considered my mating to Kieran to be a *convenience* as well," she hedged. "You see where that got us." She placed a hand over her belly and the baby growing there.

My lips curled. "I am so happy for you, Quinn. But we both know that's not my future. I'll just have to settle on being an awesome aunt to your future little one."

It was a sentence I would have voiced a month ago with a laugh at the end, because the notion of having pups of my own had never appealed to me. Yet there seemed to be a hint of longing in my voice as I spoke the words just now, one I hadn't anticipated hearing.

Most Omegas thrived on the concept of procreation, craving motherhood and the experience of nurturing a young one. However, I'd never possessed that desire before. I'd assumed it was the result of Fare and his friends fucking it out of me.

Although, a small part of me wondered what a child with Lorcan would look like. The visual passed unexpectedly—and undesirably—through my mind, giving me momentary pause.

Then I blinked it away with a subtle shake of my head.

That's never going to happen.

"I guess we'll see," Quinn replied, her response timely with my thoughts.

We wouldn't be seeing anything, but that was a debate for another time. For now, I needed to say goodbye to my best friend.

"Call me if you need anything," I told her. "And keep me updated on the search for whatever Alpha asshat is behind all this."

"I will," she promised, giving me another hug.

I walked with her through the palace and along the grounds to where Kieran stood waiting with Lorcan. We'd both moved toward them without much thought, their auras resembling glowing moons to our inner wolves.

Except that wasn't really the case for me at all. Lorcan wasn't mine. And it was time my inner animal accepted that fact.

Kieran immediately wrapped Quinn up in a hug, his lips going to her temple before he dipped to whisper something privately into her ear. I could have tried to hear the words if I wanted to, but I really didn't. Their open display of affection was enough for me.

If there'd been any question about whether or not Quinn had chosen Kieran, it was answered now.

She was over the moon for her Alpha. And it seemed he felt the same way about his Omega.

What's that like? I wondered, a hint of melancholy touching my inner voice.

A hint of melancholy that I immediately squashed because I refused to consider it more.

I preferred being alone. In charge of my own fate. *Unattached.*

My gaze went to Lorcan, his expression bored. There was no question that he felt the same as I did.

With a nod of understanding, I returned my focus to Quinn. "Fly safe. Let me know when you've arrived."

"I will," she told me. "Love you, K."

"Love you, too, Q."

We hugged again.

Then I watched as the three of them walked through the courtyard wall, out toward the waiting jet.

Lorcan didn't say a word. Didn't think anything at me. Didn't even look or acknowledge me with a goodbye. He just disappeared, his duty to Kieran fully intact, just like he'd promised.

My wolf whined inside, aware that he was leaving.

We'll get through this, I whispered to her. *We've survived much worse...*

KYRA

My wolf was moping.

I tried to convince her to go for a run, but all she wanted to do was curl up into a ball in our ice cave and pout.

This is pathetic, I told her. *We don't crave Alphas; we kill them.*

She huffed in reply. Not that she actually understood what I was saying, just how I was feeling. Shifter dynamics were unique in that we could only really communicate basic emotions and needs with our animals, nothing more.

Therefore, my wolf didn't understand concepts, such as the fact that Lorcan wasn't truly ours, or that I didn't want this mating. To her, we were now bonded to an Alpha, and she wanted to play with said Alpha.

If you're going to just pout, then—

Kyra, Lorcan interjected, causing my wolf's head to come up with interest.

Sorry, I didn't mean to bother you with all this. My animal is being obstinate.

He didn't reply right away, like he wasn't sure what to say.

I'll try to tone down the mental thoughts, I added. *I know you all are busy interrogating Alphas.* Quinn had messaged me when they'd landed in Blood Sector, and I knew from some of Lorcan's scattered thoughts that he and the others had gone into the dungeons to start questioning some of the potential culprits.

That's... that's not why I'm reaching out, he said slowly. *I need you to help me verify something.*

Oh. My wolf sat up, her ears and nose twitching as though searching for her Alpha's scent. *What do you need?*

Myon is saying that Kiana MacNamara's necklace was bespelled with a tracker for her safety, and he thinks the charm malfunctioned since it was designed for her and not Quinnlynn.

Uh, okay... I wasn't sure I believed that, and from the sound of Lorcan's voice, he didn't seem to believe it either.

He's also saying that the MacNamaras weren't actually killed, that they added another charm to the necklace to send that warning to Quinnlynn. They did it to keep her from taking a mate too early.

Who are they? I asked.

Seamus MacNamara's Elites, Lorcan replied. *Apparently, Fritz is one of them.*

Fritz? I repeated, standing now.

Yes. And according to Myon, the fabricated story about Quinnlynn's parents was Fritz's idea.

I shifted back into my human form and shadowed to my nest to grab some clothes. *That's one hell of an accusation.*

I agree.

Fritz has been a Protector in the Sanctuary for longer than I've been alive, I told him as I pulled on a pair of jeans and a sweater. *He was close to Seamus, but he wasn't an Elite, as the Elites have never been allowed on the island. Until you, anyway.*

He's now saying he has the black box, which can prove that the plane exploded due to engine failure, Lorcan added. *It all seems very convenient.*

Too convenient, I agreed, disliking that term despite its appropriateness for the conversation. *I'm going to find Fritz.*

Thank you.

I shadowed to Fritz's floor and knocked on his closed door. He'd always favored privacy, and I respected that. But right now, I wanted answers. So I knocked again before he could answer.

His blond hair was mussed with sleep as he opened the door, his blue eyes unfocused. "Fuck, Kyra. I was having a really good dream. This had better be important."

"Are you one of Seamus's Elites?" I demanded.

His gaze instantly focused, his look confirming my question without needing a response.

So I plunged right in. "Did you enchant the diamond necklace to deliver a fake message from Kiana to her daughter? About how an Alpha had killed them?"

He grimaced. "Myon's been talking, has he?"

"That means it's true? All of this has been one royally fucked-up lie?"

"A necessary one," he corrected softly. "We needed a way to give Quinn time to find the right mate."

"By sending her on a dangerous chase around the world for a killer that didn't even fucking exist? During a global pandemic?"

"The Infection didn't exist when we came up with the plan," he argued. "That... complicated things. And by then, she was already in hiding."

"This is un-fucking-believable." It also seemed implausible. Too ornate. Too *bizarre*.

He confirmed the story, I told Lorcan. *But something doesn't feel right about it.*

"Why didn't you trust Quinn to make her own choices? She wouldn't have rushed into a relationship. You know that."

"The Alpha Princes were all focused on mating Quinn for power. She couldn't trust any of them."

"And again, you didn't trust her to make that decision for herself? So you concocted a mystery for her to solve instead?" This wasn't like the Fritz I knew. He was all about Omega empowerment. "What kind of asinine misogynistic bullshit is this?"

He had the good grace to flinch. "Kyra—"

I held up my hand. "Yeah, no. We're not having this conversation right now. I'm going to let Quinn deal with you instead. Pregnant or not, she can still kick your ass."

Okay, maybe not really. Fritz had a good foot on each of us, and he was a weapons expert. He was also ancient.

But Quinn would have anger on her side. As she should. Because wow. *Wow.*

Fritz tried to say something else, but I shadowed back to my nest and locked my door. *This is insane. What the hell was he thinking?*

To let that ruse play on for over a century? Hell, to create it to begin with?

It wasn't Fritz.

It... it was like someone else had taken control of Fritz and given him this ridiculous idea. One that made absolutely no sense.

This can't be right. It's too simple and too out of character. Besides, Fritz can't enchant objects. Although, maybe he can. Maybe I just don't know him at all. I mean, it's not like we haven't spent the last century together or anything.

Myon said Fritz told him to create the enchantment, so Myon was the one with the ability, not Fritz, Lorcan murmured.

I hadn't really been talking to him so much as myself, but I didn't mind his interjection. Maybe he could make this make sense.

That still doesn't make this any more believable for me. Fritz is the last person I can think of that would take an Omega's right to choose away from her. Yet that's exactly what he did.

Lorcan didn't reply this time, but I heard him puzzling through everything Myon had just revealed to Kieran, as well as everything he'd picked up from my mind during my brief conversation with Fritz.

It's too easy, I said after a beat. *Too... contrived?*

Such as Fritz's immediate admission.

He didn't even try to explain himself. Not really, anyway. He'd just admitted to what he'd done, had given some half-hearted excuse about having to protect Quinn from the power-hungry Alpha Princes, and seemed mostly unapologetic.

Actually, that wasn't true. There had been a hint of guilt in his flinches and features, yet his words... those hadn't matched his actions.

I ran my fingers through my hair and frowned at my reflection in the mirror.

I really need a shower. My blue-black strands were all knotted from my shifting and hustling to talk to Fritz. *No. A bath,* I decided, spying the large fixture in my bathroom. *With jets.*

I wandered over to turn it on and waited for the hot water to flow. Magic enabled a lot of things on the island, constant heat being one of them. Using enchantments allowed it to be environmentally friendly, too. Win-win.

I grabbed some evergreen-scented salt—a recent item I'd acquired through a trade with one of the Omegas. My wolf approved even while I acknowledged it'd been a sign of weakness to pick this specific fragrance.

Whatever.

I was allowed to like this particular aroma. It didn't matter that it also happened to match Lorcan's natural cologne.

Steam started to billow around me as the tub began to fill. I dumped a conservative amount of salt in, not wanting to use up my stash too quickly. These types of indulgences were hard to find now that the human world had gone to shit.

There's one thing I don't understand. Lorcan's voice in my head caused me to freeze.

About...? I asked, worried that he was going to ask me to justify my bathtub salt preferences or something else related to my current task.

Or perhaps even comment on my moping wolf and how much she seemed to miss him despite it only being hours since he'd left.

Myon is saying the location enchantment must have malfunctioned, that it was attacking Quinnlynn because it wasn't actually made for her. He thinks that's why it exploded. But if he added that message charm to it, then wouldn't he have also reconfigured the enchantment to accept Quinnlynn...?

I frowned, my gaze on the pooling water. *I agree. Why add one spell without fixing the other? Unless he didn't notice?*

That seems too careless.

Just like all this seems too contrived? I countered.

Yes. As you said, it's too easy.

I nodded. *Then we're missing something.*

Yes, he repeated. *The question is, what are we missing?*

Have you talked to Kieran about it? I wondered.

No. Not yet.

What about Cillian?

He's a telepath. He's aware of my misgivings.

My lips twisted downward a little. *Does that mean he can... hear us?*

No. Our link is just our own.

The fact that he answered so quickly told me he'd already asked Cillian that question. The response made me feel oddly relieved. I didn't like the idea of anyone else knowing about our chats. They were... ours. Private. *Intimate.*

I'm going to do some digging here, Lorcan added. *See if I can't find out what's really going on. Or find proof that he's telling the truth.*

What about the black box? I asked, recalling what he'd said a bit ago about Myon having it in his possession.

Cillian is going to watch it. And while it might reveal that their plane did in fact go down due to engine failure, my intuition is firing.

Like it did with the barrier, I replied.

Like it did with the barrier, he repeated. *Was it still setting off your instincts like that when you left?*

Yes.

Oh. That... bothered me a bit. He knew something might not be right, yet he'd left anyway. Because his loyalty was to Kieran, not to the Sanctuary. And definitely not to me.

Kyra.

I turned off the water as it neared the rim. *I'm about to take a bath. You might want to leave my head now,* I told him as I yanked my sweater off.

That sounds more like an invitation to stay, he whispered back, his slightly flirtatious words surprising me.

My fingers paused on the button of my jeans, my wolf rising to the surface with renewed interest.

Enjoy your bath, mate, he added, his voice soft. *I'll check back in if I learn anything more. Please do the same.*

My throat bobbed as I nodded. Not that he could see me. *Okay,* I finally managed back to him.

Alas, his silence told me he'd already left. Or perhaps he was just hiding. We couldn't exactly turn off our link, but we could distract ourselves from it.

I removed my pants and slid into the tub, my mind rolling back to everything with Fritz and Quinn. I'd have to try talking to Fritz again later, perhaps with a clearer head, and see if I could read between the lines of his responses.

I refused to accept his answers. Mostly because it would mean I'd misjudged him for well over a century. Since the day we'd met. He was one of my best friends. Just like Quinn. But to trick her into believing her parents were murdered, just to stop her from taking a mate? That... was inexcusable.

And so not Fritz, I thought again.

I slid under the water, an instinct to scream ripping through me.

It'd been a long day.

Make that a long fucking month.

A long, messed-up life, I thought flatly and shook my head, causing water to splash everywhere.

When I finally came up for air, it was to the scent of evergreens clouding my nostrils, the aroma instantly relaxing me.

At least until a faint whiff of blood taunted my senses.

Old blood.

Like rusted iron. I frowned. *That's strange.*

Maybe I'd left some blood out somewhere. Except I could swear it was accompanied by the distinct smell of dying roses.

I flinched as old memories threatened to engulf my mind. *Black roses, dried out and dead on my pillow. Splattered with blood. His blood.*

I gagged, the odor so powerful I thought it was real.

But it couldn't be.

He's dead, I told myself. *He's fucking dead.*

And I really needed to stop letting his memory haunt me.

I leaned as close to the water as I could without inhaling it and took a deep, calming breath. *Evergreens. Safety. Warm.*

My eyes fell closed, the sense of calmness rolling over me as I recalled Lorcan's distinct purr. I'd heard it every time we'd entered the ice cave, the rumble one I'd never forget.

It was so loud in my mind, almost as though he were purring for me even now.

My Alpha, my wolf seemed to say. *My protector.*

I let her think what she wanted, not bothering to correct her this time. Because I much preferred this innocent obsession over the darkness of my past.

Evergreens instead of dead roses.

Purrs instead of blood.

An Alpha protector instead of an Alpha aggressor.

Leaning back in the tub, I finally turned on the jets. Then I let the salts chase away the lingering stench of rotting flowers.

Tomorrow, I'll talk to Fritz again.

And tomorrow, I'll go for another run. Alone. With no time spent in the cave.

NIGHT SECTOR

My wolf and I had to forget these last few weeks.
And the only way to do that would be to move forward.
The past couldn't be my present. No matter how hard it often tried. *I'm alive. I'm free. And no Alpha will ever own me again. Not even a potentially good one.*

LORCAN

A Few Days Later

"It's too easy," I muttered, the words ones Kyra had said just the other day. "We're missing something."

Cillian stood beside me in a tux, his gaze on the crowd in the ballroom.

It was coronation night in Blood Sector, marking Kieran and Quinnlynn as King and Queen of all V-Clan kind.

They'd just finished their task of greeting Alpha Princes from the various V-Clan Sectors. And now they were off to celebrate their bond, leaving everyone else to party in their wake.

I'd shadowed over to Cillian after he'd successfully chased off Ivana with a few words about finding another dance partner. She'd obliged him for now, but I fully expected her to return.

Would Kyra have wanted to dance if she were here? I wondered.

Then I smirked inside as I realized she'd sooner kick me in the balls than waltz around the floor in an elegant dress. Fighting was her form of dancing. I highly doubted she'd ever enjoy ballroom routines or fancy steps.

That was fine by me. I much preferred sparring, too.

Not that she was here to spar with. Nor would she ever be here.

Yet I couldn't seem to stop imagining her here.

I blamed my wolf. He missed our afternoon runs.

Fucking mating link, I thought, palming the back of my neck. It was messing with my head. As was my lack of sleep. Kyra's nightmares had gotten worse, causing me to wake up often to her mental screams.

I purred into her mind just long enough to pull her out of it, then I'd retreat and listen as she analyzed her dreams.

She blamed me and our *forced* bond. She thought that was the cause of her worsening nightmares. From what I'd gathered, her version of Alpha Fare kept demanding that she talk about her new mate. Yet, true to form, she refused every time. Which had evolved now into torture sessions, ones her mind seemed to be pulling from her past to mingle with the present.

"Have you heard a word I've said?" Cillian demanded suddenly, startling me.

Because no, I hadn't realized he was talking. Hell, I'd forgotten he was even here.

"That Omega is deep inside your head," Cillian mused, his expression knowing. "Maybe you should just let your wolf knot her, see if that helps cure you of the distraction."

I snorted. Two could play this game. "Are you projecting, Cillian? Is your wolf craving a certain *distraction?*"

Because I'd seen the way he'd been looking at Ivana before I'd approached. It wasn't with distaste. Quite the opposite, in fact.

Which was why he'd convinced her to go dance with another Alpha. He didn't want to crave her. But he did. And he hated that he did.

I'd always found it amusing before, never quite understanding why he didn't just knot her out of his system.

But now I understood.

One or two times wouldn't be enough. If anything, it would only deepen the desire. And that would be an even worse distraction.

"I don't *crave* Ivana or anyone else," he replied flatly. "It's just hard to ignore such a determined Omega, even if she's playing in the wrong league."

I snorted. Cillian meant that Ivana was too good for him, that she should be trying to find a mate more worthy of her affections. Mostly because he was married to his job first and had no intention of ever changing.

I felt the same.

Or... I used to, anyway. My devotion to Kieran and Blood Sector had always been absolute. It still was. Except, lately I found myself worrying more about Kyra and the Sanctuary.

Are they safe?

Has that weird disturbance made itself known yet?

Should I be there instead of here?

"She really needs to start looking for a more appropriate mate, someone who won't mind her misguided penchant for telling Alphas what to do."

My lips twitched. "I think she enjoys irritating you."

"Yes, and that's precisely the problem. She needs to find someone better suited for her childish games. Someone who will actually appreciate her unsavory qualities, such as her boldness and her misplaced confidence."

I gave him a look. *Who are you trying to convince here? Me or you?* I asked, switching to a mental conversation to save my voice.

Fuck off, he groused back. "My point is, I'm not the one hung up on an Omega, mate. I just happen to have one who is annoyingly persistent. *You* have one consuming your focus. Those are very different situations."

"If you say so," I drawled. But my mind instantly returned to Kyra, just to check and make sure she was okay.

"You fed me information about Kieran, knowing I would recommend him to Quinn," she was saying. "That's betrayal, Fritz."

I couldn't see the Omega male in her thoughts but overheard her analysis of his facial expression.

Playful Omega was her chosen description.

Fritz's voice then echoed in her mind, their conversation flowing as though I were right there with them.

"Some would call that accurate matchmaking," he told her.

"Yeah?" she replied. "And what about that bullshit murder story you concocted? What do you call that?"

That appeared to strike a nerve, or so she deduced via his clenching jaw.

It seemed she was trying to analyze both his mannerisms and his words, just to see if they matched. Mostly because she was still convinced that there was something odd about his behavior. She was adamant that he would never do what he'd done to Quinn; his decisions didn't make sense to her at all.

"*A necessary trial*" was his succinct response.

"*A trial for what?*" she demanded.

He's running his fingers through his hair, she noted. *A nervous tell. Or an exasperated one.*

"We both know Alphas can be evil, Kyra. I was trying to steer her away from the mating games by making her wary of them all."

"While also driving her toward Kieran," she pointed out.

"Because I knew he was good for her."

"And all the others were bad for her?"

"Some of them are," he hedged, his cagey response making Kyra wonder what he was hiding from her. "But Kieran was meant to be hers. They're perfect together."

"Okay, Mister Matchmaker," she drawled, unimpressed by his finagling.

"You and Lorcan are pretty good together, too," he added, making her give him one of her infamous glares.

"Are you trying to convince me to kill you? Because I gotta tell you,

Fritz, I'm already halfway there. You might not want to push me much further over that line, or I'm liable to put a blade in your heart."

He apparently grinned at that. *"Flirt."*

A nostalgic sensation trickled through her thoughts, her admiration for the male Omega palpable. Yet, aloud, she snapped, *"Get the fuck out of my room, Fritz."*

But he didn't immediately leave. The moment seemed to sober between them, and Kyra's exhaustion became that much more palpable.

"Do you think she'll ever forgive me?" Fritz asked her softly, his question hurting her heart.

"Honestly? I don't know," Kyra replied. She'd talked to Quinn before the coronation tonight, their conversation brief. Quinn didn't blame Kyra for what had happened, but my mate felt guilty nonetheless.

I should have seen signs of the truth, I kept hearing her say to herself. *Some sort of inclination that none of it was real. Assuming that's even true, anyway.*

Her frustration concerned my wolf, making him want to shadow back to her that much more and offer her support in the form of his purr.

But neither of us could allow our wolves to further their bond. Otherwise, we might do something even more irreversible than what we'd already done.

"I can't really blame her," Fritz told Kyra. *"But I did it to protect her."*

"Sometimes we don't need others to protect us, Fritz. We have to learn how to protect ourselves."

Her reply resonated in my mind, her words that of a warrior who had survived so much pain in life yet found ways to continue forward.

Although, her mind told me she thought that statement sounded like something Quinnlynn would say, not her. I disagreed. That sentiment was all Kyra.

"I'm starting to realize how true that is," Fritz admitted before disappearing.

Kyra sighed, the sound heavy and sad.

It had my wolf pacing inside me, demanding that we go to her.

But I held us captive in Blood Sector, forcing my feet to remain on the ballroom floor as I watched all of our guests celebrate the new King and Queen.

Quinnlynn had asked Kyra to come, but Kyra hadn't felt right about it. She'd said the Sanctuary needed her.

It'd been an excuse to avoid me.

And also a way to avoid her guilt over everything with Quinnlynn.

Kyra was hell-bent on fixing things by getting to the bottom of Fritz's secrets. But so far, she hadn't had much luck in deciphering his motives.

I hadn't had much luck here with Myon either. It didn't help matters that Cillian believed him. He could sense the truth of his thoughts, which made it difficult to find a starting point for my search. Everything wasn't adding up.

And still... it felt too easy, just like Kyra had said, and just like I'd said to Cillian.

I glanced at him, ready to reignite the conversation, but I found his gaze on a white-haired female near the doors.

Ivana.

She had her head down, her submission uncharacteristic of her.

Sure, she was an Omega, but she usually faced the world by meeting everyone's gaze without a hint of shyness. It was that boldness that allowed her to constantly approach Cillian. Most Omegas tittered and blushed around him. But not Ivana. She always stared straight at him as she made her demands.

Her shoulders hunched a little, then straightened as she took a fortifying breath.

Did an Alpha spook her? I wondered. *Who did you send her off to dance with?*

No one in particular. I just told her to find someone else to ask, as I'm not here to celebrate. I'm working.

Do you think someone rejected her?

If they did, I'll kill them.

I gave him a look. *Technically, you rejected her. You reject her all the time. Are you going to punish yourself?*

That's different and you know it.

But does she know it? I asked him.

He sighed, his gaze tracking Ivana's every movement. Then he frowned as she shadowed out of the room. *I'll be back.*

My lips twitched as he disappeared.

And he accused me of having a distraction.

Which, of course, I did, because said distraction was lying in bed and dreading her nightmares to come.

Kyra? I whispered.

What? she snapped back, her mental tone clearly annoyed.

I knew what she was doing. This was similar to how I'd heard her react to Fritz a bit ago. Kyra didn't like to rely on others. She only wanted to rely on herself, which was how I knew she wouldn't let me soothe her right now, even though she needed it.

I sensed unease.

I'm fine, she lied.

All right. Good night.

I didn't try to push her because I knew that wouldn't do either of us any good. Kyra had survived by taking care of herself and never relying on anyone else.

Which was why I denied my wolf's desire to go to her. She wanted to handle this on her own, and I wasn't going to force her to accept my comfort.

She would call me if she needed me.

And when she did, I would go to her.

Of that I had no doubt.

KYRA

You'll give me his name, a silky voice breathed into my mind. *Soon, too.*

I clenched my teeth, refusing to give in to this nightmare, refusing to give in to *him*.

But each occurrence felt more and more real. Like now, the frigid presence beside me seemed far too permanent. Far too *present*.

And no matter what I did, he wouldn't go away.

There was no purring in my head. No V-Clan Alpha checking in or lingering in my mind. Just me and my thoughts and *Fare*.

He chuckled, the sound ominous and cruel and reminiscent of hundreds of nights spent alone in the dark. Huddled. Shivering. *Crying.*

I'm not that Omega anymore, I vowed. *I'm stronger now. I'm free.*

Are you? Fare whispered into my mind. *Because I think you've always been mine. That you still* are *mine. Not his. Whoever he is.*

I swallowed, my eyes squinting shut. *Wake up,* I demanded.

Yes, wake up, Fare taunted. *Please. I would love for you to greet me properly. It's been so long…*

I reached for my lamp, desperate to pull myself from the darkness, to yank myself out of this nightmare. But all I found was a cold, hard object beside me.

Impossibly big.

Sturdy.

Male.

Vampire Alpha.

Fare.

This isn't real. It's a dream. I'll wake up soon.

But the air swirled around me, the Sanctuary a tangible presence.

It's my mind playing tricks on me, I told myself. *You're fine. There's no one here.*

Except my hand was still against that cold, unmoving object. And it certainly felt fucking real.

As did Fare's fingers as he brushed my hair from my face.

And his lips that he pressed to my ear in a falsely tender kiss.

The hairs along my arms danced in response to his nearness, his familiarity, his *presence. Not real. Not real. Not real.*

"Hello, pet," he greeted, his voice silky and lacking the typical gravel of my nightmares. "I think it's time for you to come home, hmm?"

My eyes flew open, the room around me light with bright color.

My nest, I breathed, my palm landing against my sweat-soaked shirt. *Thank fuck.*

Except on my pillow, right beside my head, was a wilted black flower.

And next to it was a note written in blood that read, *Let's play...*

I sat bolt upright.

The scent of blood lingered in the air, stronger than ever, and inky petals decorated my floor.

No. My heart skipped several beats. *No, no, no.* That wasn't fucking possible. This… I… I had to still be dreaming. Another twisted nightmare blending my past with reality.

"I'd nearly forgotten how appetizing your fear can be, pet." The words danced ominously around my room, whispering against my ears while the source of them remained hidden. "Dreamwalking just hasn't been satisfying enough."

Fare materialized before me, his red eyes glittering like a raging fire.

"No," I breathed. "This isn't real."

His cruel mouth twisted into a smile. The kind of smile that could easily seduce an unknowing victim for the night.

But I knew that smile.

I knew *him*.

And while he might wear a gorgeous face, he was positively ugly inside. Evil incarnate.

Dead.

"This isn't possible," I told myself more than him. "I killed you."

This is just a super creepy, horribly realistic dream.

"I've always considered you an intelligent pet," he murmured. "But it's rather unwise to open old wounds so soon after being reacquainted with a lover." He took a step closer to my bed. "It could incite feelings of anger. The need for retribution. A desire to *return the favor*."

He lifted his hand to my face to draw one cold finger across my cheekbone, the touch making my teeth chatter uncomfortably.

"I would much rather celebrate this reunion," he cooed. "After all, I've worked so hard to achieve it. All those years lying in wait. Such an intricate game to play, and it took far longer than I'd ever anticipated. But you'll make it up to me, won't you?"

His touch moved to my neck, his fingers reminding me of a snake as they slowly curled around my throat and squeezed.

I was frozen. Immobile. Lost in time.

This isn't real, I kept thinking. Except it sounded more like a hopeful plea than a confident statement.

"Oh, who am I kidding? Of course you'll make it up to me." His grip tightened even more, cutting off my ability to breathe. "It's that or lose your head, which would be such a waste."

He released me to run his fingers through my hair, his touch gentle once more. But I could still feel the burn left behind against my throat.

And it hurt more than any dream I'd ever had, telling me... confirming... *Oh, Gods... it's real...*

"You're too pretty to kill," he mused. "Too delicious to drain." Those ruby orbs danced over me. "Mmm, where do I want to begin? A bite on the neck is too romantic. The pussy would be too intimate." His gaze returned to mine. "We're on a bit of a time crunch."

He tugged at my shirt, his fingernails sharp.

The fabric seemed to part beneath his command, my body still rigid with terror.

No. It was more than that. I was terrified, yes, but I also hadn't even thought to move. To shadow. To run. To *fight*.

He's compelled me to obey, I realized, the horror of my situation deepening with each passing second.

In my nightmares, I always fought back because I could. Because I had some semblance of control.

But now... now I didn't.

Because he was here. In the Sanctuary. *In my nest.*

"Your breast would be perfect," he murmured, his pupils dilating with hunger. "Just a quick—"

An alarm split through the air, the sound sending both dread and adrenaline through my veins. *The Omegas know he's here.*

Someone must have scented him. Now they were alerting the others. Grouping together to fight.

NIGHT SECTOR

I had no idea how Fare had managed to get in here, let alone *survive*, but maybe—

Screams pierced the air, causing all the hairs along my arms to stand on end.

Because hungry growls followed those screams.

My eyes widened as Fare's mouth twisted into another grin.

He's not the only Alpha here, I realized. *But that... that's not... that's not possible.*

"I told them to wait thirty minutes. I should have known they wouldn't obey," he said with a sigh. "I guess our reunion bite will need to wait." He held out a hand. "Time to go home, pet."

Home.

Greenland.

To Fare's nest.

I tried to shake my head, to refuse him, but instead I watched my arm move as though tied to a string.

No! I shouted at myself. *Don't do this!*

Alpha Fare's eyes gleamed with triumph. "Everyone is going to be so pleased to see you, my love. We'll need to throw a party. You can provide dessert."

Ice shot through my heart, causing my wolf to growl inside. She'd been pacing endlessly, feeling hopeless.

But hearing him talk about his *friends* and what he had planned... it did something to her. It made her stand up in protest.

She was no longer a docile creature tamed by my vampire half. She had claws, and she wasn't afraid to use them.

Except she didn't demand that I shift. She demanded that I *howl.* Not out loud, but inside my mind.

To her mate.

To the other Alpha tied to my soul.

To *Lorcan.*

Fare grabbed my hand as the haunting sound roared from my mind, my wolf bellowing at the top of her lungs as my nest began to disappear around us.

Just as the world morphed from light to dark, I heard a responding growl deep in my soul.

And it sounded a lot like Lorcan saying, *Kyra...*

LORCAN

A Few Seconds Earlier

An ear-piercing howl yanked me out of my slumber, causing me to shoot upward in bed.

My wolf growled, furious and agitated. And it only took me a few seconds to understand why.

Kyra…

The howl had come from *Kyra*.

I rolled off my mattress, my fingers going to my hair as I paced my den.

Is she having another nightmare? I wondered, my mind instantly connecting to hers.

Except… except there was nothing there. No sound. No feeling. No… anything.

I frowned. *Is she in a deep sleep?*

No. No, that couldn't be it. Kyra never slept soundlessly.

Something's wrong. Something's very fucking wrong.

Cillian! I shouted in the next second. *Something's wrong at the Sanctuary. Get Kieran and tell him to meet me there. Right fucking now.*

I didn't wait for him to confirm, my wolf demanding that I shadow.

Kyra's nest materialized around me, the stench of terror immediately suffocating my senses.

Kyra! I shouted via our bond, my nose twitching as I tried to track her scent. But a nostril full of decaying roses hit me first.

There were black petals scattered all over the floor and a wilted rose on her pillow. I snatched up the note beside it, reading the blood-soaked words through narrowed eyes.

Let's play...

"What the fuck?" I sniffed the note. *Vampire Alpha.*

My hackles rose as screams penetrated my momentary confusion.

Omega screams.

Followed by Alpha growls.

I shadowed into the hallway outside of Kyra's nest. Her scent lingered here, but it was too faint to have been recent.

Where are you? I demanded, my wolf dragging me forward to search for her.

But all I could hear was the violence erupting throughout the Sanctuary.

Are you fighting Alphas? I wondered at Kyra.

Her mind remained silent. Unreachable. *Gone.*

Yet I could still feel her through our link, that tether between souls promising me that she was alive.

I'll find you, I vowed as I stalked forward.

The distinct aroma of blood, Alpha aggression, and fear littered the air, causing my inner beast to snarl with rage.

Somehow, the barrier had failed. I could sense at least five Alphas nearby.

No, six.

Make that seven, I thought as I neared Fritz's staircase.

I shadowed into the hallway to find a Vampire Alpha deep in the throes of a rut, his fangs in the unconscious Omega's neck as he pounded into him from behind.

My magic ignited as I wrapped a telekinetic rope around

the vampire's neck and *squeezed*. His resulting roar came out strangled, then disappeared as I ripped his head from his body without even touching him. Then I used another strand to shove him off of Fritz and darted forward to catch the drained Omega before he could collapse to the floor.

Fuck. He was barely alive, his body covered in sprouting bruises, broken bones, and hungry vampire stench.

I lifted him into my arms and took him back to his nest to lay him in his bed, which didn't appear to be soiled at all. He'd been pinned to a desk in the other room near his security monitors.

My healing power snapped to life as I poured as much of my essence into him as I could while chaos continued to rock the Sanctuary.

This was Kieran's skill set, not mine.

Closing my eyes, I focused on the three Alphas closest to me and attempted to telekinetically leash them.

They didn't even resist, too lost to their tasks to notice my tightening nooses around their necks. I yanked on them, holding them hostage and only then felt them react.

Feral snarls followed, the sound echoing through the Sanctuary with ominous intent.

I resecured my hold in response, then went after the other three Alphas. They were harder to control, mostly because I was stretching my talents.

One Alpha against six.

Hardly a fair fight.

For them, anyway.

Dividing my focus between two abilities strained my efforts, though, causing sweat to pebble across my brow. But I just had to give the Omegas a fighting chance, a way to subdue these bastards before they destroyed the Sanctuary.

Because I could taste their rutting intent. Their desires to pillage. Their need to mount and fuck every Omega until they'd had their fill.

These weren't tame Vampire Alphas.

They were starving. Angry. *Savage.*

Most vampires could be cruel, but this was on a different level, their auras boasting a distinct hint of insanity.

Where the fuck did they come from? How the hell did they get through the barrier?

A roar ripped through the night.

My wolf stood up and took notice.

Kieran.

I responded to him with a howl of my own, alerting him to my whereabouts. Not that he needed it. He would find me instinctively.

But first, he had an island full of intruders to slaughter.

I felt him take down the first in a handful of seconds, my invisible hold snapping as the Alpha went down.

Two more shattered in the next instant, Kieran making quick work of the vampires.

They were too far gone to their rut, too distracted by sweet Omega scents, too *mad* with lust, to pose much of a threat. If it were one Omega they were devouring, they would have grouped together to defend their prey and mark their territory. But there were too many options here for them to pick a single source to guard.

They were overwhelmed by their thirst, giving Kieran the upper hand.

Of course, it helped that I had them all tethered for him, too.

There would be no mercy. Only death.

And the sweet scent that brought to my nostrils had me grinning in response. *Victory.* Except spilled Omega blood taunted my senses with my next inhale, telling me that several of them had been injured.

Including the still unconscious Omega beneath my palms.

His breaths came a little easier now, but he was nowhere near repaired enough to wake up.

Fritz must have been caught off guard. He excelled in enchanting weapons, of which he had many stashed around his nest and his work area. I could sense them even now. Yet not one of them seemed to have been used, suggesting he'd been subdued before he could even put up a fight.

My wrist buzzed, followed by a screen with Cillian's name on it.

"Answer," I told my watch.

The screen morphed into Cillian's face, his expression furious. Kieran joined him in a flash, the call connecting all three of us.

"Six Vampire Alphas," Kieran summarized, his tone matching Cillian's expression.

"Seven," I corrected. "I killed one right before you arrived."

"How the fuck did they get through the barrier?" Cillian demanded. "Is it down?"

"It's not down," Kieran replied, his tone gentling as his focus shifted to something beside him. "Shh, you're safe, little one," he added in a murmur, his purr lightly rolling to life.

This was one of the few situations where an Alpha might purr for an Omega who wasn't his mate.

"How many injuries?" I asked gruffly. "Because I have an Omega—*Fritz*—in bad shape up here. He's requiring a lot of healing power."

"I can handle the others." Kieran maintained his soft voice, but I could see the fury burning in his gaze.

"He's right here," Cillian said suddenly.

Then Quinnlynn's face appeared beside him on the screen. "Where's Kyra?" she asked, her voice holding a note of fear. "And did I just hear you say Fritz is hurt?"

My jaw tightened. "I don't know where Kyra is. She's..." I wasn't sure how to finish that statement. *Unresponsive? Mentally cut off from me? Busy?* "Have you seen her, Kieran?"

"No," he answered, his focus still away from the screen.

"But I'll ask the Omegas where she is." He appeared to be kneeling now, the screen showcasing a bloodbath behind him. I hoped like hell that was mostly vampire blood, but I suspected it belonged to at least one Omega, too.

"Fritz?" Quinnlynn choked out, reminding me that she'd also asked about him. "Is he...?"

"He's going to be okay," I told her, wincing as he tugged on more of my energy to heal. *It's Kyra I'm worried about*, I added to myself. *Where the fuck are you, little killer? And why was your nest covered in dead roses?*

She often thought about that scent in her dreams, her mind linking it to Alpha Fare.

But he's dead, I thought, frowning. *She killed him.*

Unless...

My lips curled down even more.

What if she only thought he was dead?

Vampires were notoriously hard to kill. Severing their heads was one way to do it, but the oldest ones, the most powerful ones, could regenerate.

"Did Kyra burn Alpha Fare's remains?" I asked, cutting off whatever Cillian had just been asking.

Everyone stared at me.

"Quinnlynn. Did Kyra burn Alpha Fare's remains after she killed him?" I repeated, adding just a little more to my question.

"I..." She blinked. "I don't know. I just know she beheaded him."

Shit. I'd never thought to ask, as I'd just assumed she knew for sure he was dead.

But now her nightmares took on a new meaning.

What if they weren't just relics of her past? What if the vampire had been dreamwalking? It was a rare trait, but vampire skills varied across bloodlines. Some could teleport. Some couldn't. Some could compel their victims. Others couldn't.

And some could dreamwalk.

"*Fuck*," I muttered, picking up Fritz. "I need to check the security feeds."

Because if I was right, then Kyra wasn't in the Sanctuary at all.

She'd been taken.

Which would explain why I couldn't hear her now.

Because an ancient vampire was blocking our ability to communicate.

An ancient vampire Kyra had thought was dead.

An ancient vampire who was likely hell-bent on revenge.

An ancient vampire who has taken my Omega mate…

KYRA

"Spread your legs, Omega." The deep tone compelled me to comply, my limbs parting against my will.

Just like I'd stripped when he'd told me to.

Climbed into this bed on his command.

Lain down because he'd whispered the words.

Everything I'd done since arriving here had been a result of coercion. I had no choice. No free will. No ability to fight back.

He'd suffocated my senses so entirely that I almost couldn't even focus on my surroundings. I knew I was in a bedroom. I knew it was dark.

And I knew we weren't in Greenland, which was home to most of vampire kind.

But it was too hot here to be Greenland. Too humid. Too salty.

So where did he take me? I wondered.

Only for the thought to be immediately replaced with, *I like it here.*

No. I hate *it here,* I snapped back at myself. *I don't want to be here at all!*

You love it here, a part of me cooed back. The part of me

that had been *compelled* to behave. To *like* whatever Fare had planned.

Inside, my wolf screamed in protest.

Yet on the outside, I remained stoic.

I'd once thought Lorcan's telekinetic ability was similar to Fare's penchant for compulsion.

I'd been wrong.

Very, *very* wrong.

With Lorcan, I could at least attempt to battle his invisible hold. It was a futile fight, his power absolute. But I could at least *feel* my own resistance.

I realized now how vital that feeling was to my sanity. Knowing I could try to defend myself provided motivation to at least make an effort to escape.

Whereas Fare's compulsion smothered my fight entirely. He made me *want* to obey. To do whatever he asked. To play the part of his perfect pet.

He hummed in appreciation now, his gaze thoughtful as he surveyed my intimate flesh.

"It's just been so long that I can't decide where I want to bite you." He tapped his chin with one long finger, his red eyes glowing with interest. "I mean, everywhere, obviously. But this is a first after going so long without a taste. I need it to be perfect. You know?"

I didn't know.

Nor did I *want* to know.

Fare was a psychopath. A monster. *And very much alive.*

My one saving grace right now was his inability to actually read my mind. He could only hear the words I spoke to him, and that was only when he engaged our mate-bond link.

A link I'd thought was *dead*.

But it was very much alive. He'd simply engaged it during my dreams, when I was at my weakest. Never during my waking hours.

Otherwise, I might have sensed him.

Assuming I'd believed he was actually talking to me. I would likely have figured it was just my mind tormenting me with my past.

I shivered as Fare kneeled on the bed, his presence entirely unwelcome. But I couldn't even say that out loud. I couldn't scream. I couldn't tell him to fuck off. I couldn't voice any of my thoughts or feelings because of his fucking compulsion.

If he told me to enjoy his bite, I would.

And I hated that worst of all.

"I really have missed you, pet," he murmured. "You never break, and I admire that." His ruby orbs glittered as he gazed down at me. "I'm oh so glad Seamus left dear Fritz to clean up my remains that day. Otherwise, we likely wouldn't be here, right now, like this."

My skin burned as his eyes roamed over my nude state once more, his hunger palpable.

But it was his words that held me captive now.

Is he saying Fritz helped him live? I frowned inside. *That can't be possible.*

Fritz would *never* help Fare. He hated vampires. That was why Seamus had asked Fritz to come with him to help clean up Fare's vampire nest.

There'd been an Alpha informant working with Seamus to take down a vampire operation in Greenland, prior to the Infection. That informant and Seamus's interest in squashing the vampire nest were the two reasons I'd been able to kill Fare.

The informant had given me the knife.

Seamus had then stepped in to clean up the nest.

And Fritz had taken me to the Sanctuary.

That was how we'd met. It was also how I'd met Quinn. The three of us had become immediate friends.

So why is Fare implying that Fritz helped him?

"I forgot how emotional your eyes are," Fare mused, drawing my attention back to where he knelt at the foot of the bed. "No matter how deep my compulsion goes, your true feelings shine in those green irises of yours."

I really hoped that was true. Because that meant he could see my hatred.

"So confused and frightened," he continued. "So angry, too. I suppose I would be as well if I found out my best friend had been lying to me for a hundred-plus years."

He paused then, his expression thoughtful.

"Actually, no. I'd just find it amusing. Especially in your case. It's not like he had a choice." His cold fingers found my ankle and started tracing a path upward. "Seamus is really the one you should blame. He should never have left little Fritzy boy behind."

His chilling touch reached my calf, stirring goose bumps along my skin. *So cold. Like ice.*

"His mind was easy to reach." Those lips curled once more. "So feeble and pliable. With Seamus, I hadn't stood a chance thanks to your little betrayal. But Fritzy boy? Oh, he was so easy to compel, even while incapacitated. It was the start of a beautiful friendship, really."

Fare sighed, his expression wistful.

It wasn't real, though. None of his emotions were. Fare didn't feel anything other than pleasure in life. And that pleasure usually came at the expense of others.

"He's probably dead now." He shrugged. "Now that I have you back, I no longer need him." His red eyes met mine once more. "See, I got rid of all my distractions for you. Consider it a grand gesture of my devotion to *us*."

My stomach churned. *Fritz… is dead?*

No, Fare had said Fritz was *probably* dead.

Which meant he might still be alive.

"I want to give you all my focus, pet. Everything I am." His palm flattened against my thigh. "We have so much catching up to do."

My heart stopped beating.

"Now, where shall I bite you?" he asked thoughtfully. "Decisions, decisions."

My wolf growled inside, not at all keen on feeling his teeth in our skin. But my vampire... my vampire half whimpered. She craved her Alpha's bite. His venom. The way it would make us feel.

Because he compelled me to want it. To crave it.

And it was working.

Just not on my inner beast. She refused. She had another Alpha she submitted to, not this feral being before us now.

My wolf was leashed to my sanity, grounding me when I would have otherwise drowned.

It left me feeling conflicted. More confused than ever. *Furious.*

My head spun, delirious from my internal fight and overwhelmed by what Fare had just revealed.

He was alive because Fritz had never burned his remains.

He's been compelling Fritz.

Is that how Fare found me?

How long has this been going on?

If Fare had access to Fritz, then why did he just now come for me? Why not before?

Something wasn't adding up. Maybe his hold on Fritz had been flawed? Not as strong as he'd needed it to be?

Similar to how I feel now?

Because while my vampire side was an obedient mess, my wolf was too pissed off to submit.

"Fascinating," Fare whispered, his touch having paused near the apex between my thighs. "You're fighting my compulsion."

He cocked his head to the side, his lips curling once more.

"Oh, this just adds a new flavor to our reunion, pet. I love it. How kind of you to spice things up for us." He slapped the sensitive flesh between my legs, causing me to yelp in response.

It fucking burned.

And it was nothing compared to what I knew he had in store.

A fact he drove home by sliding off the bed.

"A bite isn't going to be enough. We need something to speed things along." He disappeared from view, not necessarily teleporting, just walking away from where I lay frozen on the mattress.

Because he'd told me not to move.

But maybe I can break the hold, I wondered.

He'd said he could feel me fighting his compulsion. Perhaps I wasn't as helpless as I'd originally thought?

"Ah, here we are." The touch of excitement in his voice had my veins icing over.

I knew that tone too well.

Feared it.

Hated it.

Because pain always followed.

"This should help move things along quite nicely," he continued as he sat beside me on the bed. "See, my pet? I've been preparing for you."

He clasped my chin with two fingers and tilted my face toward him.

My breath stilled.

A syringe.

He was going to drug me with vampire venom.

It would push me into a heat-like state, maybe even a real estrus.

My eyebrows tried to lift, a plea forming in my thoughts. But all that did was make his smile grow.

He *liked* torturing me.

And this would be the biggest torment of all.

"This should definitely help us get the party started," he said as the needle went into my arm. "And if it doesn't quickly do the trick, I have a few more doses to help ramp things up."

Heat seared my veins as the venom went straight into my bloodstream. Yet my mouth wouldn't allow me to scream.

He'd compelled me to remain silent. To take whatever he gave me and *accept* it.

My wolf snarled inside, then whimpered as the serum almost instantly took hold.

Fuck. It *hurt.* It turned my skin into liquid fire. Created an inferno in my abdomen. Jump-started my heart.

Oh, Gods... I hadn't felt this way... in... in... eons. Years. Over a century. I wasn't sure. But it... it...

I closed my eyes, the movement one of the only ones I could control.

I can't. I can't... this is... I don't want this...

Kyra... a deep voice rumbled through my head. *Where the fuck are you?*

I tried to reply. Tried to latch onto that voice.

But a new one took over. A sinister one. A cold, *realistic* one. "Welcome home, pet," he said, his lips against my ear. "Let's play."

LORCAN

Kieran met me in Fritz's security room, Jas hot on his tail. She'd been playing nurse to his doctor for the last three hours while I'd tried to recover the security feeds in Fritz's lair.

Unfortunately, all the videos stopped thirty minutes before the attack.

And only one remained.

Which was precisely why I'd messaged Kieran and told him to meet me up here. Because he needed to see this.

His dark gaze went to Fritz in the corner, his eyebrow arching in question. The unconscious Omega was lying in a makeshift bed of sheets, his body mostly healed.

His mind was another matter entirely.

Kieran would have to help with that.

But first, I needed to show him the file I'd found waiting for me on Fritz's computer. Because Fritz had absolutely known what was coming. And this video proved it.

Rather than comment, I simply hit the Play button.

"If you're watching this, then it's time. And I'm probably dead." Fritz grimaced on the screen. "This… I can't…" He sighed audibly. "I… I hope this works. And that he…"

The Omega trailed off and shook his head, his expression physically pained.

"I'm sorry," he whispered. "Just know... I tried."

Kieran folded his arms, his expression a mask of indifference. However, I knew my cousin well. He was absolutely planning Fritz's murder right now in his mind.

Because this all sounded like an admission of guilt.

And it was, just not in the way one would expect.

"Initiating emergency protocols now," a computer voice said, causing Kieran to glance at me.

Just keep watching, I told him with a look. *Trust me.*

The screen flashed from Fritz's face to black, then three displays appeared. One was of Fritz's nest. A second of the hallway. And a third of the security console room with Fritz standing by the desk.

Kieran's focus shifted to the corner of the room where a camera was hidden on a bookshelf covered with tech equipment.

Fritz stood abnormally still, his face blank.

A minute passed.

No significant movement. No words. No sound. I'd thought it was just a picture at first, except there was a slight shift in Fritz's shoulders as he breathed.

Kieran's brow furrowed a bit as he leaned forward to check Fritz's blank expression. "He's asleep."

It wasn't a question, but I nodded anyway, as I'd come to the same conclusion around this moment the first time I'd watched the video.

Another thirty seconds or so went by before Fritz stiffened, his eyes widening with what could only be described as terror.

"Hello, Fritzy boy," a silky voice greeted as a Vampire Alpha appeared beside the Omega. "It's been a while."

Fritz said nothing. *Did* nothing. But his eyes conveyed his emotions perfectly. Horror melted into fury, which dissolved into fear once more.

"Ah, this game of ours has been fun, hasn't it?" The Vampire Alpha brushed the back of his long fingers against Fritz's cheek. "Alas, your punishment is nearing an end."

"Punishment?" Kieran repeated.

I didn't reply. The video would answer him soon enough.

"Although, I will say I expected this to bring about a much faster resolution. Had I known the necklace would take this long to arrive in this little Omega haven, I would have chosen a different path."

The Vampire Alpha paused and glanced upward.

"Actually, no. I would have taken this exact same road, as it afforded me a great deal of time to torture you and my darling pet." His lips curled then, his tone and expression making my wolf snarl.

Mostly because we both knew what he was about to say and each time we'd watched had been a different form of torment for us.

"Sweet girl thinks I'm dead, that all these dreams of hers are just a lingering connection to her former mate." He chuckled, causing the hair along my nape to lift in response. "Of course, you've known the truth all along, haven't you?" He tapped the Omega on the nose. "Poor Fritzy boy, always *forgetting* our chats until you dream of me."

My teeth ground together.

A dreamwalker.

Just like I'd suspected, only I'd figured it out far too late.

"Now, we don't have much time before my friends come through the barrier. I requested a thirty-minute head start, but an island full of unclaimed Omegas is an allure I doubt they'll be able to resist for long."

He palmed Fritz's cheek, his expression borderline caring. But it was the clever mask of a blatant psychopath.

"Your punishment for trying to dispose of my remains for Kyra is nearly complete," he concluded. "I only ask that you help entertain my friends when they arrive. Alpha Dave is a fan of rare things. When I told him about my little male Omega pet, his eyes practically lit up with glee. Do show him a good time for me, yes?"

His hand went to the back of Fritz's neck. Then he roughly tugged the Omega forward and sank his fangs into the male's throat.

Fritz's mouth parted on a silent scream, the vampire's compulsive influence over him evident by the way the Omega trembled and shouted without sound.

"Fuck," Kieran muttered, the expletive the same one I'd said around this time on my first watch.

It went on for several minutes before Fare shoved Fritz over the desk. "Enjoy Dave, Fritzy boy. He'll likely be your last fuck."

He started toward the door, then paused to glance back.

"Oh, your memories are free now. Enjoy."

If evil had a grin, it was the one Fare wore now as Fritz's legs buckled.

I reached forward to pause the feed, my attention going to Kieran. "The Alphas arrive about fifteen minutes after this point. I think you know what happened next."

My cousin's jaw flexed, his cheekbones appearing that much more severe as a result. "So Fritz has been unwittingly working with Fare for... over a century?"

"Maybe even longer." I shook my head. "It's hard to say when that enchantment was put on the necklace. Before Kiana's and Seamus's deaths? Right after?"

"Whenever it was, Fare's been playing the long game. I assume you've notified Cillian already?"

I nodded. "He has Myon in custody for questioning again because I told him Fare mentioned the necklace." And we already knew Myon was involved in the enchantment.

The question became, was he working with Fare willingly or unwillingly?

My instincts said it was the latter, that if Myon was

working with Fare, it was because the Vampire Alpha had compelled him to obey. Just like Fare had done to Fritz.

I'd known something was off. My wolf had sensed it. I'd felt it, too.

"How did they get through the barrier?" Jas asked, her voice devoid of emotion despite the heavy topic at hand.

She was definitely a warrior. Just like Kyra.

You'll survive this, I thought at her now. *You'll survive, and I'll find you and watch you kill that asshole once and for all.*

Swallowing, I focused on Jas's question. "I haven't been out to investigate the barrier yet. But Cillian suspects the necklace's explosion created a back door of some kind that allowed them to teleport in."

"It also likely broadcast the island's location," Kieran muttered.

I agreed with a nod. "That's how Fare was able to find Kyra after all this time. The barrier would have let him pass as her mate. But he took it a step further by bringing along some friends."

"So the necklace had to have been doubly enchanted."

"Right. But does Myon know about it?" It was the same question I'd voiced to Cillian two hours ago.

While Myon had mentioned the locator charm, he hadn't said anything about creating a barrier entry point.

"I assume that's what Cillian is trying to determine right now." Kieran voiced it as a statement, not a question.

I dipped my chin in confirmation.

"Our best estimation right now is that the vampires had arrived via a stealth jet, then waited for the signal to teleport inside," I summarized.

It was a guess since most vampires couldn't teleport long distances. Some couldn't even teleport at all.

"Seems likely." He paused for a moment, his gaze sharpening. "Any idea where Fare has taken Kyra?"

I shook my head. "Her mind is silent. But…" I trailed off, my lips pulling tightly at the sides. "But I can feel her pain."

Whatever that bastard was doing to her was enough for her wolf to reach out with frightened yelps. But they were sporadic.

However, the agony rippling through our bond was constant.

"Then we need to wake Fritz up and find out everything he knows," Kieran said, moving toward the Omega. "We also need to come up with a defensive plan. The barrier has been compromised, and it's going to take time for me and Quinnlynn to repair it. Especially since we don't know what's wrong with it."

"You can't feel the breach?"

"No." That single word held a mountain of frustration. "The magic feels fine to me."

I frowned. Because I still sensed that wrongness from before. A hint of something not quite right.

Maybe it was the residual stench of Vampire Alpha lingering in the halls.

Or the fact that Fare seemed to have one hell of a psychic link to Fritz.

But I suspected it was more.

"Only Omegas and their mates can pass through the barrier." Kyra would absolutely have rolled her eyes at me for reiterating that statement.

But right now, it was important.

Because it gave me an idea I hadn't considered before.

A question I should definitely have asked during my initial tour, yet failed to do because I'd been too distracted by my new mate.

I looked at Jas. "How are Omegas vetted?"

She stared at me. "What do you mean?"

"Do you check the backgrounds of the Omegas before

you let them stay? Or do you just grant access to the Sanctuary to anyone who can pass through?"

Kieran had knelt beside Fritz, but he glanced up with interest now. His expression told me he, too, hadn't considered this before and was also annoyed by that realization.

"Well, yeah. We're a safe haven for all Omegas. We give all of them a home."

"But do you check to see if they're mated?" I pressed.

She frowned. "Only unmated Omegas or Omegas running from their mates come here. They're all brought here through operations designed to save Omegas in need. And we never disclose the island's location to outsiders."

"How do you verify that?" Kieran demanded. "Or do you just take everyone at their word?"

Jas swallowed, the first hint of unease breaking through her otherwise stoic expression. "We've never had a reason to question anyone. Omegas look out for each other."

As a general rule, I agreed.

But there were always outliers, those who didn't follow the rules. That was why security checks were put in place. Trust had to be earned, not freely given.

"We need to bring Quinnlynn into this conversation," Kieran said after a beat. "But first..." He pressed his palm to Fritz's head and grimaced. "I see why you haven't finished healing him."

"It wasn't for a lack of trying," I admitted.

Kieran hummed. "This is going to take a bit. Call Cillian. Tell him I want a meeting scheduled for tomorrow with the Alpha Princes in Blood Sector. We need to have a very serious conversation about the future of the Sanctuary."

KYRA

What day is it?

Where am I?

Who am I?

A bundle of nerves. Hot. Cold. Alone. *Wet*.

It was an inferno in here. Musty. Humid. *Wrong*.

My wolf whimpered in my head. Then she growled as another shot of liquid fire ripped through my veins.

A cruel laugh followed.

Words, too. Something about it almost being time.

I writhed. Begged for relief. Moaned for comfort.

Kyra, a deep voice growled into my thoughts. *Tell me where you are.*

My wolf told me to reply, but my mind couldn't fathom the words. Because I had no idea where I was. Somewhere balmy. An island, maybe. But not the right island. This wasn't home. This was hell.

Fight, that masculine voice said. *Fight his compulsion and talk to me.*

My animal whimpered in reply. She longed to obey that command. But my vampire side was in charge right now.

I curled into a ball as flames engulfed my body.

I *needed*. What I needed, I couldn't say. All I knew was that I felt empty. Alone. In pain.

But that voice continued to whisper through my thoughts.

I'm coming for you, he promised. *Don't stop fighting now.*

I closed my eyes and pictured an Alpha with piercing black eyes. Square jaw. Thick, dark hair. A perpetually arched eyebrow. Concealed hunger in his gaze.

My thighs clenched.

If he were here, he would give me what I needed. What I desired. What I *craved*.

But he wasn't here.

Something cold touched my skin instead. Something unwelcome.

"I can feel him in your mind," that unwelcome presence said against my ear. "Tell me who he is, and I'll give you what you want."

No, my wolf snarled, snapping me out of my delirious state for one horrifying moment.

A damp world of greenery and rocks formed around me, the *room* I was in suddenly revealing itself.

I'm in a cave, I marveled. *A forest-like one. Not my favorite one. No ice. Too hot. So humid.*

Good, Kyra. What else can you tell me? that masculine voice asked.

"Who is he?" the other one demanded, his fangs sinking into my throat in the next breath. *"Tell me who he is."*

My wolf snapped her jaws inside me, refusing to give him what he wanted. *No*, she seemed to repeat. *Fuck. Off.*

Kyra...

My animal quieted, *that* voice one she liked. *Mate*, she thought. *Alpha.*

Yes, he replied. *I'm here, little killer. Help me find you.*

I tried to latch onto that voice, to fight the other one near my ear. But another searing bite rendered me speechless.

Your mind is your own, that soothing tone said. *Lean on your wolf. She'll guide you.*

His purr followed, the sound rumbling through my mind and providing momentary relief from my burning veins.

Lorcan, I breathed.

I'm here. Tell me how to find you.

I... I'm not in Greenland. I'm somewhere tropical. In a cave. I can smell the ocean. That was the source of the salt and the humidity. *I think it's an island.* I couldn't say why. That was just my instinct. Probably because of all the water.

Can you shadow? he asked.

But the other presence cut me off before I could reply, his incisors sinking into my breast.

More venom flooded my veins.

Heat and madness.

He demanded that I give him a name. An identity. A way to find the *intruder* in my head.

But he wasn't an intruder.

He was my wolf's mate. My true Alpha. The one I'd learned to trust in such a brief period of time.

The one who never forced me. Never took advantage of me. Never *drugged* me.

"Who is he?" Fare demanded again, my mind temporarily clear despite the fire growing within me.

Why didn't Fritz tell you? I wondered. *If he was your source, the one who helped you find me, then why didn't he give you this information?*

Something wasn't adding up.

Had Fritz fought Fare's compulsion? Like I was doing now?

Before, I'd struggled to battle Fare's control over me, my body and soul addicted to his bite. But I'd found a way to focus long enough to stab him.

I'd found that focus within my wolf.

Because she'd never been bound to him. Never mated him. Never *craved* him.

And now she desired another. A better Alpha. *Lorcan.*

Fare growled, his bite turning vicious as a needle pierced my arm at the same time. *"You will tell me what I want to know,"* he snarled, his anger unusual.

He typically played games. Laughed at my torment. Taunted me with affection before throwing me to his hungry friends.

This fury was new, almost territorial in nature.

Alphas didn't normally like to share. But he'd always passed me around to the vampires within his nest. He'd even suggested there would be a welcome party to rekindle those old moments.

Yet now he seemed positively savage over the concept of sharing me with another mate.

I held on to that realization as a scream tore free from my throat. He was drowning me in his venom. Forcing my vampire instincts to flourish and come to the forefront of my mind.

He wanted me to go into heat. To lose myself to my *need*. To become a brainless toy he could use for pleasure and blood.

The more he pushed into my veins, the more muddled my thoughts became.

But that purr never left. It hummed in the back of my mind. A constant reminder that I wasn't alone. That I was more than a vampire.

I'm part wolf.

And wolves... have claws.

LORCAN

Two days.
Fourteen hours.
And twenty-seven minutes.

That was how long Kyra had been missing. How long a maniacal Alpha had had her in his possession.

I paced her nest, a screen following me as I walked.

Kieran and Quinnlynn were engaged in their second day of meetings with all of the Alpha Princes. They spent most of the first day asking questions about sector security, all under the guise that Kieran had experienced a breach to his territory.

He hadn't been lying.

He just hadn't told them what part of his territory had been compromised.

After several hours of discussion, Quinnlynn had cleared her throat, her decision clearly made. Kieran had left the choice up to her, saying he would respect her wishes on how to proceed no matter what she decided.

There were enough mated Alphas in Blood Sector for Kieran to reallocate a few to the Sanctuary for protection. But he'd pointed out that the pool of candidates would be wider if they invited the Alpha Princes to send in their own candidates.

In the late morning hours, Quinnlynn had informed them all that the security issue Kieran had mentioned wasn't in relation to Blood Sector but in relation to the Sanctuary. Then she'd explained what her family magic had protected for almost a millennium.

That topic had been the final discussion point before dispersing for an afternoon of rest.

Now that the Alpha Princes had been given a chance to process the information, they were all seated around a conference table in Blood Sector, debating on how to proceed.

"At least now we understand why you were drilling us about our sector security all night," Alpha Cael had said as yesterday's meeting adjourned. "Good to know we've earned your approval."

"It wasn't about my approval. I needed to know if you could be of any use to our situation," Kieran had replied flatly. "And my mate had to decide whether or not she could trust you all with her family's centuries-old secret."

While I hadn't been there in person, I could tell that decision hadn't been easy on Quinnlynn. She'd presented the information in a calm, concise manner, but her dark eyes had held a hint of concern.

The Sanctuary had been hers to protect, and she seemed to be struggling with sharing that responsibility. Kieran would help her, though. It wasn't about her being unable to do it on her own; it was about her not having to be the sole guardian.

Her mother had had her father.

Now she had Kieran.

Me.

Cillian.

And a roomful of Alpha Princes.

"Tell us what you need," Prince Lykos said, getting straight to the point of today's meeting. His shock of white hair and silver eyes matched his sector's name—*Glacier Sector.* "You have our full support."

Prince Cael and Prince Tadhg nodded in agreement.

The other three Alpha Princes at the table simply stared at Quinnlynn, expectant. They weren't nodding, but the fact that they were giving her their undivided attention told me exactly what I needed to know—they were deferring to the Omega Queen to make decisions for the Sanctuary. Which was precisely as it should be.

Kieran also gave her his undivided focus, his chin inclining just a bit in encouragement. *Tell them what you need,* he seemed to be saying.

I already knew what she intended to say, as the three of us, along with Cillian, had discussed it last night.

The barrier rules were clear: Omegas and their mates could pass through. No one else.

That was why I'd remained in the Sanctuary—I was mated to one of the island inhabitants. It didn't matter that Kyra wasn't here; she had a nest here. A safe haven. And that was enough for the magic to let me through.

However, since the enchantment was still unstable, I'd chosen to remain here as the island's guardian while Kieran handled things with Quinnlynn and the Alpha Princes.

And now they were going to detail our plan.

A plan that revolved around the relocation of certain Alpha and Omega pairings.

It would have to be voluntary, of course. And the pairings would need to be evaluated prior to being offered homes in the Sanctuary. But the idea was to move at least a dozen couples into the Sanctuary, with the Alphas having the sole role of protecting the Omegas within the barrier.

Quinnlynn outlined it all, then waited for the Alpha Princes to comment.

"Who will serve as the Sanctuary Alpha?" Prince Cael asked after digesting the information. It was the same question Cillian had posed after we discussed this plan as a group.

"Technically, Kieran," Quinnlynn informed them.

But like Cillian, Prince Cael was already shaking his head. "You need a Sector Alpha who can lead the others. It's simple pack dynamics. Otherwise, the Alphas on-site will eventually clash over their roles. Having someone in charge will help smooth the waters and provide a clear hierarchy for decisions."

"I agree," Alpha Tadhg said, his gruff voice low and growly. He was the largest Alpha at the table, his hulking size paired with a bald head and intelligent green eyes. "And it needs to be someone who can keep the others in line. If not, his position will be challenged."

"For now, Lorcan will be acting as Sector Alpha," Kieran announced, his words nearly making me wince. Fortunately, I'd already known to expect them. We'd had this conversation when I'd chosen to remain as the Sanctuary's Protector.

It might be temporary.

It might not be.

That remained to be seen.

The fact of the matter was that I had a duty to Kieran and this island fell under his responsibilities. As the only one of his Elites with the ability to cross over the boundary, I was duty bound to be here and protect the Sanctuary's inhabitants.

I leaned against the wall of Kyra's quarters and stared at the screen, aware that every Alpha Prince had turned their focus toward my projected image in the room.

"You accept this responsibility?" Alpha Cael asked.

I lifted a shoulder. "I'm mated to the Sanctuary's second-in-command. It's a logical step." We hadn't yet told them that said second-in-command was missing. We'd address that topic next.

"He's also more than powerful enough to tame a handful of Alphas," Kieran added. "I think we can all agree on that."

No one at the table attempted to debate Kieran's words. They simply nodded in agreement.

I was powerful enough to be one of them. Cillian was as well. The only reason we didn't have *Prince* attached to our titles was because we didn't have sectors of our own to manage.

"So you need Alpha-Omega pairings," Prince Cael said, drawing the conversation back to the initial request. "I assume these applications should be sent directly to Lorcan for review? Or should we send them to both of you?"

"You can send them to Quinnlynn. She will review first, then pass on her approvals to me and my Elites for review," Kieran replied.

Prince Cael nodded again before dragging his fingers through his dark brown hair. "Now, shall we discuss the security incident that provoked this need?"

Cillian cleared his throat. He'd been seated to Kieran's left, while Quinnlynn sat to my cousin's right. "To understand that, you'll need a bit of history."

Kieran inclined his head, giving Cillian permission to proceed. As he was the one who'd spent the last few days rummaging through Myon's and Fritz's thoughts to gather pieces and put them together, it made sense for him to explain.

"As Queen Quinnlynn has already explained, the Sanctuary provides refuge for those who need it," Cillian summarized. "What she's not yet mentioned is that prior to Seamus's death, he and his Elites targeted Alpha clans or nests known to be harboring unwilling Omegas. They killed those Alphas and invited the Omegas to recover in the Sanctuary."

These were all details Myon and Fritz had provided. However, Quinnlynn had added a few of her own. While she hadn't known the full extent of their missions, she'd befriended several of the Omegas who had come to the Sanctuary as a result of her father's expeditions.

Kyra had been one such friend.

"As you can imagine, that line of work created a few enemies," Cillian continued. "One of those enemies was Alpha Fare."

A few of the princes exchanged glances, clearly familiar with the infamous vampire.

"It seems King Seamus made a grave error in assuming a beheading had been enough to incapacitate the ancient Vampire Alpha. He left one of his Elites behind to handle the cleanup while he saw to an Omega's injuries."

Kyra, I thought, having heard the official story now.

She'd earned her title as an Alpha killer after Fare's death. Only, what the V-Clan world didn't know was that she'd had some help on the inside from another Vampire Alpha. One who had provided her with a blade that she'd used on Fare.

During an intimate moment.

Something I really didn't want to think about.

Fortunately, Cillian had pulled the occurrence from Fritz's mind and didn't elaborate on the incident, just provided the essential details.

"Unfortunately, the Elite he left behind was susceptible to Alpha Fare's compulsion," Cillian went on. "Also, unfortunately, that Elite was one of the island's sole Protectors."

The Alpha Princes exchanged glances again.

"He's an Omega," Kieran said, aware of what the princes were likely wondering. "Fare's been using him for over a hundred years. He's a dreamwalker. However, his compulsion only went so far."

Cillian nodded, then explained what he'd learned from Fritz's mind.

Fare had compelled Fritz to lie about the remains, to say he burned them when he hadn't. He'd then left a strand of compulsion in Fritz's mind, one that had allowed Fare to maintain a link to Fritz—one Fritz could only remember when

Fare activated the link. Meaning every time Fritz dreamt of Fare, his memories returned. Then he'd forget it all when he woke up.

"He didn't immediately activate the link," Cillian went on. "He waited until a few years after Seamus wiped out his nest, ensuring everyone thought he was dead. Only then did he start reaching out to Fritz in his dreams. However, as I said, his compulsion had limits."

He meant that literally.

As in Fare's mental hold on Fritz had been fragile due to their physical distance. Which meant Fare had needed to be very careful about what he'd made Fritz do.

He'd known Kyra had been taken to a safe house of some kind, one he'd thought was in Blood Sector. And when he'd tried to ask Fritz about it in the dreams, Fritz would automatically wake up. It hadn't taken Fare long to realize that Fritz's loyalty to the safe haven was stronger than Fare's compulsion.

So he'd gone about it in a different way, instead using their dream sessions to learn more information about Seamus's operations. The key players. *Elites.*

Which was where Myon came into play.

V-Clan wolves were known for their secrecy, our identities ones we rarely allowed others to know outside of our world. We preferred to be mysterious to outsiders. Unknowns. *Ghosts.*

But Fritz had given Fare enough details in those dreams for him to find another source—*Myon.*

However, unfortunately for Fare, the source he'd attached himself to didn't know the location of the Sanctuary. Just that it existed, why it existed, and that it was protected by MacNamara magic.

So Fare had compelled Myon to enchant Kiana's necklace. Seamus had already placed a locator charm on it—something that had been done to protect Kiana MacNamara. However, it was only supposed to ignite in an emergency.

But then Myon had changed the spell to track her every movement.

He'd also added a code that would cause it to light up like a beacon when she reached the magical barrier of the island.

"This was over a century ago," Alpha Lykos marveled, his eyes widening as Cillian told the tale.

"He played the long game," Cillian replied. "He also indirectly killed the MacNamaras."

Quinnlynn flinched, causing Kieran to immediately rest his arm over her shoulders. "They realized the necklace was bespelled and crashed their own plane."

"Fare met Myon at the scene." Cillian's tone was bitter, mostly because he'd been the one to review and validate the black box just a week ago. Which we now knew had been manipulated by Fare. "He compelled Myon to think it was an accident and gave him a black box as proof. Then he handed him the MacNamara diamonds and told him to add a new enchantment, one that would cause the jewelry to explode when they reached the Sanctuary."

"Yes, and then he forced him to forget all about it," Kieran added flatly.

Cillian nodded. "And told him to work with Fritz on how to handle the situation with Quinnlynn."

He went on to explain how Fare had used his dream connection to Fritz to *suggest* that Alphas couldn't be trusted, to plant seeds of doubt about what really happened with the MacNamaras, and urged him to ensure Quinnlynn didn't take a mate too quickly.

The whole purpose hadn't been to send her on a mission throughout the globe, though.

The point had been to scare Quinnlynn into running back to the Sanctuary for safety, with the expectation that she would take the MacNamara diamonds with her.

"They would have exploded when they hit the barrier,

killed the last living member of the MacNamara line, and taken the enchantment down with it," Cillian concluded.

"But why go that far when all he really needed was the location of the island?" Prince Tadhg asked, his brow furrowed. "He was mated to Kyra, right? I assume she's been living in the Sanctuary all this time?"

Cillian hadn't revealed her name as part of the conversation, but her reputation as Fare's killer had made her a bit infamous in Alpha circles. So I wasn't surprised that Prince Tadhg knew her identity.

"He didn't know the parameters of the magical barrier," Quinnlynn murmured. "He thought it had to be down for him to pass."

Because Fritz had never told him anything about it. Anytime Fare had asked about the Sanctuary, Fritz had woken up and forgotten all about the dream. And Myon hadn't been able to detail anything about the enchantment.

It also seemed that after the years, Fritz had started to realize that something was going on in his head. That was when he'd made that prerecorded video and set up a fail-safe to turn on an auto-record feature in his personal areas should he ever switch off the island security feeds.

Because he knew he would never do that willingly.

"What happened next?" Prince Cael asked.

Kieran explained how he and Quinnlynn had discovered that the diamonds were draining her power and how he'd taken them off of her and through the barrier. Then he'd thrown them over the ocean just before they exploded.

"The only reason it didn't detonate upon her initial arrival was because she'd shadowed into the Sanctuary originally," Cillian added, explaining what he'd learned from Myon. "The spell was cast to only activate if physically taken through an enchanted boundary; it didn't factor in shadowing."

"Which essentially saved Quinnlynn's life," Kieran commented. Then he went on to say what had happened the other night, how the vampires had slipped through the magical enchantment and attacked the island.

There were four casualties.

And over two dozen injuries.

All caused in a matter of minutes.

Which was what had necessitated these meetings. The Sanctuary had been compromised, was *still* compromised, and needed protection.

"There's one thing I don't understand," Alpha Lykos said slowly. "If the necklace exploded outside of the barrier, then it wasn't taken down, right? The vampires had the location, I assume from the detonation, but how did they get in?"

"That's something we haven't determined yet," Cillian admitted.

"And why Lorcan is there instead of here." Kieran glanced at me on the screen before returning his focus to the Alpha Princes. "The Sanctuary is compromised. Which is why we need your help."

My chin began to dip in agreement, only to tighten instead as Kyra's roar ripped through my mind.

I grabbed my head, my wolf snarling in response to her animal's agony.

Kyra!

A sequence of moaned words that I couldn't decipher followed, her mind seeming to fracture from whatever that bastard was doing to her.

"*Fuck,*" I breathed, going to my knees.

I was vaguely aware of Kieran and Cillian saying something through the screen. But I couldn't hear them over the howling in my mind.

Her wolf was *pissed*.

Talk to me, I demanded. *Tell me what's happening.*

She'd been silent for hours, our connection seeming to come and go. But it felt particularly strong right now.

Kyra. I forced a purr to underline my words, sensing her need for comfort. *I'm here, little killer. I'm here.*

V-venom, she whispered. *F-forced... H-he... heat...*

I swallowed. *He's forcing you to go into heat.* I hadn't known what he'd been doing to her for days, but had suspected he might be doing something like this. I'd spent countless hours scouring maps while trying to determine her location. But there were too many uninhabited *hot* and *humid* islands. I could spend decades searching them all.

Cillian had questioned Myon and Fritz endlessly about where Fare might be, too, but neither of them knew.

There'd apparently been a Vampire Alpha providing information from the inside when they'd initially taken down Fare's nest. But they had no idea how to even reach him now.

He likely wouldn't be useful anyway.

I need you to fight back, I told Kyra. *I know you're scared. I know you're hurt. But you're stronger than you realize. Your mind is your own. Fight his compulsion. Shadow. Escape him.*

She whimpered in reply. *C-can't...*

You can, I countered, my dominance underlining those two words.

Her wolf whined, her mental voice quiet.

Come on, little killer. Shadow home. Shadow to your nest.

No response.

Kyra.

Silence.

Kyra, I need you to snap out of it, I demanded. *You're stronger than this. Don't let that bastard win.*

Still nothing.

But I *felt* her lingering. Sensed her wolf trying to connect. To listen to her Alpha.

Shadow to your nest, I repeated, my dominance ringing through each word. *Shadow to your nest right fucking now.*

KYRA

SEVERAL MINUTES EARLIER

EVERYTHING'S BURNING.
 So hot.
 So painful.
 So much need.
 I mewled, my limbs shaking, my heart racing, my world *ending*. It was too much. Not enough. Everything all at once. And nothing at the same time.
 Oh, Gods, what's wrong with me?
 Too much sensation.
 More.
 Please!
 My inner wolf snarled, trying futilely to snag my attention. She was pissed and I didn't know why. All I knew was that *desire*.
 I tossed and turned, the sheets beneath me rough instead of soft. The fabric abraded my tender skin, causing me to flinch and whine in protest.
 "Bad Omegas don't get nests," a cruel voice said. "They get fucked on concrete instead."

My shoulder bit into something hard, the world tumbling around me.

Vaguely, I was aware that I'd just been thrown onto the floor, the cold stone digging into my side.

My inner beast snapped her jaws, furious at the treatment. No. Furious at *me*.

I blinked. *What's wrong with you?*

Cold fingers dug into my hips, yanking me onto my back and forcing my legs apart. "Almost ready, pet. Just *give me his name.*"

Whose name? I wondered dizzily. *I... I don't want to talk. I want—*

"Give me his name!" the Alpha shouted, his grip leaving my hips for my throat. Where he *squeezed*. "*Now*, Omega."

My wolf roared in response, refusing to give him what he wanted. She didn't care how much pain he inflicted; she wouldn't relinquish her control to him.

I tried to understand, attempted to focus. She seemed to have taken over my mind. Controlling my human form like I could her wolf form.

Impossible, I mumbled, delirious. *How...? Why...?*

Fare growled, the sound going straight to the apex between my thighs. He'd bitten me there several times, forcing me to take his venom while he injected me over and over with those syringes.

He kept telling me to stop fighting him. To stop fighting my *heat.*

I... I didn't know how to stop.

My wolf wouldn't allow it. Not quite. Not...

I swallowed as his fangs bit into my thigh, causing my wolf to howl again, this time in agony. Each shot of venom threatened her hold over my mind, making it that much harder to remain in control.

Kyra, that soothing voice whispered.

Mmm, Al... Lor...? It came out in a jumble. *Kn... hmm?*

I frowned inside, unsure of what I was trying to say. Something about his knot? His voice? His Alpha prowess.

Oh, Gods, thinking of him ignited an inferno in my core. *Yes. Yes, please.*

"That's a little better," the unwanted voice cooed. "But I want more slick."

He growled on those last two words, forcing my body to comply. Making me wetter. More needy. *Readying me for...*

...happening.

Hmm? I thought, confused by the single word from another voice. The one in my head. The one I craved. Had I missed more of what he'd said? I hoped not. I really liked his voice.

Kyra, that voice purred. *I'm here, little killer. I'm here.*

My wolf whined, wanting him to be physically here and not just in my mind.

Because we were going into heat.

Wait, no. My vampire side was. Because... because...

V-venom, I thought. *F-forced... H-he... heat...*

My eyes tried to fly open but barely even fluttered. I couldn't... I had no control... I...

He's forcing you to go into heat, Lorcan surmised.

I know! I tried to snap back. But all that came out was a whimper. A needy fucking whimper.

Followed by a growl from my wolf.

And another bite from Fare, this one on my hip bone.

I jolted, the pain tearing through my senses and making me vibrate with furious need.

Fuck. Fuck. Fuck.

I need... you're scared... hurt. But you're... Your mind... own. Fight... Sha... Escape...

His words came to me in pieces.

C-can't... I tried to reply. *Can't hear...*

You...

His voice disappeared, leaving me alone once more. My

wolf huffed, irritated and determined, only for another shot of venom to shoot through my veins.

Gods!

Fare growled something in my ear, his knot pressing into my stomach.

Wrong. Mate.

Not. Mine.

Do. Not. Want.

A blast of compulsion threatened to undo my thoughts, to rewrite my desires.

Only for a low internal growl to take over my mind. The growl of a true Alpha. Of *my* Alpha.

Shadow to your nest, he demanded. *Shadow to your nest right fucking now.*

My wolf perked up, responding to her chosen Alpha's command.

Fare cursed.

And the world faded around me.

It was a blur of sights and smells and colors. Then the familiar perfume of *home* hit my nostrils.

"Kyra," a male breathed.

My male.

My mate.

My Alpha.

I turned into his arms on a sob, my insides igniting with renewed fire. I *needed* him. His knot. His purr. His strength.

But he was wearing too many clothes.

Too much fabric.

My fingers turned into claws as I swiped at his sweater, then pressed my nose to the bare skin below.

Blood tinged the air. *Alpha blood.*

I'd cut him with my claws. Left marking scratches down his chest and abdomen.

Mine, I thought, leaning forward to lick up his decadent essence. *Mine. Mine. Mine.*

NIGHT SECTOR

He said my name, but I was too busy playing with his belt to hear him.

Knot. Knot. Knot.

"*Kyra,*" he growled.

Alpha, I thought back at him as I reached the button of his jeans.

He grabbed my wrist, his opposite hand going to my nape to squeeze it gently. "Stop," he demanded.

My brow furrowed. *Alpha?* Was he rejecting me? Rejecting my wolf? *Why?*

"You don't really want this." His grip tightened a little on my neck. "I won't knot you like this."

What? I blinked, my legs shaking from the effort it took to stand. I wasn't even sure how I'd landed on my feet, let alone ended up here.

All I knew was I wanted *him*. My Alpha. My beast.

I tried to twist my hand away from his, to resume my methods. But he held me captive.

My wolf growled, irritated. *Knot. Now.*

I shadowed to his back and swiped my claws against his jean-clad ass.

He snarled in response. *Kyra.*

Alpha, I returned.

You're high on vampire venom.

Mmm. I didn't care what I was high on. I just knew I needed him. My Alpha. My knot.

I tugged at his torn pants, determined, only for him to disappear and reappear behind me. I spun, intrigued by his playful game, and suddenly found myself on my back.

In my nest.

Yes, yes. I arched into his much bigger form as he held me down, his hands on my shoulders.

"I refuse to bind you with my power. Not after everything you've been through."

My wolf ignored him, and I did, too. All we wanted was

his knot. His power. His *thrusts*. I wrapped my legs around him, ready for more. But those damn jeans were still in the way, the fabric abrasive against my sensitive flesh.

Off, I told him as I pressed up into the impressive bulge hidden beneath his pants. *Jeans. Off.*

No.

Now, I demanded. *Off.*

No, he repeated, his voice underlined with Alpha authority.

Which only made me writhe even more, because *mmm*, dominance. Alpha. *More*.

He sighed, his head falling to my neck as he inhaled deeply. *Fuck, Kyra. You're killing me here.*

Knot me.

His growl vibrated my bare chest, tightening my nipples and igniting a fresh wave of slick between my thighs.

I'm not going to knot you, little killer. I can't. He pressed a kiss to my thundering pulse, his rumbling growl turning into a purr. *But I'll take care of you. Heal you. Protect you.*

His words didn't make any sense. Why wouldn't he knot me? My wolf wanted him. *I* wanted him. *Needed* him.

Without his knot... I... I would... *hurt*.

Burn.

Lose myself to the fire.

I blinked, confused. Dizzy once more.

There was a roar in my head, one demanding that I... I return... but I didn't want to return. I wanted to stay here. Stay in my nest. Stay with my Alpha.

Unless...

Am I...?

"Kyra." The purr underlining my name had me looking up into a pair of black irises. So beautiful. Like obsidian stones. Glittering with hunger. "Focus on me, okay?"

"Yes, Alpha."

"Lorcan," he corrected me.

My brow furrowed, uncertain as to why that mattered. "Knot me."

He pressed his face into my neck again, his vibrating chest alluring and comforting. A wave of warmth spilled from his aura into mine, the energy making me gasp and moan at the same time.

It felt… good. Soothing. *Healing*.

But it was followed by an explosion in my lower belly, one that created a maelstrom of sensation. Heat. Pain. Cramping. Shivering.

I trembled in response, my core tightening around nothing, my insides demanding something else. Something more intense. Something *hard*.

I grabbed his shoulders, my thighs clenching around him as another blast of his potent energy hit my senses.

A moan tumbled from my lips, my center pressing up into his groin as more of that fire seared through my veins. *Alpha…*

Lorcan, he returned.

Mate, I tried again.

He shuddered, his lips a ghosting presence against my pulse.

Bite me, I urged him.

No.

Knot me.

No.

I whimpered. He was rejecting me. Rejecting my wolf. It didn't make any sense. My body was made for this, for *him*.

And everything *burned*.

Only he could fix it. Only he could help turn my world right-side up. *Please…*

He sighed, more of his power rolling over me as his mouth moved along my throat, kissing me gently, leaving behind an exquisite mark of adoration.

I gyrated beneath him, loving the feel of his mouth on me and begging him for more.

More skin. More tongue. More *teeth*.

But all he did was shower me in his essence, hitting me with wave after wave of intensely soothing heat. All the while, he kept me pinned to my bed, his mouth lingering against my throat.

I panted beneath him, this foreplay moving along too slowly for my liking.

Yet something about his touch... his *power*... had me yawning. I tried to keep my eyes open. Attempted to speak. To ask him for... for something else...

However, the world started to slip away.

Pushing me into darkness.

Starless night.

Alone.

To suffer... in the cold.

I'm here, he whispered after a beat, his voice bringing with it a blast of heat. *I'm right here.*

Where? I asked.

Holding you in your nest. His palm flattened against my abdomen, confusing me. *Just sleep, Kyra. It'll help.*

Help what? I breathed, my body resembling an inferno of need. Trapped in this inky abyss. Unable to see. *Alpha?*

Shh, he hushed. *I'll give you what you need.*

More of that warmth washed over me, flooding my insides with foreign sensations. *Alpha...*

It's okay, mate, he promised me. *Sleep for me. Just for a little bit. Then I'll reward you.*

Reward?

Yes.

My wolf seemed to like the sound of that. She might not understand the term, but she understood his voice. The sensual promise within it. The cause and effect of pleasing her Alpha to get what she needed.

It was enough to calm her.

NIGHT SECTOR

Quiet her need.
Just for a bit.
Long enough... for a nap.

LORCAN

Fuck.

I'd never been this hard before in my godsdamn life.

Kyra's mewls and words played over and over in my mind, driving me nearly mad with *want*.

Bite me. Knot me.

Those two requests had nearly undone me.

But I couldn't take her like this, not when she wasn't *her*.

She'd been severely drugged. Which had ironically worked in my favor, as it seemed forcing her into a false heat had made her wolf crave the mate she desired most, thus allowing her to break whatever compulsive hold Fare had had over her mind.

I'd been stunned by her arrival, then immediately aroused by her scent and her lack of clothes. It was the stench of vampire on her that kept me grounded. And the bite marks all over her thighs and pussy that kept me from falling into any sort of rut.

She needed a bath.

A long night of rest.

Purring.

Proper care.

Healing.

I hit her with another wave of my power, attempting to soothe her inner ache. I knew she had to be burning with desire, her false heat in full effect thanks to Fare's fuckery.

Omegas were half out of their minds during heat cycles, craving their Alpha's knots more than oxygen itself. However, Kyra had made it *very* clear that she didn't want me to help her through her heat. She might have changed her mind now that she was in a forced cycle, but I wouldn't take advantage of her mindless state.

When I fucked her—because it would be *when*, not *if*—it would be with her mind fully intact.

It would be with her begging me for entirely different reasons.

Writhing and wet and willing to *fight*.

Because I wanted *my* version of Kyra. My little killer. The one who'd kept plotting my demise shortly after our mating.

Not this wounded version.

Oh, she hadn't lost her survival instincts. The fact that she was in her nest with me wrapped around her now proved that. She'd fought Fare's compulsion and won. And now I had a telekinetic leash wrapped around her, just in case he tried to yank her back to him.

If he did, I'd be following right along.

And I would end him.

My wrist buzzed, alerting me to an incoming message. I'd already shot Cillian a text to let him know Kyra had returned. It'd been quick, my focus on her more than my typing skills.

Is she all right? was his reply.

No. She's been bitten at least a dozen times. And there are track marks in her arms. The bastard forced her into a heat. I sent the full report back to him while my jaw clenched in fury.

My healing essence should be able to drag Kyra out of this, but it was going to take time. Hours, maybe even days.

Fucking with an Omega's cycle could have lasting impacts.

And those impacts were rather unknown at the moment, mostly because Kyra was a hybrid. V-Clan Omegas went into month-long estruses. I had no idea what Kyra's typical cycle looked like.

Fuck. Any idea where he is? Cillian asked.

No. But if he shows up here, he'll regret it. I wouldn't, though. I would happily rip off his balls and feed them to him.

Cillian didn't immediately reply, giving me a moment to send another wave of healing power through Kyra's sleeping form.

Her mind was mostly blank apart from a few needy mewls. I hated doing this to her. But it was the only way to provide her with a semblance of comfort.

Energy shimmered nearby, an incoming Alpha presence making my wolf growl low in warning.

It disappeared in the next breath, but my instincts remained on alert, my beast prowling beneath my skin.

My Kyra. My Omega. My mate.

She hummed in her sleep, her little rump bumping up against my throbbing knot.

I cursed under my breath, my muscles tight with barely restrained need.

This little Omega had gotten under my skin. Burrowed her way into my heart. Secured herself to my very soul.

It went beyond our wolves dancing, and directly to our spirits, this bond cementing us together for eternity.

Each passing day made it more and more difficult to remember why I didn't want this. Why I'd never desired a mate.

Apologies. The message scrolled through the air, the sender Kieran. *I didn't realize you would be... territorial.*

She's mine, I typed back, my wolf still agitated by Kieran's brief appearance near Kyra's nest. His leaving immediately had been the only thing that had kept my animal from charging out the door to challenge him.

Understood, he replied. *I'll keep my distance. But I'm here to guard while you see to Kyra's needs.*

I swallowed, my wolf still very close to the surface. Probably because I had a delicious Omega snuggled up against me. Vampire stench aside, she smelled divine.

Spicy blood oranges, ripe for the tasting.

Fuck.

I pressed my nose to her neck, inhaling deeply.

I desperately wanted to taste her. Nibble every inch of her. Kiss her. *Bite* her.

She was covered in another Alpha's cologne. *A vampire.* My wolf growled, hating his scent on her. Hating his marks. His claims. His venom poisoning her blood.

I wanted him gone.

Erased.

Replaced.

This Omega was *mine*. And I would not share her with that psychopath.

Hell, I wasn't sure I could share her with anyone.

Which was a huge fucking problem since Kyra didn't want a mate.

I pressed my mouth to her pulse, noting the normal heart rate. It was much better than before.

However, now my heart was the one racing. I wanted to slaughter her vampire mate. Kill anyone who so much as looked at her. Shred anyone who dared take her away from me.

"Fuck," I muttered, the visceral need to slaughter drowning me in a wave of intense aggression.

My knot pulsed. My beast raged. My insides smoldered.

Mine, I thought. *This Omega is mine.*

She just didn't know it yet.

I wrapped her up in my power, soothing her with both my healing ability and my purr.

She snuggled into me in her sleep, her contented sigh pleasing me immensely.

Kyra might not want a mate. But she officially had me for eternity.

I would just have to show her what that meant.

In the end, it would always be her choice.

But it was my job to be the right choice for her. The ideal mate. The one she could rely on. Trust. Admire. Maybe even love.

And in return, I would give her everything I could.

I would be enough. Be what she needed. Cherish her. Stand by her. Even let her lead, within reason.

All she had to do was give me a chance.

Maybe we'd discuss that when she woke up.

Or maybe I would wait until a more appropriate moment.

Regardless, my mind was set. I didn't care if it was her heat seducing my thoughts or if the events of the last few days had fundamentally altered my instincts.

The decision had been made.

Omega Kyra was mine.

And Alpha Fare was a dead man.

KYRA

Evergreens.
Wolf.
Alpha.
I rolled in the scents, reveling in the way it coated my bare skin. It was all over my nest. All over *me*.

But there was an underlying aroma of dead roses that tainted it all. *Dead roses dusted in rust.*

I shivered, not caring for that cologne. I wanted more of the evergreens.

My wolf sniffed, my nose searching until I found the source.

Hard. Hot. Male.
Mmm.
I nuzzled his chest, my palm sliding along the firm ridges of his abdomen and down to his hips.

My lips curled down, confused by the fabric there.

It was soft. Silky. Mildly acceptable. Except I wanted him naked, not clothed.

I kissed his chest, my tongue darting out to taste his skin. Only, my lips found a hint of something more there. Something delicious. *Blood.*

My mouth salivated, my stomach churning violently with *need*.

When was the last time I fed? I wondered deliriously. *Where even am I right now?*

Oh, but it didn't matter. This Alpha had what I craved. What I desperately required.

"Please," I whispered, asking him for permission, *begging* him to give me a taste.

I knew better than to bite without asking. Alphas were territorial. They only gave what they wanted to give. If I tried—

"Take whatever you need, Kyra," he said, his words punctuated by a low rumbling purr. "My blood is yours."

My eyes darted up to his, noting the sincerity in their dark depths. *Is this a fantasy?* I wondered.

It can be, if you want it to be, he returned, obviously having heard me.

Thank you, Alpha.

Lorcan, he replied.

My brow furrowed, not understanding his correction. But I was too hungry to ask for clarification. I needed to taste him. To bite him. To *feed*.

But where? I mused. *Where shall I….?* I trailed off, a memory nagging at my thoughts.

"*Now, where shall I bite you?*" a Vampire Alpha had asked recently. "*Decisions, decisions.*"

I swallowed, my appetite slowly dissipating.

Fane.

Images of a needle flashed through my mind, followed by his mouth. That cruel smile. His fangs in my flesh.

I jolted upright, my hands going to my hips and then my thighs. The marks were gone, my skin clear. But I could still feel his touch there. His greedy pulls. His taunts.

A gasp left me, my nest suddenly feeling all sorts of wrong.

My body defiled. *The scents...* I rolled out of the bed, desperate to fix it, needing to... to... be rid of *him*.

"Kyra." The Alpha in my nest said my name with a purr that had my knees threatening to bend. It was such a soothing sound. So perfect. So... *hypnotic*. "Tell me what you need, and I'll give it to you."

"I..." I blinked at the room, searching for the foul scents. A vision of rose petals replayed in my thoughts, along with a note... "The flowers...?"

"I threw them away," the Alpha said, sounding disgruntled. Yet his purr remained. That beautiful, loving sound.

I want more of it, I thought dreamily. *Between my thighs. Against my throat. During a kiss...*

But I couldn't do that right now. I needed to fix my nest. Remove the dead stench. The wrongness.

It's all fucking wrong.

I growled, furious by my sullied sheets. My marked skin. The cologne ugly and repellent.

A shower, I realized. *Yes. Yes, that's what I need.*

I started toward the bathroom but paused as the purr behind me grew softer.

The Alpha wasn't following.

No, no. He had to come, too. I... I needed his purr. His aroma. *His blood.*

He slid from my nest, his expression emotionless as he stepped forward.

Had he discerned my needs from my actions? Or had he read my mind?

I wasn't sure. Nor did I care.

What mattered was his presence, his protection, his alluring fragrance.

I moved toward him to press my nose to his chest, my inhale deep and purposeful as I indulged in his essence. Even that hint of blood on his skin was heavenly.

Wrapping my hand around his, I pulled him with me toward the adjoining bathroom and started a shower. The tub was too small for him, let alone both of us. So a shower would have to do.

He said nothing as I prepared the water, finding the right temperature. Then I stepped inside and stared at him expectantly. He needed to remove those boxer shorts. I wasn't sure why he had them on anyway.

When did he put them on? I wondered. *Or… wait… wasn't he wearing… jeans?*

Everything from the last few… however long it'd been… was muddled together. Reminiscent of a dream.

Actually, it still very much felt like a dream now.

But at least I wasn't on fire anymore.

Just hungry. *Make that starving.*

His jaw ticked, his dark eyes staring down at me with a whirlwind of emotions. "Who am I?" he asked me after a few seconds.

My eyebrows came down, the question not making sense to me. "Alpha."

He shook his head. "Lorcan."

There was that word again.

Rather, his *name*.

Lorcan, the Elite, I thought.

My wolf rumbled in approval inside, reminding me of a time she'd played with her Alpha on the ice. Rolling around. Bumping his side. *Curling into a ball to snuggle in the ice cave.*

The water rained down around me as the memories spun through my mind.

Only for a more recent moment to take over next. *Me on the bed. Spreading my legs. Ruby-red eyes. Fangs.*

I shuddered and grabbed the soap, suddenly feeling the need to scrub at my skin. *Wrong. Wrong. Wrong.*

The Alpha stepped in with me, his boxer shorts still in place.

Such a tease. Because I could see the outline of his impressive knot and I *very much* wanted a taste of it.

But I needed to rid myself of this stench first.

Clean myself. Bathe in the scent of this Alpha. *Bite him.*

He took the soap from me and lathered it against my skin, helping me to chase away the odor of the other Alpha. The wrong one. The one who made my stomach twist with dread.

I swallowed as this Alpha went to his knees, his gaze intent on my thighs, his touch purposeful yet hot. It made me want to draw his hands up higher, right to the apex between my legs.

But he was methodical. *Thorough.* Creating suds and washing them away, then repeating the motion until, finally, he pressed his nose to my skin and inhaled. His eyes held mine the whole time, hunger smoldering in those inky depths.

Slick immediately pooled in my core, responding to that look. That *need*.

Because *oh, yes, please.*

I drew my fingers through his thick hair, yearning to feel him. Hold him. *Guide him.*

"Tell me my name, Kyra," he whispered, his words sounding almost pained.

Alpha lingered on my tongue. But I was beginning to understand what he wanted. What he was trying to ensure I knew.

Him.

Lorcan.

The Elite... I'm mated to.

I stared down at him, my tongue thickening in my mouth.

He'd pulled me back from Fare. Saved me from a fate I didn't even want to think about facing. Because I'd been in heat.

Yet now... now I was... still in heat. But not quite. On the fringes of it, I supposed. Leaving the heart of the cycle.

Hence my hunger.

No, actually. That was because of Fare. He'd taken a lot of my blood. Too much. Without providing any in return.

I was famished.

Dying of thirst.

But there were other things I craved, too.

Like Lorcan. On his knees. With his mouth against my thigh.

Not biting. Just... kissing.

He held my gaze as he did precisely that, leaning forward to taste the skin he'd just finished soaping and rinsing. My eyes nearly closed in delight, the sensation so all-consuming that I almost forgot how to breathe.

His hands ran up my opposite leg then, his touch repeating the same ministrations—removing Fare's stench. His marks. His existence.

Lorcan... was replacing him.

Showing me what it was like to be cherished. Respected. *Mated.*

I'd been in the throes of my heat, and he'd... rejected me. Sort of. I'd felt his need. Could smell it. Yet he hadn't tried to knot me at all. He'd put me in some sort of sleep state, his healing power helping to chase away the remnants of Fare's venom.

Lorcan had taken care of me.

Held me.

Purred for me.

He was still caring for me now, with each stroke of his fingers, chasing away Fare with individual caresses against my skin.

I shivered despite the heat of the water spray, my body slickening for very different reasons than my heat.

Lorcan was seducing me. Perhaps not on purpose, but his touch was... *hypnotic.* Perfect. Exactly what I needed.

I tightened my hold in his hair as he moved his fingers up

to my hip bones, his thumbs completing little circles against my skin.

"Where else did he bite you?" he asked, his voice low as he finished with my hips—his nose having brushed against each one when he was done.

"My breasts," I told him. "My... clit."

His nostrils flared, his gaze going to my shaved mound. "Only your clit? Nowhere else down here?"

My throat worked as I slowly shook my head. "He bit me multiple places down there."

Lorcan's jaw ticked, his thoughts raging with murderous intent.

He would have to stand in line. Because now that I knew Fare had survived, I fully intended to murder him all over again.

And this time, I would remember to bring a fucking match.

Mmm, there's my little killer, Lorcan mused into my mind.

I almost snorted, but his touch... went... to my overheated center. He gently applied soap, his movements meticulous as he lathered away Fare's invisible marks.

And replaced them with his own.

My legs trembled, my fingers clenching in his hair.

I hadn't been with an Alpha in over a century. These last however many days with Fare didn't count. He hadn't knotted me. He'd only bitten me. He'd been waiting until I was too incoherent for words to fuck me.

His friends hadn't even entered the room.

Yet there were still hundreds of memories I longed to have erased. *Replaced.*

It could be the residual moments of my heat driving my needs, but deep down, I knew it was so much more than that.

Somewhere along the way, Lorcan had touched a piece of my soul. Maybe with those afternoon runs. The way he'd cuddled my wolf.

Or perhaps it was just *her*, my animal, knowing that this was right. Knowing that he was meant to be ours. Choosing him as her mate, not because we'd been forced into this mating of convenience, but because he'd proved himself worthy to her.

Then he'd proved himself worthy to *me* by not knotting me when he easily could have.

He'd respected me.

He'd protected me.

He'd *healed* me.

And now, he seemed to be claiming me.

With each touch, I felt more and more like I belonged to him.

His palms went to my hips again as he leaned in to scent my mound and lower to my clit, his nose skimming my skin along the way. His exhale touched my slick folds, sending a quiver up my spine.

"Lorcan," I whispered, my legs suddenly weak.

"Mmm," he hummed. "Say it again."

"Lorcan."

"Good girl," he breathed, the words right against my sensitive nub. "Do you want me to more thoroughly remove his bite, little killer? Replace it with my tongue, perhaps?"

"Yes," I admitted. "Yes, please."

"Tell me to lick you."

"Lick me," I repeated automatically, warmth spreading along my skin. "*Please.*"

LORCAN

My knot throbbed, my groin tightening with *need*.

That vampire's presence lingered on my Omega, his memory tainting her mind, his fangs leaving invisible claims all over her creamy skin.

I wanted him gone. Dead. *Replaced*.

My wolf snarled in agreement. Fare had no business being between me and Kyra. No purpose residing in either of our thoughts.

This was about me and her. Our wolves. Our bond. Convenient or not, it had grown. Into what, I wasn't sure.

But I wanted her.

Hell, I *needed* her.

My cock had been hard for three fucking days while she'd healed. Three fucking days of having her naked body pressed against me. Three fucking days of hearing her little mewls and smelling her delectable slick.

Then she'd woken up and sniffed me like I was her favorite perfume.

And now she was wet. Freshly clean. *So beautifully swollen.*

I held her gaze as I leaned forward to lave her clit. Her

pupils dilated, her wolf staring down at me with stark approval.

My inner beast gazed right back up at her, his low growl rumbling in my chest and making our mate's legs shake in response.

An Alpha could use that sound to make his Omega wet between the thighs, to help encourage a rut. But Kyra was already soaked, her pussy lips glistening with arousal.

I slid my tongue along her slick folds, indulging in a thorough taste.

Kyra's grip tightened in my hair, her body trembling. "Lorcan," she breathed.

"So good," I praised, pleased that she kept saying my name. It told me she wasn't lost to her heat any longer, that she was actually aware of what we were doing.

And it meant she wasn't thinking about *him*.

I sealed my lips around her clit, determined to give her sensual gratification rather than pain. She deserved to be adored. Worshipped. *Pleasured*.

Her mouth parted on a gasp, her hips undulating toward me as I suckled her hard little nub.

My name left her lips again, this time on a pant as she leaned back against the tiled wall behind her. Both her hands were in my hair now, her fingers gripping my strands tightly as she rocked herself into my face.

It was so fucking hot to watch her writhe. So alluring to feel her slick against my lips. And absolutely perfect to experience her flavor on my tongue.

I wanted more. So. Much. More.

My tongue flattened against her as I released one of her hips and drew my hand down to her thighs. Goose bumps met my touch, her body quaking beneath my attentions.

I slid my palm upward, my fingers teasing her opening.

She arched off the wall in response, her body seemingly

desperate for me to own her. Claim her. Mark her inside and out.

I gave her what she wanted, slipping two fingers inside her and curling them in a way I knew would drive her mad.

She moaned, long and loud, the sound one I would forever remember. Because *I* did that to her.

And it was *my* name that rolled over her tongue.

She was close. I could feel it in the way she clenched around me. The way her grasp became violent. The way her nipples beaded into hard points.

I wanted her to come. To explode on my tongue. Mark me with her scent as I claimed her with my mouth.

Scream my name for me, little killer, I murmured. *Let everyone know your Alpha is on his knees for you.*

Her limbs shook in response, her fingers locking in my hair.

And then she flew apart on an orgasm that rocked through our bond, making my knot *ache* for her.

Intense waves of ecstasy rippled between us, her climax explosive. Beautiful. Positively divine.

I lapped at her weeping cunt, loving her citrusy flavor.

Then I smiled as she started to come again, her Omega pussy primed and ready for its Alpha. She needed more than just my tongue, her sheath clenching around my fingers in a silent demand for my knot.

But I forced her to fall apart like this once more, needing to remove any and all traces of that vampire from her body.

When she finished wringing my fingers, her body was replete from three subsequent orgasms.

But that sense of gratification wouldn't last long.

Pleasing her had unleashed her wolf. And her wolf was *hungry*. As was her vampire.

My Omega still needed blood.

She also needed my knot.

I kissed a path up her body, then paused at her breasts as I recalled what she'd said about Fare's bite.

Retrieving the soap I'd discarded earlier—when my attention had gone to licking Kyra instead of cleaning her—I refocused my efforts on her chest.

Her nipples were hard little points, begging for my mouth. But I washed them first, three times with soap and water.

Only then did I give those needy buds my lips and teeth.

I didn't bite. I only nibbled. Kyra's body deserved reverence. Teasing. *Love.*

I sucked her nipples into my mouth and rolled them with my tongue. She moaned in response, her touch sliding to my shoulders to hold me against her.

Once I finished with her tits, I continued on my path upward, my nose leading the way.

Fare had left his scent against her neck, his claim all over her throat.

I fixed it with soap and water. Then I kissed away each invisible bite, re-marking Kyra as my own.

By the time I reached her mouth, she was a sensual goddess of need and desire. Her catlike eyes gleamed with intent, her fingers digging into my shoulders.

"Knot me," she demanded.

"Who am I?" I asked her, my fingers going to my boxers as I waited for her reply.

"My *inconvenient* mate," she snapped, making my lips twitch. "Lorcan. An Elite. A soon-to-be-dead Alpha if you don't put your knot inside me right fucking now."

I chuckled, my boxers disappearing in a flash. "I'm going to have to fuck that attitude right out of you."

"You can try," she replied.

My hands went to her hips, my wolf roaring in expectant victory. "Tell me if I go too hard."

"You won't."

"You underestimate how much I want you, little killer." I lifted her off the ground. "Wrap your legs around me."

She did, her movements compliant and yet urgent at the same time. Her thighs *squeezed* my hips, demanding that I enter her. Fuck her. *Claim her.*

I shifted to align my cock with her entrance. I'd read from her mind that it'd been a very long time since an Alpha had last fucked her. So I attempted to ease myself in slowly.

But the little vixen undulated her hips and forced me deeper, faster, by pressing herself into me.

A moan left her lips, her head falling back against the wall as she shut her eyes.

None of that, I thought, my hand going to her jaw. *Look at me while I fuck you, Kyra.*

Her lashes fluttered as she obeyed, her passionate stare drugging my instincts.

I slammed into her fully, loving the way she released a little gasp at my size and power.

I could worship her and destroy her at the same time, something her mind was encouraging me to do.

More, she was demanding. *Harder.*

I pulled out to the tip and drove into her again, forcing her to take all of me, claiming her irrevocably, *mating* her.

Her nails scratched down my back, her hips pushing into mine.

But there was one thing missing. Something vital. A piece of her I still needed to possess.

Her mouth.

Kyra's nostrils flared as I captured her gaze, her pupils resembling huge black diamonds.

I held her stare as I brushed my lips over hers. Then I teased the seam with my tongue. She invited me inside with a gasp, her body opening to me in every way.

I didn't hesitate to accept her invitation, to possess every part of her.

Her mouth.
Her tongue.
Her breasts.
Her pussy.

I laid my claim over every inch of her, my punishing thrusts forever marking her as *mine*. My kiss devastating her for future men—of which there would be none. My roaming hands leaving invisible traces all over her skin.

Mine. Mine. Mine.

My wolf snarled in agreement, demanding that I sink my teeth into her neck to renew our mating bond. But I held him back. Kyra had been bitten enough these last few days. I'd give in to my beast's desires another day.

Because there would be another day.

Hell, there'd be more fucking tonight.

"Squeeze your pussy around me," I told Kyra. "Mark me like I'm marking you. Make me knot you. Make me *claim* you."

Her nails turned into claws against my shoulder, her lips curling against mine. "I want to make you bleed."

"Then do it," I snarled as I fucked her against the wall. "Rip me apart. Bite me. Do whatever you want."

Her sheath clenched around me, clearly liking that notion.

But she didn't rake her claws across my chest like I'd anticipated.

Instead, she bit down on my lip. *Hard.* And soothed away the ache with her tongue.

A groan left her as she imbibed some of my blood. A feral noise followed, then she did it again. Even harder.

I gripped the back of her neck, squeezing to show dominance. But I didn't stop her from biting me. My savage little killer needed an outlet, and I happily provided it to her.

Our kiss turned messy, my blood pooling between us as she greedily swallowed.

She pulsed around me, her orgasm nearing. I thrust into

her, urging her along, aware that her impending explosion would force me over the edge with her.

My knot pulsed in expectation, my balls tightening.

So good, I thought, loving the way she gripped me. *So fucking good.*

Kyra's nails embedded themselves in my shoulder again, her body tensing against me. "Lorcan!" she screamed as she fell apart on a powerful wave, her body clamping down around me and demanding that I follow her into oblivion.

A roar tore out of my throat as my knot shot forward, securing me to my Omega and sending us both into a violent spiral of euphoria.

It overwhelmed every aspect of my being, darkening my sight, shooting fire through my veins, drawing growls from my chest.

So fucking intense.

So amazingly perfect.

Kyra panted, her body shuddering from the onslaught of pleasure drugging her being.

Her forehead went to my shoulder, her little tongue gingerly stroking the bloody indents she'd created with her claws.

"Drink from me," I whispered to her. "I can feel your thirst."

She shivered, her mind telling me how thankful she was that I'd offered again. She'd been afraid to take from me before. But I told her with a thought that my offer was indefinite. She could bite me whenever she needed to. I would never reject her.

Her incisors bit into my neck, her resulting moan going straight to my balls and making me want to knot her all over again.

But I hadn't yet finished coming inside her, my knot unleashing my claim in the most intimate way imaginable.

She'd be sensing my seed inside her for days.

And when that sensation started to disappear, I'd just fill her up again.

I wanted her drenched in my cum. Saturated in my essence.

You're mine now, little killer.

Yes. Till death do us part, she mused tiredly back at me.

I chuckled. *Is that a threat?*

Probably.

Excellent, I told her. *Violent foreplay is my favorite.*

Then it's a good thing I have a lot of knives.

Mmm. A good thing indeed, I whispered back at her. *But first, I need to knot you again.*

In my nest, she told me. *I need... your scent. In my nest.*

I pressed my lips to hers, my kiss gentler than before. *I would be honored to scent your nest, Kyra.*

She smiled, the motion a bit shy. *Thank you, Alpha.*

This time, I didn't make her say my name. She meant the title as a compliment. An endearment of sorts. And I welcomed the sentiment.

Just as I welcomed the opportunity to mark her nest.

Over and over again.

Until both of us were too exhausted to move.

Only then did I pull her into my arms and whisper, "I've changed my mind. I do want a mate. I want you."

But she was already asleep.

Her mind beautifully quiet.

"Sweet dreams, little killer," I told her, my purr igniting at her back. "There will be no nightmares today. Or ever again. Because I'm here. And I'm here to stay."

KYRA

Lorcan stood beside my nest, his knot an engorged distraction I tried to ignore. But it was right there in front of my face, too huge for me to miss. So, really, he couldn't blame me for staring at it.

In typical Lorcan behavior, he arched his eyebrow. "See something you want?"

"Yes," I admitted. "But I'm not done yet."

I bent to retrieve one of his recently worn shirts—he'd been staying in my nest while I was gone, waiting for me to come back—and added it to the corner of my nest.

All traces of Fare were gone, completely replaced by Lorcan. At least in my nest.

My mind would take time. Fortunately, I'd spent the better part of the last century overcoming my experiences with Fare.

What he'd done to me this last week had paled in comparison to our history. I could handle his venom. And it seemed I could handle his compulsion, too.

Something had clicked during my forced heat. Some sort of switch I hadn't realized I possessed.

I'd told Lorcan about how my wolf seemed to take over,

her fury providing me with the strength to overcome Fare's mind control.

I couldn't feel him now, likely because he wasn't actively trying to engage me.

This definitely wasn't over. But I felt more confident. More in control. More *alive*.

I'd escaped him.

That meant I could do it again.

Although, Lorcan seemed pretty fixated on not leaving my side until Fare was dead. He hadn't voiced that opinion aloud, but I'd overheard it in his thoughts.

Along with several other proclamations he hadn't mentioned out loud yet.

Like the one about staying in the Sanctuary. Indefinitely.

Things were evolving between us. I wasn't sure how I felt about it, just that it felt right.

Neither of us was trying to label it.

And I liked that.

My wolf was content, too. Especially because her Alpha kept purring for her. Like right now. All that rumbly goodness vibrated behind me as I bent to fluff one of my many pillows.

While I hadn't said anything out loud, Lorcan knew how important my nest was to me. Particularly as Fare had never let me keep one.

This had been my safe haven for over a century. I'd never allowed an Alpha inside it.

Lorcan had been the first one when he'd shadowed us here after the sparring match outside.

Then Fare had arrived and defiled my space, just like he always had. Except Lorcan had cleaned up the mess in my absence.

Afterward, he'd stayed here while protecting the Sanctuary.

He'd also been trying to find me, something I'd realized when he'd shown me the map he'd put up on the hallway wall outside of my nest. There were pins everywhere noting potential locations for Fare's nest, all based on what I'd told him and his instincts.

He and Kieran had also sent out information requests to their allies in other sectors around the world, hoping someone could provide a lead.

Lorcan's purr intensified as I crawled out of my nest to grab more clothes from his basket. This time I took a pair of boxers and used it to prop up one of my pillows. Then I went back for a pair of lounge pants. They were black and smelled like evergreens tinged with sensual male. I inhaled happily and added them to my growing pile of Lorcan-scented items.

He didn't move while I worked, just stood there waiting to be used or called upon.

I sprawled out in my nest and rolled around, my inner wolf and vampire both content in a way I hadn't felt in a very long time.

Sighing, I slid to the back and looked expectantly at my mate. "I'm ready for your knot, Alpha."

His lips curled as he placed a knee on the mattress. "Where do you want it, Omega?"

I spread my legs, my thighs already slick in anticipation. "Here."

"Do you want my tongue first?"

I considered it for a moment, my lip catching between my teeth. Then I slowly shook my head. Because no. I wanted him inside me. Knotting me. Spilling his masculine scent all over our nest.

It would complete my project, complete *us*.

He crawled over me, his dark eyes holding me captive beneath him as he settled between my legs, his cock hot and heavy against my center. "That might have been the most painful three hours of my life, watching you prance around naked while working on your nest."

"Even more painful than my heat?" I asked, arching up into him.

"*False* heat," he corrected. "And that experience had been different. I wasn't allowed to touch you then."

"And now?"

"And now..." He slid into me in a measured thrust, his engorged length filling me deliciously. "And now you're *mine*."

I moaned as he pulled all the way out and drove into me again, his thick shaft stretching me with each punch of his hips against mine.

It was unlike any of my previous encounters, primarily because this one was very much consensual. Both parts of me craved Lorcan, even my vampire half. He made me feel complete in a way I hadn't anticipated, his wolf placating mine in a manner I hadn't realized I needed.

Mating of convenience it is, I mused, my body rising to meet his. *So convenient. Better than convenient. Pretty damn amazing, actually.*

Fucking spectacular, he corrected, his mouth claiming mine.

I moaned as his tongue slid between my lips, his motions rivaling that of his movements below.

Plundering and worshipping.

Taking and giving.

Owning and nurturing.

I wrapped my arms around his neck, lost to our embrace, loving the way he handled me. It wasn't tender at all, his methods very much treating me as his equal rather than something breakable. Which was exactly what I needed.

My trauma was in the past. The only way to erase it was to be grounded in the present.

I didn't want to be seen as fragile, but strong. And his pace told me he knew that. He respected that. He *liked* that.

I bit down on his lower lip, drawing blood and allowing it to flow over my tongue.

He growled in response, his wolf pleased by my mark. It

kept healing, which made me want to bite him often, just to ensure my vampiric kiss never left his skin.

This male was mine.

If any of the other Omegas here thought to claim him, they were in for a world of hurt. Because I would not share him. Not ever.

He groaned, the sound sending shivers down my spine. *I'm not going to share you either, mate,* he whispered into my mind. *You're mine.*

So you keep saying.

Then allow me to prove it, he countered, his mouth going to my neck.

I froze as he sank his teeth into my skin, hard enough to make me bleed.

But he didn't drink. He simply left his imprint there, the impact oddly... soothing. *Another memory chased away*, I realized. *Replaced by Lorcan.*

He lapped at the wound, his inner beast growling in approval. However, he didn't push me to take more. Didn't shove any venom into my veins. Didn't force me into an unwilling heat.

Because he wasn't a vampire.

He was a wolf.

My wolf.

My Alpha.

And he didn't believe in taking me by force. He wanted my willing participation, my pleasure.

I pushed my hips up against him, taking him deeper, needing to feel everything. His knot. His rapture. His *seed*.

Fill me, Alpha, I demanded. *Mark me as yours.*

His mouth returned to mine, his growl all Alpha male. He liked the idea of possessing me. It was a drive he didn't bother to fight despite his feelings about having a mate.

I understood because I felt the same.

I embraced my instincts, loving the way it felt to be taken by such virility. Cherished. *Owned*.

My nails bit into his back, my wolf needing to lay claim to him as well, as I licked the blood from his lips. It was a mixture of our essences, providing a decadent flavor that intrigued my inner vampire.

I'd thought only a Vampire Alpha's blood could sate my Omega needs, but it turned out that Lorcan was more than capable.

In fact, he was exactly what I craved.

Strong. Caring. Dominant.

Every aspect of him was desirable and had been from the beginning. I just hadn't wanted to admit it to myself or to him.

His palm wrapped around my nape, his Alpha prowess taking over as his opposite hand went to my hip. He took over in every way, fucking me in our nest with a force that took my breath away.

There was no holding back.

No gentle movements.

Just pure Alpha aggression.

And I loved it. Yearned for it. *Needed* it.

Each thrust further drove my past from my mind, exchanging it with thoughts of Lorcan. New memories. New experiences. Redefined expectations.

I panted beneath him, my thighs clamping around him as I held on for the ride. My center throbbed for him, my clit rubbing him each time he propelled himself forward.

It was intense.

Perfect.

Arousing.

His knot was right there, pulsating against my flesh, the thick bulb pure Alpha male. I wanted it inside me. Securing us together. Driving us to new pleasurable heights.

I'd feared this for so long. Terrified to let another Alpha inside me like this.

But Lorcan was different. He was *mine*.

Yours, he whispered. *Now come for me, mate. Squeeze my knot and take me over the edge with you.*

I arched into him on a moan, his demand echoing through my spirit and tugging on my nerve endings. I wanted to please him. Earn his praise. *Earn his knot.*

My limbs tensed as the maelstrom inside me threatened to burst. It made my stomach *twist* with need. Intense. Overwhelming. Passionate.

Lorcan's tongue tamed mine, his mind urging me forward. *Now, mate,* he demanded. *Come for me now.*

Hearing him repeatedly say *mate* into my mind lit a fire in my veins. It made me feel treasured. Respected. *Claimed.*

My heart skipped a beat, my breath stalling in my lungs. *So much. Too much.* It was overwhelming. Hot. All-consuming.

I clenched around him, my lower half bowing off the bed as the flames lit up my nerve endings from head to toe.

His name echoed from my lips, only to be swallowed by his resulting growl. So animalistic in nature. Feral. *Commanding.*

Warmth exploded through my insides as his knot shot forward, claiming me in the way only an Alpha could.

Rapturous vibrations pulsed through my being, rendering me useless beneath him. Motionless. Lost to my incoherent screams. *Satisfied.*

Oh so intensely satisfied.

Over and over again.

Unending pleasure. Ecstasy personified.

This was what mating with an Alpha should feel like, a profound meeting of souls on a plane of nonexistence. An out-of-body experience. Oblivion. The restructuring of reality.

I clung to him through it all, reveling in the euphoric waves licking at my core, causing me to spiral into unending bliss.

Lorcan.

Kyra, he returned, his voice holding a note of reverence as he kissed me soundly. *Mate.*

I shivered, my arms looping around his neck once more. They'd fallen during my climax, my body having gone through some sort of spiritual episode. It was as though I'd died and come back to life, but only in the best way.

His tongue grounded me, assuring me that I'd never actually left, that it'd all been just a pleasurable affair.

Our mingled scents reached my nose, my nest feeling more complete than ever before.

I inhaled deeply and sighed. *Evergreen. Alpha. Oranges. Dead roses.*

My brow furrowed on that last one.

Wait... My eyes flew open, my limbs freezing.

"What is it?" Lorcan asked, his handsome face hovering right above mine, his knot still lodged deep within me.

I opened my mouth. Then closed it.

And inhaled again.

Dead roses.

They were gone. They weren't here. *How...?*

I searched my mind, my wolf beginning to pace, agitated.

"I—" A sharp pang tugged at my heart, causing my body to jolt beneath Lorcan as my shadowing ability attempted to engage against my will.

My eyes widened, my arms tightening around Lorcan.

No! I shouted, fighting the urge to disappear. *No, no, no!*

Lorcan growled, his power wrapping around me in a telekinetic hug that forced me to remain. But my mind was insistent.

Come to me, I heard Fare whisper. *Come to me right fucking now.*

No, I snarled back at him, my mind fracturing beneath his command and my body's inability to comply.

Now! Fare demanded.

Everything faded in and out, light and dark, my eyes focusing and blurring.

No, I whimpered, my mind at war with my body, at war with Fare, at war with my very existence.

Lorcan said something above me, but I couldn't hear him. I could barely breathe. The need to shadow was consuming my being. But I couldn't. Lorcan wouldn't let me. Yet Fare demanded it.

I suddenly felt strained.

Caught between two battling Alphas.

Two conflicting demands.

Two strong personalities.

Two ancient beings.

Ripping me in half. Shredding my wolf and vampire spirits.

Agony splintered inside as I tried to fight them both, to make my own decisions.

My nest. My safe haven. My Alpha. That was what I wanted. What I needed. *This is my life. My soul. I'll do what I want!*

Cruel laughter echoed in my thoughts, Fare mocking my attempt at refusing him.

Only for him to snarl in the next moment as Lorcan sent a blast of healing energy directly into my mind.

I flinched, the power momentarily blocking Fare from my thoughts. But I knew it wouldn't hold. He'd implanted some sort of anchor in my head. A back door that allowed him access to control me.

Or at least to command me to shadow back to him.

I buried my head in Lorcan's chest, greedily inhaling his scent, needing to feel whole again. Needing to remind myself that I was *here*, with *him*.

His arms were around me, his being protecting mine.

But it wouldn't last long.

I could feel Fare clawing his way through.

Only for Lorcan to hit me with another explosion of his healing power.

His growl rumbled through my chest, followed swiftly by his purr.

No, both at once.

My mind whirled, fighting to understand.

He's talking, I realized. *He's talking to someone in a growl.*

But the purr was all for me.

A beacon. Another type of anchor. One I appreciated. One I *needed*.

Healing energy battled with compulsion in my head while Lorcan grounded me in reality, allowing me to look at him once more.

He'd rolled us to our sides, his knot no longer attached to me.

His palm was on my face, his eyes on mine.

"We're going to kill him," he promised me. "We're going to find him and kill him."

I blinked, suddenly exhausted. *Let me know how that goes,* I thought drowsily at him, my eyelids drooping.

Oh, no, mate, he whispered back to me. *I'll have a front-row seat. Because I'm going to watch you kill him. Then I'm going to hand you a match so you can burn his remains.*

I swallowed, his image a nice one in my head.

Killing Fare once and for all would be... a very good dream.

The fact that he wanted me to do it made it that much better.

Rest, he added. *Kieran will be here soon to help me drive Fare out of your mind. Then we'll start hunting.*

LORCAN

Kieran stood in the hallway, his focus on the map, while his healing essence surrounded Kyra.

"She already started unraveling his compulsion on her own," he'd said upon arrival, his admiration evident. "Unless you did that?"

I'd shaken my head. Because no, I hadn't. That had all been Kyra's doing.

Kieran had nodded then and begun unweaving Fare's compulsion from her mind, just like he'd done for Myon and Fritz.

It would go faster if he could touch her, but he knew better than to try to enter her nest. Especially with me standing nearby.

Our mating might have started as a platonic business transaction, but it had evolved into something much more primal. Kieran undoubtedly sensed that in the way my wolf prowled just beneath the surface.

"I'm still waiting for a few return calls," he told me conversationally. "But I have enough information from some of our allies to cross certain locations off your map."

He listed the island names, giving me something to preoccupy my mind while Kyra healed.

Then he informed me about which Alpha-Omega pairs would be relocating to the Sanctuary this week. There were four sets, all of them from Blood Sector.

"I can't stay here much longer," he added. "My wolf misses his pregnant mate. As do I."

I glanced through the doorway, my eyes falling on Kyra's prone form in her nest. An image of her being pregnant with our pup flirted with my thoughts. That would certainly not happen anytime soon, but maybe one day. If that was what she wanted.

However, if that day ever came, I doubted I would have the strength to leave her side.

Which was a realization that made me frown.

Kieran had shadowed here out of duty, his need to protect his mate's Sanctuary likely the motivator he'd required to justify leaving Quinnlynn.

I would do the same for Kyra if I had to. But I wasn't sure I could do it for him.

And that was the cause for my frown.

At some point, my loyalty had shifted.

Kyra was now my priority, not my cousin.

"You don't approve of my Alpha-Omega choices?" Kieran asked, his midnight irises scrutinizing me.

I shook my head. "No, those pairings are adequate. I assume Quinnlynn already approved them."

"She did," he confirmed. "But your expression displays doubt."

"Because your comment about missing your mate made me realize I couldn't very easily leave mine," I told him. I'd always been blunt with my cousin. Though, we rarely spoke. Well, *I* rarely spoke. Mostly because I never had much to say.

However, lately that had changed.

Because of Kyra.

"I rather gathered that." Kieran ran his knowing gaze over me. "You realize this decision will make your new title permanent, yes?"

"I do." Because Kyra would never want to leave the Sanctuary. I'd deduced that from her thoughts. This was her home. She'd dedicated her life to these Omegas, and nothing would take her away from them.

I would never desire to change her mind.

If she wanted to nest here, we would nest here. And I would help her lead by keeping the Alphas in line.

"Have you spoken to her about it?" he asked.

"Not yet." I'd filled her in on bits and pieces over the last day, but we'd mostly spent our time between the sheets. Or on top of them. Or in the shower. And once against the door.

"Does she know about Fritz?"

"She knows he's alive." She also knew about Fare's compulsion because the vampire had bragged about it. "The one thing she didn't understand was why Fare had never asked Fritz for information about me." As apparently Fare had drilled Kyra for my name.

Yet she'd never given it.

Which was a good thing.

Because if she had, he'd likely be on the run right now. It was best for him to assume I was a regular Alpha. That would give him confidence. Play into his ego. Ensure he stayed put long enough for us to find him and kill him.

Of course, today's display of power might have served as a warning regarding his competition.

Which made finding him soon all the more imperative.

"Did you explain how the dreams always ended if Fare asked about anything to do with the Sanctuary?"

I nodded. "I told her that was why he couldn't ask about her—she's part of the Sanctuary. And it wasn't like he could implant random ideas about her that would make Fritz talk."

That seemed to be how Fare had controlled the Omega—via idea stimulation.

Such as his idea to turn off the security feeds.

And his idea to manipulate Quinnlynn.

Although, technically, her parents had been killed by an Alpha after all. Just not a V-Clan Alpha.

Kieran hummed, his focus returning to the map. "She's almost fully healed."

"Thank you."

"No need to thank me. You would do the same for me if you could." His midnight eyes flicked back to me. "You realize that just because you're the new Sanctuary Sector Alpha doesn't mean you're not still one of my Elites, yes?"

"Forever enslaved to the Blood Sector King."

"We are blood, after all," he drawled.

I rolled my eyes but found my lips twitching upward at the sides. "Have you finished repairing the enchantment?" I wondered aloud, aware that he'd finally discovered the problem yesterday.

He inclined his chin. "Yes, now that I've finally mastered the magic, I was able to fix it."

"So the breach was related to the diamonds?"

"It was," he confirmed. "That was the real reason why the jewelry had to touch the barrier. I finally figured it out when I found the back door."

"So we don't have a mole in our midst."

"Not that I'm aware of, but Jas is still re-vetting everyone. She took your comments seriously."

"Good." Just because someone was a certain designation didn't make him or her automatically innocent. "But about the magical barrier, does that mean the explosion wasn't just meant to kill Quinnlynn, but to create the back door?"

I wanted to be sure we'd covered all our bases and didn't have any other potential security concerns on the island.

"Yes. It seemed to be the backup plan, one Myon didn't

know about. The spell he cast was one Fare had given him, not one he concocted from memory. Of course, that makes me wonder how Fare acquired that information."

True, I thought, frowning. "He's ancient. It could be any number of old acquaintances." But whoever it was had to be a V-Clan wolf. Because only V-Clan pack members understood our magic.

"Yes," Kieran repeated, his palm going to his nape as he stretched his back, the movement telling me he was more exhausted than he was letting on.

It seemed fixing the enchantment had taken a lot out of him. Given that it was a protection spell that hid an entire island, I wasn't surprised.

"She's healed," he murmured, his eyes falling closed. "You can wake her up now."

Rather than wake her, I simply removed my healing essence from her mind, granting her the option to stir on her own.

Then I turned toward the map while we waited. "Has Ander gotten back to you yet?" I asked, referring to the Andorra Sector Alpha. He was an X-Clan wolf who had access to some of the world's best technology.

Of course, it wasn't as good as ours, but he had surveillance in areas we did not.

"His last message said he might have a lead, but he hasn't confirmed it yet. I'll let you know as soon as I hear from him." He checked his watch. "In the meantime, I think I'll go call my mate, give her an update on things here. She'll be pleased to know Kyra is in good hands."

"Very good hands," I heard her murmur from the other room. "Excellent hands. Alpha hands. *Lorcan* hands."

My lips curled at the drunken slur in her words. "Someone is high on healing magic."

She hummed happily in response while Kieran smirked. "Have fun," he told me, shadowing out of the hallway before my wolf could even consider the fact that it was *his* magic Kyra was enjoying, not mine.

She's healed, I told my beast. *Don't start snapping your jaws now.*

He huffed, his irritation mild, but one look through the door had him perking up with interest, the altercation forgotten. Because his Omega was sitting up in her nest, looking perfectly rumpled.

And very naked.

I'd covered her with blankets before Kieran had arrived, careful to hide her beautiful form.

A ridiculous concept, really, considering we were both shifters who had to be nude before we could change into our wolf states.

But that didn't stop my possessive instincts from flaring in her presence.

"What did Kieran do to me?" she asked dreamily. "I feel... *free.*"

"He unwove every strand of compulsion Fare has ever implanted in your mind," I said as I stepped into the room.

The door shut softly behind me, closing us in her safe space.

She stretched her arms over her head, her breasts moving sensuously with the display. It didn't matter that I'd just knotted her an hour ago. My cock was hard and ready for more.

And her scent told me she felt the same way.

I prowled toward her, my jeans disappearing along the way. I hadn't bothered with a shirt or shoes, aware that my cousin had seen me in various states of undress several thousand times over our long lives together.

Kyra fell back into her nest as I climbed on top of her, her eyes lighting up with promise. "We're going to need to talk about all the changes happening around here," she said. "Including this role of *Sanctuary Sector Alpha* that I overheard Kieran mention. But I want you to fuck me first."

"You heard us talking?"

"I did. Sort of. Like a dream, but not a dream." She frowned then. "That was real, right? You telling him you... you can't easily leave your mate?" There was a hint of insecurity in her voice, one that rivaled her thoughts.

Because I had left her before.

On the jet with Quinnlynn and Kieran.

And while I'd been gone, Fare had taken her.

She didn't blame me. She understood why I'd left with my cousin and his mate. But it left her wondering now what had changed.

So I let her hear my mind. The conclusions I'd drawn after hearing Kieran talk about his pregnant mate. How I'd realized that I couldn't leave Kyra. How my loyalties had changed.

I'm not sure when that happened, I admitted. *Perhaps... the moment we mated. And it's just slowly evolved from there. But I know how I feel now. I'm here to stay, if you want me.*

I ensured she could hear how I wouldn't force her to accept me. How I was okay with not labeling this for now. How I understood that this was a lot for us both. A significant change from our initial agreement.

But it was no longer about *convenience* to me.

This mating was real.

My wolf's infatuation was resolute.

And my desire to be hers was unconditional.

I wanted her. End of discussion.

The question was, *Do you want me, too?*

I do, she whispered back, her green eyes intense and no longer dreamlike. *I want you, Lorcan. As my mate.*

Are you sure?

Her head moved in a little bob. *I'm not sure what it means. I'm not sure where it'll lead. But my wolf... she's chosen you. And... and I have, too.*

The hesitation in her mind seemed to be about finding the

right words to explain her feelings, not her uncertainty over keeping me.

She wasn't one who often articulated her emotions, something I very much understood. Because I was the same.

But for her, I would try.

And I sensed that same resolve within her.

We were in this together. Convenient or not, we were mated for eternity.

Till death do us part, she murmured, a smile reaching her eyes.

You really do like that phrase, I teased her. *Still plotting to kill me?*

Probably.

Then you'd better prepare for my knot, mate. Your penchant for violence makes me hard.

You're already hard, she pointed out.

Mmm. Then I guess you'll be getting my knot sooner rather than later.

Foreplay is overrated, she returned.

I chuckled. *Then you haven't been doing it right, little killer. But don't worry, we have an eternity to work it out.*

I'll sharpen my blades.

How about we start with your claws?

Oh, now that, I can do. Her nails bit into my shoulders. *Like this?*

Yeah, just like that, I whispered. *Now hold on tight, mate. And don't be afraid to make me bleed.*

LORCAN

Kyra yawned, her naked body snuggled tightly into my side.

She'd been insatiable, her healed mind freeing her from several hooks in her past. The memories were still there, but Fare's influence was gone.

No more nightmares.

At least, none that I'd heard since she'd returned.

But I suspected they were gone for good. Knowing Kieran, he'd implemented some sort of safeguard to keep Fare from accessing Kyra's subconscious.

I kissed her forehead as she yawned again, her legs intertwined with mine. I could definitely get used to this. Sleeping in a nest. Cuddling. Having a naked Omega pressed up against me all day and night.

She nuzzled my chest as if to say she agreed. Or perhaps she was just enjoying my purr. She seemed quite content with the soft rumble, which was why I'd been purring for her for the last few hours while she slept.

Kieran and Cillian kept sending me updates, which prevented me from falling asleep with her. It seemed we might have a lead on Fare's whereabouts, and I was waiting for the latest details to come through.

Remember how that jet of Omegas went down over Exiled Sector? Cillian had asked an hour ago.

Yes. It was something we'd only heard about recently.

Quinnlynn had been helping a bunch of Omegas survive hell down in Bariloche Sector for the last century. Kieran, Cillian, and I had helped a bunch of X-Clan Alphas dismantle the hierarchy and kill the Sector Alpha a few months back.

Most of the injured Omegas had been sent to Andorra Sector.

But one plane hadn't made it.

A plane piloted by one of the Alphas we'd worked with to dismantle Bariloche Sector.

Enrique survived, Cillian had informed me shortly after my reply. *He's on Venom Island and has been in touch with Ander.*

Did the Omegas survive? I'd asked, frowning at my watch.

Some of them, yes, he'd typed back. *They escaped in pods all over Exiled Sector.*

I'd grimaced. That was quite possibly the worst place for a bunch of Omegas to randomly drop from the sky.

Exiled Sector housed some of the worst of Alpha kind. The beings there had all been cast out of their own sectors for villainous crimes or heinous acts.

How Enrique had managed to contact Ander was a mystery to me. Technology on those islands didn't exist. At least, not that I was aware of. The Alphas there were positively feral, living in overgrown forests like animals rather than humans.

Enrique is going to check the other islands, see if he can find Fare, Cillian had added. *The location matches Kyra's description. It also seems like the kind of place a supposed dead man would hide.*

I'd agreed.

And now I was waiting to hear more.

Rather than attempt to rest, I started scrolling through some of the candidate pairings Kieran and Quinnlynn had forwarded my way for the Sanctuary. They were starting to come in from the other sectors now, the Alpha Princes having carefully selected a few of their most trusted Alphas to apply.

Right now, the Sanctuary was still mostly a secret. But we all acknowledged it wouldn't remain that way for much longer.

Prince Cael had apparently suggested a coming-out party, saying it might be a good way to help introduce some of the Omegas to V-Clan sector life.

Quinnlynn was still thinking about his idea. From what Kieran had told me, she was talking to a few of the Omegas in the Sanctuary for their opinions on it.

There were a lot of changes coming.

Some of them would be easier to embrace than others.

Moving Alpha-Omega pairs here would be the first step.

Broadcasting their presence to the V-Clan sectors would be the second.

Unfortunately, it came with the territory of adding protection to the boundary walls. One couldn't guard something he didn't know about. And it took more than a handful of Alphas to properly protect a sector, especially one full of coveted Omegas.

I ran my fingers through Kyra's dark hair, smiling as she nuzzled into me again. My gaze was on the screen, reading through the application about a pair of V-Clan mates. The Alpha had telepathic skills, though not on the same level as Cillian. Still, that would be useful.

And his mate was apparently a weaponsmith.

That could definitely be a good fit. *Kyra'll probably like her.*

Oh, I definitely will, she replied, causing me to glance down at her.

She was reading along with me. *Shopping for a new Omega?*

My lips twitched. *No. I rather like the one I've been force-mated to.*

She snorted in reply, then lifted her finger to swipe back to the Alpha. *He's not bad-looking.*

A growl rumbled in my chest. *Careful, Omega.*

Her giggle echoed around us, her green irises alight with mischief. *Or what?* she taunted.

Or I'll—

My phone began to ring, cutting off my playful—or maybe not-so-playful—threat.

Cillian's name flashed across the screen, causing me to pick up with the video display turned off on my end. My Omega was naked and not for his eyes to see.

His face appeared in front of us, while the screen facing him would be black. If it bothered him, he didn't comment on it. Instead, he got straight to the point.

"Fare's on Outcast Island," he said. "Apparently, he's their equivalent of a Sector Alpha."

My jaw ticked. "That's going to make him harder to kill."

"But not impossible," Cillian pointed out.

"No, certainly not impossible." But we were going to need some help.

"And I know some X-Clan Alphas who owe us a favor," he added.

"How soon would they be available to help?" I asked.

"I don't know, but I'll ask."

"Do," I replied. Then I looked down at my Omega. "You'd better start sharpening those blades. We have an Alpha to kill."

KYRA

Three Days Later

There was a strange sort of irony to my position, sitting on a stealth jet, hovering a few hundred yards from the shore.

Primarily because Fare and his vampire friends had been doing exactly this less than two weeks ago, only their jet had been lingering over the chilly Greenland Sea rather than tropical Caribbean Sea waves.

Lorcan stood beside me, a lethal Elite dressed from head to toe in green camouflage. I wore a similar outfit, only I'd opted for a tank top, while he had on long sleeves. My arms were coated in war paint, as was my face. Lorcan's, too.

All of us were prepared to disappear and reappear on Outcast Island, a notorious Exiled Sector island known for its feral inhabitants.

It seemed vampires had taken over this specific territory, which was why we'd chosen daylight to attack, not night.

The sun might not harm them, but it was very bright. And vampires didn't enjoy shiny lights.

I checked my legs for my knives. It was a habit, one that had the corner of Lorcan's mouth lifting beside me. Because yeah, I'd done this about seven times since we'd arrived. But I wanted to make sure I had all my toys.

He only had a hatchet on him, something he was bringing to deal with overgrown greenery. He'd be using his telekinesis as his primary weapon.

Maybe his fangs and claws, too.

The objective was to kill Fare and anyone who got in our way.

"From what I've gathered, Fare is Sector Alpha. But he doesn't have a lot of loyalists," Enrique had told us upon our arrival. He hadn't joined us for the mission, something about having other priorities he needed to deal with on Venom Island.

His scent had told me those *priorities* might have something to do with a pregnant Omega mate.

Alpha Ander hadn't joined us for similar reasons. He'd sent his brother Sven along instead. The burly blond Alpha had taken one look at Kieran and sighed, "You again."

Lorcan's amusement had fluttered through my mind even while he'd remained outwardly stoic.

What's his deal? I'd asked.

Not my story to tell, he'd replied.

But I'd caught bits and pieces from his mind.

It seemed Kieran had offered to help avenge Sven's mate while in Bariloche Sector. But he'd been rather *flirtatious* by Sven's standards, making him dislike Kieran on sight.

Jonas, the X-Clan Alpha with Sven, appeared to have similar feelings. He'd straight up glowered at Kieran when we'd met up on the coast of Venom Island.

"How's my darling Riley?" Kieran had asked the Alpha.

"Fuck off," Jonas had snapped back at him.

"That good, yeah?" Kieran had drawled. "Hmm. Perhaps I'll pay her a visit soon. Compare notes."

Jonas had growled.

Lorcan and Cillian hadn't reacted at all, neither of them

thinking of the other Alpha as a threat. But I'd again heard a thread of amusement in Lorcan's mind.

My cousin is very good at making friends, he'd told me, his sarcasm evident.

I see that, I'd replied.

"Shall we?" Kieran had said to the X-Clan Alphas.

"I thought you'd never ask," the third and final member of the X-Clan Alpha party had said. His name was Kazek, the Alpha of Winter Sector.

Of all the visiting Alphas before us, he was the one Lorcan had identified as our biggest threat.

I was the only Omega. But none of the Alphas had questioned my presence here. If anything, they seemed to respect it.

Six of us crouched on the jet now while Sven piloted from the cockpit. "Next time we do this, I want a stealth jet as payment," Sven had said when Lorcan went over the controls with him.

"Next time?" Kieran had prompted.

Kazek had grinned, confirming Lorcan's assessment of him. "Should we invite them along to Copenhagen next time?"

"Drop them in the middle of a nest?" Sven had asked. "Yeah, I'd enjoy that."

Cillian and Lorcan had snorted. Kieran had just looked mildly intrigued.

However, all signs of amusement were gone as we surveyed Outcast Island now.

"Ready?" Jonas prompted.

"Always," Kazek replied, several guns strapped to his body. "Who wants to shadow me to shore?"

X-Clan wolves didn't have teleportation or shadowing abilities, meaning one of us would have to take them to the island from here.

Kieran grabbed Kazek's wrist, the two of them disappearing in a blink.

Lorcan looked at me and nodded toward Jonas. "I'll take him. Meet me on the shoreline. Don't go in alone."

"Yes, *Alpha*," I told him. But inside, butterflies fluttered around in my belly.

We're doing this. We're really doing this.

We are, Lorcan agreed, grabbing Jonas. *Meet me on the shore. Now.*

He disappeared with the words.

Cillian went to the cockpit for Sven. The jet was in a hover status, hidden from view. We'd have to shadow back up to it, but that wouldn't be hard to do.

I left them to work out the details and shadowed to shore, just like Lorcan had demanded.

My flat boots touched the sand a few feet from where he stood. Jonas, Kazek, and Kieran had already disappeared.

Lorcan and I soon followed, darting into the overgrown greenery lining the beachy shore. I couldn't remember the original name for this island. It was one of the Caribbean islands, though. White-sand beach. Palm trees. Lush greenery. Humid. *Hot*.

My nose twitched as I took in the familiar scents. *This is definitely where Fare brought me.*

Do you think your wolf can track him?

I nodded. *Yeah.*

That was the plan. Because all of us suspected that Fare would sense my arrival as his mate. So the point was for me to go hunting with Lorcan while the others made themselves scarce. They were backup. I was the bait.

It should scare me, but I was too pissed off to feel fear.

My wolf was in charge right now, her furious energy forcing my legs to move as she led me by my nose.

I was still technically in control. However, I gave her free rein, similar to how I typically operated in animal form. It was a different way to exist, one I'd only ever done one other time —when I'd escaped Fare. But it made sense to try it again now.

I trusted her to keep me safe.

To protect my vampire half.

To *fight*.

We moved deeper into the underbrush, the green leaves kissing my painted skin and marking me as one with the island. It would do very little to disguise my scent, something Lorcan worried would give me away before Fare could make his move.

We were on an island full of savage Alphas. One whiff of my Omega perfume would send them all running.

They wouldn't care that I was mated. *Twice*. They'd want a piece of my flesh, their animalistic needs overriding basic human thought.

That was why they lived here.

They were too feral for their home sectors.

If they surrounded me, I'd have to shadow. Assuming I could.

Kyra. Lorcan paused, his nostrils flaring as he looked slowly to the left. I froze beside him, waiting to pick up on whatever he'd just scented.

Then I heard the subtle *crack* of broken bones, followed by a gasp of pain.

Lorcan had a vampire in his clutches, one he was breaking with his telekinetic powers.

Leaves rustled as the Alpha crumpled to the ground, momentarily incapacitated. *Momentarily* because Lorcan hadn't popped his head off. He was reserving his strength for bigger threats.

He inclined his head after a moment, gesturing for me to continue.

My wolf picked up the pace again, the island aromas flourishing around me. There were definitely a lot of Vampire

Alphas on this island. But I was only trying to find one in particular.

Where are you? I wondered as a stray vine caressed my arm. *What cave are you hiding in?*

I thought you'd never ask, a voice replied.

My brow furrowed. *Fa—*

The world around me vanished, my shadowing ability igniting without my permission. Lorcan's growl echoed in my mind, but his power failed to hold me in place.

What...? He'd leashed me. I shouldn't be able to...

I blinked, the world becoming clear once more, my vision obscured by a male chest.

Oh.

It was then that I realized I hadn't shadowed at all.

I'd been teleported.

By Fare.

It hadn't been a vine caressing my arm, but a Vampire Alpha.

Fuck.

I'm coming, Lorcan promised me.

Hurry, I replied as Fare took a step back to reveal my new surroundings.

It wasn't the cave he'd originally taken me to, but a metal container of some kind.

Except no, that wasn't quite right.

We were surrounded by water here.

I could hear it banging against the steel walls.

A boat, I realized. *He teleported me to a boat.*

"I'm so glad you returned," Fare cooed. "But it's rather poor form to show up with your new mate."

I took a play from Lorcan's handbook and cocked a brow at him. "Oh? You suddenly don't want to share?"

Some of the amusement in his features died, his red eyes glittering with a dark emotion. "Did I say you could speak?"

"No. I didn't realize I needed permission to have a voice."

Those ruby irises smoldered. "I see we need to go back to basic training." His palm wrapped around my throat as he pushed me up against the wall of the ship, his grip crushing my windpipe as he stared deep into my eyes.

My wolf snarled in response. *No,* she seemed to be saying. *We. Do. Not. Bow. To. You.*

She wouldn't submit.

So neither would I.

And he responded by tightening his grasp even more.

I couldn't breathe. But it didn't matter. My wolf and I refused to bow.

Fare snarled, the emotion one I rarely saw from the psychopath. He was usually all charm and grace. But it seemed he didn't appreciate his Omega challenging him.

A growl rumbled from his chest, the sound one that would have brought me to my knees mere weeks ago. Yet all it did now was irritate me. Because that growl wasn't the right growl. It didn't belong to *my* mate.

It belonged to a monster from my past.

A relic I'd failed to burn.

A vampire I longed to kill.

He pulled me away from the wall, just to slam my back up against it once more. The impact shot pain down my spine, my lungs begging to breathe.

Kyra. Lorcan's voice held a note of urgency.

But I couldn't focus on him. I had to pay attention to the vampire before me. The furious being only inches away from my face. "You're displeasing me, pet," he warned.

Good, I thought.

"I don't know what's happened to your mind, but I will fix it." His nose went to my cheek as he drew his touch all the way to my ear. "No matter how long it takes." His lips descended to my pulse, his intent clear.

My animal bristled inside, her wrath boiling through my blood. *No,* she was saying again. *No!*

I shadowed behind him on instinct, causing him to roar with rage. "*Stop. Shadowing.*" His compulsion pierced my mind like a knife, the need to do exactly what he said rendering me momentarily winded.

Only for my inner beast to roar in reply, her jaws clamping down on his mental leash and shredding it. I gasped, my lungs burning in response to the sudden influx of air.

I can breathe.
I can shadow.
I can... shift.

All those blades tucked into my pants no longer seemed to matter. They were sharp. They were fun. But they were nothing compared to my *claws*.

Fare darted forward, intent on grabbing me once more, but I shadowed to his opposite side, my fingers stretching into talons.

He didn't seem to notice, too fixated on catching me. His mouth was practically salivating, his eyes wild with his outrage.

I used it to my advantage, dancing around him like I'd done to Lorcan during our first sparring lesson.

This is who I am, I thought. *A powerful Omega. Half wolf. Half vampire. Strong. Independent. An Alpha killer.*

Fare spun with me, his hands gripping me, only for me to escape again.

This was an Alpha who adored his games, but only when he was in charge of them. He *hated* that I was playing with him now, riling his temper, forcing that charming facade of his to melt away.

Left. Right. Front. Back.

He caught me by the shoulders, his aggression flooding the ship's cabin. I shadowed before he could throw me up against the wall or onto the ground again.

I purposely let him grab me in the next phase, my claws ready.

He shouted as I slashed them across his chest, my wolf howling in victory.

But I didn't give her a chance to celebrate, instead shadowing behind him to claw at him again.

I disappeared from view entirely to shred my own clothes, the movements fast and masked by my stealth abilities.

Then I fully shifted into wolf form and lunged at the enraged Vampire Alpha.

He tried to snatch me by my shoulders, but they weren't the human ones he'd anticipated.

His eyes widened just as I caught his throat between my jaws.

Fare's arms instantly came around me, his strength threatening to shatter my bones, but I wouldn't let go of his neck. I had to destroy him. Kill him. *End him.*

Lorcan was shouting in my mind.

But I couldn't hear him over my animal raging.

Bones cracked as Fare fought back in earnest, his much larger size playing to his advantage. But I had a death grip on his throat, and I wasn't letting go. No matter what.

My wolf shook her head, treating his neck like a chew toy while he crushed our sides. I couldn't breathe, but neither could he. Blood poured into his throat, audibly choking him.

Ribs punctured my lungs.

My spine threatened to snap.

But my animal and I held on, determined.

Until finally we heard a *crack.*

One that ended in Alpha Fare's arms slowly falling away from our body. Everything hurt. I still couldn't breathe. My vision was darkening. But I had to remove his head. Had to sever his neck. Had to *finish this.*

I released his throat just to chomp at him again. And again. And again. Until I could no longer see. No longer focus. No longer *feel.*

He'd better be almost dead, I thought, delirious. Alone.

Drowning in… in blood. *His* blood. From biting his throat. I just needed to burn him.

Light a match.
Sink the ship.
Kill him.

I shuddered, the world going cold around me. The opposite of a fire.

Because there's no air here. I tried to blink open my eyes, to process my surroundings. But there was nothing to see. Nothing to sense.

Nothing… at all.

LORCAN

Kyra! I shouted, my wolf raging inside.

She wasn't responding.

There are too many fucking boats out here, Cillian snarled into my mind. *This is going to take forever.*

I ignored him, already shadowing into each one, my nose leading the way.

Kieran followed my lead, doing the same, leaving the X-Clan Alphas to investigate on foot. It would take too long to shadow with them.

I jumped between ships, furious when I found each cabin empty.

I was about to check my tenth or twelfth one when Jonas shouted, "Incoming!" A gun appeared in his hand at the same time Kazek opened fire, a nest of hissing Vampire Alphas running onto the sand in full-on attack mode.

Fare must have initiated some sort of alarm.

My wolf snarled, furious by the influx of scents near our wounded Omega.

Where are you? I thought at her, aware that she wasn't conscious enough to respond.

I shadowed into six more ships, my nose coming up blank each time. *What if it's not in the ocean?* I asked Cillian. *What if it's in one of the lagoons?*

Go. Search. We'll keep looking here.

I darted inland, choosing to shadow instead of run, as it was faster.

But each lagoon I found was empty. No boats. No signs of my mate.

She couldn't be that far, though. Fare was a vampire. They couldn't teleport more than a few miles.

Still searching, Cillian told me.

I didn't reply, my lack of commentary confirming I was doing the same.

Every few minutes, he provided a useless update.

No sign of Kyra yet.

The X-Clan wolves are holding their own against the vampires despite their lack of magical abilities.

I pushed onward, my wolf determined. But every corner came up empty.

With a frustrated sigh, I paused in the middle of the greenery and just... closed my eyes. My mate was nearby. I could feel her. I just had to *find* her.

She'd transitioned into her wolf form. I'd felt her shift.

Removing my clothes, I opted to do the same and set my beast free. He sniffed the air, his motions cautious, curious.

Then his ears twitched.

Followed by his nose.

And we took off on all four paws, running across the island at impossible speeds. I wasn't sure what he'd picked up on, but I let him lead, trusting him to find our mate.

Just like Kyra had trusted her wolf to defend her against Fare.

Minutes passed, my lungs burning from sprinting at top speed. But I had to find her. Help her. *Protect her.*

Still no sign of her, Cillian told me. *Kieran had to join the wolves. There are too many fucking vampires.*

My wolf took off up a hill, toward a waterfall. Then paused at the edge, my focus shifting down to the beat-up box below.

It wasn't exactly a ship.

But an old shipping container.

I shadowed down on instinct, landing with a thunk on the metal box. And immediately caught the scent of Kyra's blood.

She's here, I snarled.

Of course, I couldn't say where *here* was. I shadowed into the box and found her crumpled form near a wall. She'd shifted back into human form, her naked body covered in a litany of bruises. *Kyra!* I darted forward, only to pause when I noticed the mutilated pile of vampire meat beside her.

She'd not only chomped through Fare's neck, but she'd also done a number on his face.

But given our history, it was clearly not enough to end him for good.

My jaw ticked as I shifted back into human form. I'd wanted to give Kyra the honor of torching his body, but we didn't have time to enjoy a bonfire. I needed to heal her and get the fuck out of here, as evidenced by Cillian's growing commentary in my mind about there being *too many fucking vampires* on this island.

I crouched beside her, my healing ability kicking in on instinct. She was barely breathing, her rib cage smashed completely in from that bastard *crushing* her.

I was willing to bet he'd done it with his arms.

But she'd certainly paid him back in kind with her teeth.

Her face was covered in his blood.

If she hadn't been beaten to a pulp, I'd almost call her ferocious state alluring.

I pulled her up into my arms as I engulfed her with my

healing essence, forcing her to accept as much of it as she could without causing her too much pain.

Sometimes healing too quickly could be agonizing; it was a delicate balance.

Lor-Lorcan? she whispered, clearly sensing my presence despite still being unconscious.

I'm here, little killer, I told her. *You're okay.*

F-Fare? she asked. *D-dead?*

His head has been ripped off, I replied. *But he needs to be burned.*

L-light the m-match, she whispered. *F-finish him. F-for me.*

She knew I'd wanted to watch her end him.

But she must have picked up on the urgency to get off this godforsaken island in my mind. Or perhaps she didn't want to risk him piecing himself back together again.

I'll burn him, I said as I cradled her against my chest with one arm and pulled a lighter out with my free hand. I'd intended to offer it to her as a gift, but there was no time.

He needed to die. For good.

I knelt beside him with the lighter and flicked it to life against his shirt. It wasn't going to be enough. We needed an accelerant.

The fabric started to burn, charring quickly and spreading while I searched for something flammable.

The container seemed to be mostly empty.

I shadowed out with Kyra and set her carefully on top of the box, then went to find a bunch of kindling from the forest area nearby.

Most of the leaves were wet. The branches, too.

I need something fucking flammable, I snarled to no one in particular. With a growl low in my throat, I turned back toward the container.

And froze as Cillian appeared with Kazek.

"I hear you might need some help," Kazek drawled. He was covered in blood and appeared quite pleased about it.

"Hair is pretty flammable." He tossed a bag of heads at my feet. "Use those. And the thing in the bottom."

Cillian said nothing.

I just blinked at them, then grabbed the bag and shadowed it into the container to dump the remains all over Fare.

My lips curled when a can fell out last.

Propane.

I had no idea where the crazy X-Clan Alpha had found it, but I didn't care. I opened the contents and doused all the remains, smiling as they burned bright in response to the accelerant.

Then I shadowed out, grabbed Kyra, and met Cillian at the top of the waterfall. *How did you find me?* I asked him.

Locator charm, he drawled, looking at my hatchet.

My eyebrows lifted. *You put a locator charm on me?*

I didn't trust you not to go all rogue on us.

When have I ever gone rogue? I demanded.

He lifted his shoulders. *Newly mated and all. Instincts are weird. I've learned that from watching Kieran these last few months, figured you'll be just as difficult as him.*

My jaw ticked.

But given how I'd run off through the woods on my own to find Kyra... he might not be wrong.

"We need to go," Cillian said aloud, his tone bored.

Kazek nodded, holding out his hand.

They disappeared, leaving me with Kyra.

I curled her naked form against my chest, just now realizing we both stood nude in the forest. Fortunately, there were blankets back on the jet.

I shadowed us directly into the bedroom chamber rather than into the belly of the jet and immediately searched the closet for something to put on.

An oversized shirt for her.

Jeans for me.

Then I laid her on the bed and refocused on her healing.

Kieran joined me in the next second, his outfit completely intact without a single speck of blood on it.

Typical, I thought. "Help me," I whispered aloud.

He nodded, saying nothing as his hand hovered over my mate.

I lay on the bed beside her, holding her as he worked.

Her breaths almost immediately evened, causing my wolf to purr in approval. I closed my eyes, ignoring everyone else on the jet, focusing entirely on my mate.

My future.

My Omega.

I was only vaguely aware of Kieran leaving after he finished, all of my attention on Kyra's strengthening form.

You did so well, I told her softly. *I'm so proud of you. My little killer.*

Her snort echoed through my thoughts, her mind conscious while her body continued to heal. *Little.*

Do you prefer Alpha killer as a title? I mused.

I do, actually.

Okay, my Alpha killer. I kissed her temple.

Maybe just "mate," she whispered back on a mental yawn.

Mate, I repeated.

Your mate.

My mate, I agreed.

My Alpha, she replied, still asleep. *Will you purr for me?*

Always. I pressed my nose into her neck. *Do you want me to take us back to your nest? Instead of staying on the jet?*

Fare's dead? she asked softly.

He's dead, I confirmed. *For good this time.*

Then yes, she breathed back at me. *Please take me back to* our nest.

I smiled. *Our nest,* I repeated.

Yes.

I like the sound of that, I admitted.

Me, too, she agreed. *Alpha.*

Omega, I returned as I engaged my shadowing ability to take us home.

To the Sanctuary.
To our future.
To our *nest.*

KYRA

Lorcan stared down at me with a mixture of emotions, his wolf pacing in his gaze. Arousal mingled with fury and pride in his mind, his beast impressed by my kill while simultaneously pissed that I was covered in another Alpha's blood.

His nostrils flared as the water poured around us, the droplets swirling with red streaks over my pale skin. Thoughts of fucking me against the wall played out through our bond, Lorcan torn between knotting me and bathing me. Maybe both at the same time.

But the idea of tasting another Alpha on my mouth had him holding back.

I'm not afraid of your beast, I told him.

You should be. He's raging inside.

I know. It's intriguing my wolf. My animal was practically jumping up and down in anticipation, fully ready to bend over and present her rump for his knot.

Hell, she'd been that way from the moment he'd shadowed us back into my nest. But one look at the blood coating my skin had caused Lorcan to drag me into the shower first.

Where he'd started staring at me with all those emotions swirling in his dark gaze.

His muscles flexed as he attempted to restrain himself, his hands curled into fists at his sides. Adrenaline coursed through our veins, the fight too recent.

Kieran's power had healed me quickly, but I was still technically mending inside. That was the reason for Lorcan's hesitation now. He didn't want to risk hurting me.

However, I wasn't breakable.

Maybe a little bruised. Sore, too. But still extremely capable of handling his hungry wolf.

I ran my fingers through my damp hair while he watched, his obsidian irises smoldering with dark interest.

He wanted to grab a fistful of my hair and yank me into his chest. Capture my lips. Punish me with his tongue. Then force me to my knees and fuck my mouth until he came so hard that his seed coated my face. He wanted to erase Fare's essence. Ensure only his own fluids marked my skin.

But another part of him wanted to go to his knees instead, press his mouth to my clit, and lick me until I could no longer stand.

My warrior. My goddess, that side of him was whispering. *She needs to be worshipped. Praised. Adored.*

I wasn't sure which fantasy appealed to me more. I wanted both. I wanted everything.

Lorcan cleared his throat and grabbed a bottle of shampoo, then lathered the suds into my hair. His movements were gentle. Too gentle. Especially as he combed his fingers through my wet strands, the touch tentative rather than dominant.

"I'm not going to break," I told him.

"You're still healing," he replied gruffly. "And there's still blood on your neck." A growl caressed those last two words.

He grabbed the showerhead and repositioned it to wash

the offending mark away. Then he watched forlornly as it slithered down the drain.

His wolf saw the blood as a trophy of sorts. An award for my bravery.

Yet he needed to remove it, the stench of another male driving him mad.

His muscles flexed again, drawing my attention to his bare abdomen and the delicious display of sinewy strength. I wanted to trace all those defined lines and flat planes with my tongue.

The last of the blood disappeared, but the other Alpha's cologne remained, something Lorcan's mind told me more than my own, as his wolf despised the scent.

He grabbed the soap and started washing my face and neck. Four rounds of lathering and rinsing later, he still wasn't satisfied.

I finished cleaning my hair while he worked, his hands roaming over my body with dark determination. He needed me to be clean. Unmarked. *His.*

Yet nothing satisfied him or his wolf.

His frustration grew, his aggression mounting with each passing second.

My wolf danced inside in anticipation.

Yet the damn male restrained his inner beast, refusing to indulge in his possessive desires.

Because he didn't want to risk hurting me in my delicate state, like I was some sort of fragile doll that needed to be handled with care.

My gaze narrowed as Lorcan lifted the soap a fifth time, like he thought that would fix the issue.

The scent was gone. What he needed to do was *replace* it with his own.

I caught his wrist, halting his movements before the suds could meet my skin. "Knot me," I demanded.

That eyebrow of his arched upward. "You need to finish healing first."

I scoffed at that. "What I need is my Alpha's knot." I needed his claim. His seed. His rough hands on my body. His teeth in my flesh. "Knot. Me."

He grabbed my nape with his free hand, his grasp dominant. "Not yet." *I'll injure you in this state.*

I snorted. *I'll heal.*

Kyra.

Lorcan. His hard cock met my belly as I stepped into him. "Knot me."

"No."

My wolf snarled in annoyance. She didn't appreciate him denying her needs, especially when his animal shared her desires.

I didn't appreciate it either.

I could more than handle his aggression. In fact, I craved it.

Kyra, he repeated, sounding tired. *You were attacked by a sadistic Alpha. I'm not about to unleash my wolf on you while you're still healing.*

Maybe that's what I want, I countered. *Maybe that's what I need.*

His animal wanted to erase Fare's scent from my body, while I needed him to help erase Fare from my mind. All our history. All those memories. All the terrible things he'd done. I wanted them gone. Removed. Replaced by Lorcan.

His reservations were all wrapped up in the fact that I'd been injured, that he'd struggled to find me on Outcast Island after my mind had gone silent.

But I was here. Alive. *And perfectly fine.*

Holding back was almost insulting to everything I'd been through. I was strong. A fighter. And more than capable of taking on Lorcan's beast.

However, it seemed he needed a reminder of that.

A reminder that I wasn't some broken Omega living in fear of Alphas. I'd never been that female. I'd always fought back, even when drugged out of my mind on vampire venom.

And I wasn't about to stop now.

I pulled back to look at Lorcan, my eyebrow lifting to match his favorite expression.

Then I shadowed out of the shower to where I kept one of my favorite knives in the other room. I didn't care that I was about to splash water everywhere. I'd clean it up later. Right now, I needed my Alpha to see me as an equal. His partner. His *mate*.

His responding growl vibrated up my spine, exciting my inner animal.

Come get me, she seemed to think at him.

He appeared in the room with me, his expression guarded. "Kyra—"

I didn't let him finish, choosing to shadow around him with my stealth abilities intact, and attempted to stab him in the side. He moved with impossible speed, countering my action before I could strike. His palm snagged my dagger, the sharp metal cutting through his skin like butter. But that didn't stop him from yanking the weapon out of my hand.

Rather than pause, I shadowed and went for another knife hidden in my nest. I threw this one right at his back.

He spun in time to catch it in midair, his responding snarl going straight to my core. My name echoed through the room as I went for a third blade, his command that I stop only encouraging me to push him that much harder.

I'm not a flimsy toy, I snapped at him. *I'm an Alpha killer.* I went for a fourth knife before shadowing toward him, intent on drawing blood.

Only to find myself suddenly pinned in my nest with a very hungry Alpha pressing me into the sheets. "*Stop,*" he ordered.

"*No,*" I bit back, thinking about his response in the shower to my demanding his knot.

His chest rumbled as I attempted to shadow out from beneath him, his telekinetic power holding me in place while his palms secured my wrists over my head.

But blood coated his hands, making his grip slippery.

I purposely squirmed, the sensation of his essence on my skin placating my raging wolf.

New scent. New mark. My Alpha.

However, we needed more.

His mouth. His knot. His *seed.*

I didn't wait for permission. Didn't bother asking again. I simply lifted my head and grabbed his lip between my teeth.

And bit down.

His responding growl vibrated against my breasts, causing my nipples to bead into sharp points. Slick pooled between my legs, my stomach clenching with exquisite expectation.

Yes, yes, I thought, my thighs wrapping around his bare hips. *More.*

I rocked up into his throbbing erection as I licked the blood away from his mouth.

It wasn't enough.

I needed *more.*

I bit him again, only this time I moved my face to the side to press my cheek against his bleeding lip. My wolf purred inside as her Alpha's essence marked her skin.

We were making a mess. A beautiful fucking mess.

Lorcan whispered my name, his restraint hanging on by a thread.

The knives were still in my hands, despite his grip on my wrists. I dropped them in the sheets above my head and attempted to shadow again.

His mental hold was resolute, his much stronger frame keeping me pinned beneath him.

But his bloodied palms made it possible to slide my wrists

up and down. His essence painted my skin, pleasing me immensely.

"Grab my throat," I told him. "Replace his touch. His scent. *Reclaim* me."

Lorcan released a low sound, one that rolled through me, touching my senses and lighting my blood on fire.

Then, ever so slowly, he complied.

Warmth caressed my skin, his natural scent engulfing me in a forest of evergreens. I sighed happily, my lower half rubbing against him in earnest.

If he wasn't going to fuck me, then I'd just use his knot for my own pleasure.

He groaned as my slick heat met the base of his cock, my clit throbbing with the need for release. The bastard had insulted me and my wolf with his assumptions that I might break, that I couldn't handle his beast.

Sure, he'd just wanted to protect me. Which was a noble concept. One I would normally respect in an Alpha.

But not *my* Alpha.

He should know better.

You were barely breathing just thirty minutes ago, he snapped into my head.

I'm breathing just fine now, I snapped right back as I arched up into him. *Either take care of me or I'll take care of myself.*

His beast raged in his head, his grasp tightening around my throat. *Careful, Omega.*

No, I repeated. *I don't want* careful. *I want* you, *Alpha.*

His forehead met mine, his exhale warming my face. "*Fuck*, Kyra."

"That's what I want, yes."

He huffed a humorless laugh in response, his head shaking a little against mine. But it wasn't in denial so much as resignation. "Tell me to stop if I'm hurting you."

KYRA

Lorcan didn't give me a chance to disagree—because no, I would not be telling him to stop, even if it hurt a little—and captured my mouth with his own.

Blood and lust flavored our kiss, fueling my yearning and deepening my hunger for him. *More, more, more*, my wolf panted. *Knot, knot, knot.*

But Lorcan seemed hell-bent on taking his sweet time exploring my mouth with his tongue. When I tried to demand that he move it along, his palm squeezed my windpipe, forcing me to accept his pace, his touch, *his dominance.*

I'd been topping from the bottom, or that was what his mind told me. And he was about to correct that behavior with his own form of sensual punishment.

Because he was the Alpha here.

While he would let me lead almost anywhere, he refused to submit in the bedroom. Even when I was doing *exactly* what he craved—fighting him.

The conundrum in his mind made me dizzy with fury, enticing me to battle him all the more.

His chest vibrated with both displeasure and approval, the

mixture exciting my instincts. I pressed up into him, my insides aching for his cock. His thrusts. His *knot*.

"*Lorcan*," I growled against his mouth.

"Hush, Omega." He kissed me again, even slower than before, his tongue so damn thorough I nearly forgot my own name.

And yet, it left me panting. Needing. *Lusting*.

He was trying to kill me with his mouth, his grip on my throat unrelenting, his other hand still around my wrists.

Every part of me burned. My lungs. My veins. My core.

A whimper left my wolf, the sound escaping my lips.

I felt so incredibly powerless, so ridiculously aroused, that I couldn't form words. Only sounds. Snarls. Whines. *Moans*.

His thumb traced the column of my neck, pausing over my raging pulse as he pressed his groin into mine.

"You submit so beautifully," he praised against my mouth. "Every part of you is yearning for me, yielding to my touch, *obeying* my command. All the while, your mind pushes the boundaries of my dominion, your desire to rebel an absolute fucking turn-on."

His lips whispered across my cheek to my ear, where he nibbled the lobe.

I shuddered as he bit down, hard enough to draw blood.

It hurt, but then his tongue soothed the ache, his lack of venom leaving me oddly relaxed beneath him. His teeth went to my neck next, his mouth replacing his thumb against my pulse.

Another bite had my legs clenching around his waist and a moan leaving my lips.

This time, he pulled my essence into his mouth and swallowed.

It had me freezing beneath him, memories instantly assaulting my mind, only to be replaced by the soothing touch of his tongue that followed.

No venom.

Because he's not a vampire.
He's a V-Clan Alpha. My *V-Clan Alpha.*
Yes, I am, he confirmed into my mind, his mouth sealing over my pulse once more. *You taste amazing, mate.*

I trembled in response, my body reigniting with another fiery wave of need. *Lorcan...*

He pulled on my vein, his bite imprinting on my very spirit. *Mine,* he was saying with each swallow. *My Omega. My mate.*

His evergreen aroma washed over me, the cologne a mixture of our blood and my slick. It created an intoxicating fragrance that left me writhing beneath him. If he didn't knot me soon, I'd combust.

Please, I begged him as he returned his mouth to mine.

He hushed me once more, instead torturing me with slow licks of his tongue against my own while his cock pulsed against my damp heat.

Too much. I pressed up into him. *It's too much. And not enough. Please, Lorcan...*

He nipped my lip, his palms around my throat and wrists unyielding. I was trapped beneath him, his power ensuring I couldn't shadow, his body possessing mine in the most delicious way.

An Alpha needing to tame his mate. To reprimand her wolf for pushing his limits.

To reward her for being brave enough to challenge him, he corrected me as his hips shifted against mine.

I gasped as he filled me in one harsh thrust.

To remind her that she's his mate, he added, pulling back to the tip.

His grip on my throat cut off my scream as he drove back in with even more power. *Fuck,* I breathed, the fullness unlike anything I'd ever felt. Which didn't make any sense. I'd *felt* him before. And yet, he seemed impossibly thicker now.

And that much more in control, too.

To ensure she knows he respects her as his equal, Lorcan continued, his hips punishing mine. *But that it's his responsibility to care for her. Protect her. Never push her too hard.*

He relaxed his grasp, allowing me to gasp in a much-needed breath. *Push me,* I argued. *I can handle you.*

"I know you can," he whispered against my lips. "But that doesn't mean you should have to, Kyra."

I want to, I countered. *You're my mate just as much as I'm yours. My beast* wants *to accept yours. Let us do that, Lorcan. Let us have every part of you.*

He growled deep in his chest, his animal demanding that he accept our offer.

My wolf could feel his longing to be free, his desire to let his aggression out to play, his *need* to possess his mate.

It would be feral. Hard. *Beautiful.*

Lorcan cursed, his control slipping. *Kyra...*

Stop fighting us, I demanded. *Give me everything. Please, Alpha. Stop holding back.*

Another rumble left him, the tether securing his control seeming to snap.

I yelped as the world shifted, my stomach abruptly hitting the mattress as he spun me beneath him. I wasn't even sure how he'd done it, just that suddenly my rump was pressed into his groin and his palms were on my hips, pulling me upward until I had no choice but to balance on my hands and knees.

And then he was inside me.

Filling me.

Commanding me.

Owning me.

His mouth went to the back of my neck, subduing me immediately.

So dominant. So Alpha. So mine.

He bit down, his wolf driving the feral action. My animal answered in kind, bowing down, submitting, all the while urging him onward by pushing back against him.

It was a dance of mates.

A savage meeting of our hips while our souls joined as one.

I hadn't realized how weighed down I'd felt, my spirit having been divided in two with one half belonging to a Vampire Alpha and the other half longing to connect to a V-Clan Alpha.

But now... now I was simply Kyra.

A hybrid Omega with one mate. *Lorcan.*

The *right* mate.

The right Alpha.

I squeezed around him, demanding that he fill me, complete me, *knot me.*

He purred against my neck, hearing that demand and finding it impossible to deny me. Mostly because he didn't want to. He'd made his point with that slow kiss.

Now it was time to *fuck.*

His primal need matched my own, his carnal thrusts hitting that deep spot inside me, the one that called for more slick, more moans, more *passion.*

I screamed his name, shamelessly telling the whole world whom I belonged to.

He groaned in kind, announcing his possessive intent and ensuring everyone knew I was his and he was mine.

This felt like the true beginning for us, our real mating, the one not driven by our vows to others but by the vows we wanted to make to each other.

No more ties to my past. No more Fare. *No more nightmares.*

Only the present. With Lorcan. And dreams of our future.

My fingers dug into my sheets, my back arching as each of my nerve endings lit up in warning.

So hot.

Too hot.

Close.

Oh, so close...

Lorcan bit down on my nape again, his knot pulsing as he violently took me from behind. I didn't need any other stimulation, no stroke to my clit or his hands on my breasts. His mouth and knot were enough, the dominating position giving me exactly what I craved.

My vision went dark as my world exploded, my limbs shaking from a sudden climax that I felt all the way to my toes.

Lorcan purred into my mind, his wolf pleased with my reaction to his claim.

Then that purr morphed into a deep rumble as he picked up his pace even more.

My insides clenched around him.

I was still riding the wave from my first orgasm and quickly crescendoing into another.

Lorcan's palms seared my hips, his mouth warm against my nape, and his cock... Oh, Gods, *his cock*. It was throbbing. Pounding. *Thick*.

I pulsed around him, my lips parting on a garbled scream against my sheets as Lorcan exploded inside me.

Fuck, he growled into my mind.

Yes, I hissed back, tumbling over the edge into oblivion with him.

Our bodies joined, his knot securing us together and throwing us both into a euphoric spiral that lasted for minutes. Maybe even hours.

I wasn't sure.

All I could feel was pleasure.

So. Much. Pleasure.

Oh, Gods... I forgot how to breathe. How to blink. My lungs were on fire. My sight black. My body... replete. Sated. Exhausted.

Lorcan collapsed over me, his muscular form cradling mine as he took us both to our sides. He wrapped one arm around my lower belly, his groin tucked snugly against my rump as he continued to come inside me. Each hot spurt pulled me into another orgasmic whirlpool, the sensations causing my stomach to tighten as rapturous pulses shot through my veins.

I hummed, moaned, sighed, and breathed his name. Over and over. It was like being swathed in a tornado of bliss.

Lorcan kissed my neck, his purr returning with a vengeance as he whispered praises into my mind. He told me I was strong. A fighter. His perfect mate. Then praised me for accepting his wolf, telling me how good it felt to unleash his strength, how much he loved knotting me and biting me.

I replied in kind. Although, my words were a little jumbled. Maybe not even coherent.

Hell, I was barely awake by the time his knot subsided.

My eyes were closed, my limbs limp. I might have also been snoring a little.

At least until I heard Lorcan say, "I'm only answering because you've called me three times in a row."

My brow furrowed, my eyelashes fluttering open. *Hmm?*

Cillian, he replied. *Don't worry, the video isn't on.*

"Yes, you're very welcome for flying all the way to the Caribbean and taking on a rabid nest of vampires while you hunted their equivalent of a Sector Alpha," Cillian drawled.

Lorcan grunted behind me. "Like you didn't enjoy the chaos."

"I'm not quite sure I enjoyed it as much as Kazek and Sven seemed to, but that's not the reason for my call."

"Then I suggest you try reaching a point quickly before I hang up," Lorcan returned.

"You left me and Kieran behind on the jet, Lorcan. Then Kieran took a page from your playbook for Mates Gone Insane and shadowed back to Blood Sector. So now I'm an hour outside of Andorra Sector on a jet that I'm supposed to magically get home." Cillian paused. "Perhaps you've both forgotten, but I'm not a pilot. And I can't just leave the stealth jet behind for Sven."

"Maybe you can. He seems to like it," Lorcan murmured, his mind telling me that the last thing he wanted to do was shadow to Andorra Sector, just to fly the jet back to Blood Sector. "It would be a really nice way of saying *thank you* for helping us with that vampire problem."

Cillian scoffed at that. "And what do I get out of it?"

"Not having to wait in Andorra Sector for me to come save your ass?" Lorcan offered.

The other Alpha huffed. "You know what? I no longer feel bad for the real reason I called."

"You mean we haven't arrived at the point yet?" Lorcan asked, sounding irritated.

"Kieran wants to have an official meeting with Ander and the other X-Clan Alphas in ninety minutes," Cillian said, his tone all business and no longer playful. "He and Quinnlynn are going to tell them about the Sanctuary, and he wants you and Kyra to join via conference call."

Lorcan cursed as the line went dead.

And I was suddenly no longer tired. "Kieran *what?*" I demanded. "He can't do that."

"It sounds like he and Quinnlynn have already decided to," Lorcan muttered, his knot slipping out of me. "We need to be on that call."

"No shit," I agreed, shadowing out of my nest to stand.

Only, my knees gave out in the next breath and I found myself in my Alpha's arms, my head against his chest. He must have anticipated my movements, probably because of our mental link.

"We need another shower," he said, his gaze on my neck. His wolf released a low grumble of approval as his nostrils flared. *Mine,* I heard him think. *Definitely mine.*

Because I was covered in his blood, sweat, and cum.

My animal preened in response, pleased with his physical claim.

But the human part of me very much agreed that I

needed a shower. Especially if we were about to join a video call.

Of course, we had ninety minutes.

Which meant we had more than enough time to play in the shower.

I just needed to be able to walk first. Or maybe kneel.

Yes, kneeling sounds good, I decided. Because that meant Lorcan could replace whatever was left of the Vampire Alpha's scent on my face… with his own *essence*.

Lorcan's pupils dilated. *Are you offering to put your mouth on my knot?*

I'm promising to do a lot more than that, I told him, my lips curling. *Now shadow us to the shower, Alpha. I want to take my time exploring you with my tongue.*

Then we'd meet with Kieran and the others.

And talk about the Sanctuary…

KYRA

My legs bounced with nervous energy, my stomach tied in knots. It felt strange to be faced with so many Alphas, discussing a place I'd kept secret for so long.

Alphas don't belong in the Sanctuary, I thought. *It's our sacred island.*

However, Quinnlynn didn't seem all that uneasy about it, her expression neutral, businesslike.

I hadn't been privy to the conversations since the vampire attack, mostly because I'd been with Fare on Outcast Island, but it seemed Quinn had made some decisions in my absence.

As the Blood Sector Queen and enchantress of the Sanctuary's magic, I trusted her implicitly. I just wished I knew more about what she was thinking and planning.

Especially since I was her second-in-command.

We would need to have a long conversation about the future after this call, just to make sure I understood my role in all this, and to ensure I agreed with her plans. Because if I didn't, I wouldn't be a very good second anymore.

Lorcan reached for my hand to give it a squeeze as he focused on the screens before us.

We were sitting in his former guest room in the Sanctuary,

as we needed a private space for this call and we hadn't wanted to use our nest. That was our private place, one we would never share with the world.

So we'd opted to shadow here, uncertain of where else to go. The Sanctuary didn't exactly have conference rooms. However, I suspected that was about to change.

Actually, a lot of things were about to change.

One screen showed Cillian sitting at a glass table in Andorra Sector with Kazek, Sven, Jonas, and Ander—an intimidating, dark-haired Alpha who didn't seem to know how to smile.

A fifth X-Clan Alpha lingered in the background. *Elias*, I thought I'd overheard. Given his standing position right behind Ander, I suspected he was a lieutenant of some kind. Or perhaps he was Andorra Sector's second-in-command.

Regardless, he remained quiet.

Which could be because Kieran was the one doing most of the talking from Blood Sector. He was on the other screen with Quinnlynn, the two of them explaining the Sanctuary and what it meant for the world.

I swallowed, uneasy about this development. Mostly because I knew X-Clan Alphas weren't like V-Clan Alphas. They had a tendency to take what they wanted, no questions asked.

But these were the Alphas who had taken down Bariloche Sector earlier this year. The Alphas who had been caring for the Omega slaves that had been rescued in the process.

Kieran, Lorcan, and Cillian had helped.

Although, I knew their primary goal had been to capture Quinnlynn. She'd been there helping to heal Omegas as best she could.

Those Omegas should have come back here, which was what Quinnlynn and Kieran were beginning to negotiate now.

They hadn't been able to address it previously without

revealing the Sanctuary. But it seemed they'd decided that it was time to share this secret with the world.

I wasn't sure how I felt about that.

It won't be with the world, Lorcan whispered into my thoughts.

They're talking about announcing our presence to all the V-Clan Sectors.

Yes, and V-Clan wolves are thought to be mostly extinct. However, we both know that's not true. He glanced at me, his obsidian gaze holding a touch of warmth. *Our kind knows how to guard secrets, mate.*

We're meeting with X-Clan wolves, I pointed out. *Not V-Clan wolves.*

We're meeting with trusted allies, he replied. *Allies who have everything to gain by keeping this secret safe.*

His mind elaborated a bit more on that, letting me know that Andorra Sector was notoriously low on their Omega population. They wouldn't want anyone else to know about the Sanctuary, mostly because they would want to have potential access to Omega mates.

I frowned at that last part.

Most of the Omegas here don't want an Alpha mate, I told him. *That's why they're seeking sanctuary.*

Most of the Omegas here have only ever experienced Alpha aggression, he countered. *Given their histories, it's not surprising that they would shy away from the prospect of mating. But that doesn't mean the right Alpha won't intrigue them to reconsider.*

He gave me a pointed look then, causing me to snort in my mind. But it was more of an amused snort than anything else.

Because he was using *me* as a case study.

I was forced into this mating, remember? I told him.

Hmm. And how has that forced *mating worked out for you, Kyra?* A slight purr caressed my name, causing my wolf to sigh inside.

Not fair, I muttered back at him.

Don't you want to offer the other Omegas a chance to find something similar, should they so desire it? he pressed, not letting the conversation thread go. *At the very least, they deserve an opportunity to see that not all Alphas are monsters.*

He thought about Ashlyn and some of the others, how they'd timidly approached him about sparring lessons and other Alpha-related questions.

They'd definitely been curious about him, much to my irritation.

My Alpha, I thought, my wolf huffing in agreement.

Lorcan's thumb traced a small circle against my wrist. *Your possessiveness pleases my beast.*

You thinking about other Omegas does not please my beast, I countered.

Are you going to accuse me of shopping again?

Maybe.

He released my hand to wrap his arm around my lower back, his palm going to my hip to give it a squeeze. *When this call is done, I'm going to knot that ridiculous thought right out of your head, mate. And I won't stop until I'm convinced it's gone for good.*

My thighs clenched. *That might take a while.*

I'm patient, he replied, his grasp tightening. *And I'm thorough.* A low growl underlined that last word, stirring all sorts of ideas in my mind.

Me on my knees. Him on his knees.

His knot pulsing against my tongue.

Him grabbing my hips and driving into me from behind.

Coming all over our nest. *Again.*

Being covered in his seed.

Marked by his teeth. Claiming him with my fangs.

I swallowed, my skin practically on fire. I was seconds away from demanding that we shadow back to our room when the Andorra Sector Alpha cleared his throat.

I froze, certain he was about to call me out on my sordid

thoughts. Because surely they were written all over my face, which was entirely inappropriate for this meeting.

Thank Gods they're not physically here, I thought, my cheeks burning even more.

Because if they were here, they'd smell my slick.

And that... that would be embarrassing.

I would never allow them the pleasure, Lorcan vowed into my mind. *Your pussy is mine, mate. Only mine.*

That delicious growl underscored his words, igniting a fresh wave of need within me. *Lor—*

"I have a suggestion," the Andorra Sector Alpha interjected, his tone deep and commanding. He hadn't spoken much since the call had begun, his expression contemplative while he'd listened to Kieran's explanation of the Sanctuary and recent events.

"We're all ears," Kieran drawled, his nonchalant demeanor a stark contrast to the X-Clan Alpha's quiet dominance.

"We recently welcomed ten Ash Wolf Omegas into our sector. As you can imagine, they were nervous. Especially as they came from Shadowland Sector, which is nothing like Andorra Sector."

Yes, I could imagine that going from essentially living in the wilderness of Shadowland Sector to the high-technology atmosphere of Andorra Sector would be a culture shock.

Not to mention the different pack hierarchy and the rules that came with it.

Those Omegas must have been terrified, I thought. *X-Clan Alphas are not known for their patience or kindness.*

Lorcan didn't comment, his mind telling me that he agreed with that assessment.

"We hosted a welcome party for the Omegas to get to know the Alphas of our sector," Ander continued. "The purpose was to gently introduce the Omegas to our society, and to also give them control over their own fates. Therefore, our Alphas were only allowed to court the Omegas who desired the courtship."

What if they didn't want courtship at all? I wondered.

"Did any of the Omegas choose not to take a mate at all?" Quinn asked, obviously following a train of thought similar to mine.

"Yes," Ander replied. "Two of them have not yet found a suitable mate."

"And they won't be forced to?" she pressed, the question one I pondered as well.

"They're being encouraged to, but not forced. And by 'encouraged,' I mean, they are receiving offers from Alphas that they can either accept or decline."

Quinn arched a brow. "And what if they would prefer living in the Sanctuary without a mate?"

"As we didn't know about your Sanctuary until an hour ago, I can't answer that question."

"Would you consider offering it as an option for them?"

He stared at the screen, his golden irises flashing. "Doing so would require me to let my Alpha council know about the Sanctuary's existence. Until you and your mate have decided on a path forward, my hands are tied."

Quinn's lips parted, clearly ready to fire something back at him. Probably about the notion of him telling his Alpha council. Or maybe the fact that his response felt like a fucking cop-out.

However, Ander held up a hand, telling her with a look that he wasn't done speaking.

"But," he continued, his intense gaze intent as he drew out the word. "If you decide to include Andorra Sector in your reveal, then yes, I believe we would be able to offer them the option. Same with the other Omegas we've been caring for from Bariloche Sector."

Quinn's mouth closed, her expression turning thoughtful.

"We would also be interested in offering up a few Alpha-

Omega pairings for Sanctuary protection," Ander added. "Assuming you would be inclined to accept X-Clan Alphas as Protectors. We might not have magic, but we're by no means weak."

"That much was proved in Bariloche Sector and on Outcast Island," Cillian murmured, his attention momentarily going to Kazek and Sven before settling on the screen. "It's certainly worth considering."

Kieran nodded. "We have a lot to think about where the Sanctuary is concerned." His focus went to us. "What do you think, Lorcan?"

"I think Quinnlynn and Kyra need to ask the Sanctuary Omegas for their opinions," Lorcan replied without missing a beat. "They need to trust their Protectors. Otherwise, it'll be a moot point."

If I could purr, I would right now. Because Lorcan's response demonstrated his respect not just for Quinn but for me as well.

Despite his Alpha dominance, he wasn't trying to make any decisions on the Sanctuary's behalf. Neither was Kieran for that matter.

Actually, none of the Alphas at the table seemed to be telling us what to do. They were just providing options and ideas.

Like the welcoming party.

The concept of broadcasting our existence to V-Clan kind, and maybe even part of X-Clan kind, still left me uneasy. But deep down, I understood that the purpose was to bolster our protection here.

Unfortunately, the breach had proved that the barrier might not always be enough. And while I hadn't spoken to the impacted Omegas yet, I'd heard through Lorcan's thoughts that some of them weren't taking it well.

They were scared. Unsettled. Insecure. All things I didn't want anyone to ever feel.

Bringing in some mated pairs might help. It would allow the Omegas here to meet some safer Alphas, ones not interested in taking a mate because they already had one they cherished.

Alphas like mine, I thought, earning me a squeeze from the male at my side.

"We can ask about adding different types of Protectors," Quinn said. "I've already spoken to a few Omegas about the concept of a reveal. I'll ask them how they feel about potential courtship options as well."

My eyebrow inched upward, taking on one of Lorcan's favored expressions.

Quinn's word choice of *options* made me wonder if any of the Omegas she'd spoken to had already expressed an interest in potentially meeting Alpha mate candidates.

We would need to have a conversation after this meeting adjourned.

"You could change the name of the Sanctuary, make it less obvious what the island actually is, and just claim it as a new V-Clan territory."

Everyone in the Andorra Sector conference room looked at Kazek, seemingly surprised by his suggestion.

My brow furrowed.

Lorcan sat silently beside me as he considered the other man's words.

"What?" Kazek glanced around before focusing on what I assumed was the screen depicting Kieran and Quinn. "Surely you've already considered that option. It's what I would do in this situation—claim the territory, put a powerful Alpha in charge, and then not tell anyone other than allies what actually exists there."

Silence.

"It's not like we host gatherings often or anything," he added. "No one would expect to be invited, and only a challenging Alpha would show up unannounced, which will happen anyway if someone wants to take the Sanctuary. At least this way, it's less appealing. What Alpha wants to rule an island in the middle of the Arctic Circle?"

He has a really good point, I said slowly. *Have you or Kieran already discussed this?*

No. We hadn't considered renaming the island. Our focus was more on how to reveal it.

"Your reveal party could be about the formation of the sector rather than broadcasting news about an Omega safe haven. It could also be a way to debut any Omegas who might be looking for a mate." Kazek shrugged. "That's what I'd do. Well, that and I'd send a message to make sure no one ever challenged me."

That last part seemed to be directed at Lorcan.

Sven snorted. "You'd probably build a bunch of Infected pits along the border to keep everyone out."

"Naturally," Kazek drawled, his casual demeanor reminding me a bit of Kieran. Although, both men possessed very different types of dangerous auras.

Quinn cleared her throat, her eyes meeting mine on the screen. "I think we have a lot to talk about."

"Yes," I agreed. "We do."

"Well, this has been an enlightening conversation," Kieran murmured. "I think we all have a lot to consider."

"Do we want to discuss what happened on Outcast Island?" Ander interjected, his dark brow cocked upward in a way that reminded me of Lorcan. "Or shall we table that discussion for later?"

"I think Cillian can handle that debrief," Kieran told him. "It was mostly a bunch of savage Alphas who needed to be put down."

"And a handful of sane ones in the dungeon we found," Sven added, causing my brows to come down.

A dungeon? I asked Lorcan.

But he was wondering the same thing. *They must have found that when we were searching for you.*

"Were there any Omegas in the dungeon?" I asked, my heart skipping a beat. *Did Fare have another toy he called a mate? One I didn't know about?*

Sven shook his head. "No. Just a few Vampire Alphas. We didn't stick around to ask a lot of questions, just freed them and watched as they began slaughtering their own kind."

Oh, I thought, frowning. I had no idea who that could have been, but I wasn't sure I wanted to know, either.

Kieran cleared his throat. "If there's nothing else, then we'll be in touch once we make some decisions." He paused, waiting for anyone to speak up. When no one did, he added, "I hear we're leaving behind a stealth jet. Consider it a token of our gratitude." His gaze went to Lorcan as he said it, then his screen went black.

Cillian snorted on the other screen and shook his head, but he was smiling. "Playbook for Mates Gone Insane," he muttered. "Remind me never to take an Omega mate."

"I'll remind you that you said that when you finally give in to Ivana's needs," Lorcan countered, his finger hovering over the End button. "Talk soon."

The screens went dark, his final two words making me wonder if he meant he'd be issuing that reminder to Cillian soon or if he just meant it generically.

Given what I heard in his mind about Ivana's persistence where Cillian was concerned, he meant the former.

I think I want to meet this ballsy Omega, I told him.

Perhaps you will during your next blood run, he replied, his gaze holding a spark of mirth as he glanced at me. *I believe she's been assigned to help prepare it for you.*

My forehead crinkled. *What?*

"You think I don't know about your penchant for stealing our supplies, mate?" he asked, that damn eyebrow of his inching upward. "It was one of the first things I overheard in your mind after biting you."

"Oh." I pinched my lips to the side. "I'm not apologizing."

"I didn't ask you to." He brushed his mouth against my cheek. "But I've already made provisions with Cillian to have a quarterly shipment prepared for the Sanctuary. So no more stealth runs into Blood Sector."

"What if I enjoyed those stealth runs?"

"Then we'll go on one together," he returned. "I can show you some of my favorite places to run. Maybe even find an ice cave or two to snuggle in."

My wolf sat up in expectation at that idea, presumably understanding the promise in his voice. "I'd like that."

"Me, too." He nuzzled my neck and pulled back. "But first, we should call Kieran back and talk to him and Quinnlynn about the Sanctuary."

"Yes," I agreed. "I have questions."

"I know." He typed into the screen created by his watch and hit Call when he found Kieran's name.

It rang once before he answered, he and Quinn still in the same conference room from moments ago.

"We thought you might want to talk," Kieran drawled. "I'll give Quinnlynn the floor. She can fill you in."

LORCAN

Two Weeks Later

I FOUND Kyra standing in my old den, her lips curling down at her reflection in the mirror.

She wore a black dress, the back of which opened to the base of her spine.

It was sexy as fuck.

But then, everything she wore was sexy to me. Mostly because I enjoyed fantasizing about ripping it all off.

Jeans. Sweaters. Towels. Now dresses…

My knot pulsed, ready to play. It'd been a few hours since I'd last been inside her, as she'd spent the earlier part of this evening with Quinnlynn preparing for tonight's event.

"I look ridiculous," Kyra muttered. "Why do these things always require formal attire?"

I stepped up behind her, my hands going to her hips as I stared into her eyes in the mirror. "You look stunning, Kyra," I corrected her. "And honestly, I don't know. I think it's the whole royalty aspect of it all."

Kyra snorted. "It's *royally* dumb." She turned in my arms, her palms landing on my chest as her gaze danced over me.

"Although, I'm really not complaining about how good you look in this suit."

My lips twitched. "Is that a compliment?"

"Do you want a compliment?"

"No," I lied.

"Then it's not a compliment," she returned, her green eyes glittering knowingly. *I'll just allow my slick to let you know how I feel about you in that suit instead,* she added mentally, her citrusy aroma taunting my senses.

I pressed my already hard cock into her abdomen as I grabbed her nape with one hand, my opposite still on her hip. *The feeling is mutual, mate.*

She started to smile, but I interrupted her by kissing her soundly, suddenly feeling the need to mark her as mine. Swollen lips would do just fine, as would my scent all over her svelte form.

A giggle broke free from her mouth as I rubbed my jaw along her neck, then up over her cheek. *Are you going to piss all over me, too?* she teased.

Don't tempt me.

Do it, and I really will kill you, Alpha.

And now you're taunting me with foreplay again, I sighed into her mind. *I'm going to walk around with an erection all night in front of all those eager Omegas...*

Kyra grabbed my shoulders, her nails digging into the fabric of my black jacket. *There will be no shopping tonight.*

I chuckled and kissed her throat. *I've already acquired my desired Omega, mate. I don't have the sanity or yearning to take another.*

She hummed, the sound holding a teasing edge to it.

Are you ready for tonight? I asked her, taking our conversation to a more serious topic. *Because there's no going back after this.*

After several lengthy conversations with Kieran, Quinnlynn, and several Omegas from the Sanctuary, we'd made the decision to rename the island and take Kazek's recommended approach—creating a territory under a new name, one that the outside would see as any other V-Clan Sector. However, those inside the circle would know the true purpose of the island.

I should be asking you that question, Kyra murmured. *You're about to be crowned as an Alpha Prince.*

With you as my Omega Princess, I countered.

Oh, I just get to be the fancy ornament. You're the one who has to defend your title.

I snorted. *Pretty sure you'll be helping me defend it, mate.*

Yes, but the world doesn't know that. I'm just a breakable little doll who exists solely to take an Alpha's knot. She batted her eyes demurely at me, the look so exaggerated that I couldn't help another chuckle.

Anyone who has ever met you would know immediately that that's a lie, Kyra.

Yes, but those who know us won't be our enemies, she pointed out. *To the outside world, I'm a docile, sweet, pliable little Omega. The perfect weapon, really. Because they'll never expect me to bring out my claws.*

True, I conceded. While her status as an Alpha killer might be known among the V-Clan Alphas, it wasn't necessarily known outside of our kind. She truly was an ideal weapon to help protect our new territory. And I couldn't be more relieved to have her by my side.

Especially tonight.

Not because I needed her as a secret weapon right now, but because I needed her to be my mate. To help me navigate the social circles and accept my new role as Alpha Prince.

I'd spent a millennium being an Elite, hiding silently in the shadows and protecting my cousin.

Tonight, I would be stepping out of the shadows and right into the spotlight.

Fortunately, I wouldn't have to stand there long.

After the new V-Clan territory was introduced, Quinnlynn and Kieran would take the stage to make a much more profound announcement. One that would absolutely steal the show and keep it off of me for the rest of the night.

The Alphas all knew it was coming, the rumors having begun earlier this week after Prince Cael had let a few key details slip to the right individuals.

It'd been purposefully done.

And now everyone was clamoring for details about the twelve Omegas who might or might not be in the market for mates.

When Quinnlynn and Kyra had gone back to the Sanctuary to debate options, several Omegas had perked up at the notion of *courtship*. Many of them weren't ready, but a handful had expressed interest in testing the waters.

Which had resulted in the creation of the Eligible Omega Mates, a courtship program Kieran had agreed to lead in Blood Sector. Quinnlynn was technically in charge, with Kieran managing the security around the event.

Alphas could apply for Omega mates.

And Omegas could decide if those Alphas qualified for courtship.

Omegas could also leave the program at any point, deciding instead to remain unmated. Just as Alphas could also choose to leave the pool of applicants if no longer interested in taking a mate.

I didn't envy Kieran and Quinnlynn the task of running the program. Of course, Kyra and I would likely be involved at certain points, as the purpose of all this was to bring most of those mated couples back to the island, thereby helping to bolster the Alpha population while ensuring the comfort of the Omegas involved.

"The Sanctuary Omegas accepted you more quickly because you were mated to me, and they know me," Kyra had pointed out during the discussions. "While it's a good idea to bring in mated pairs, both the Omega and the Alpha are new to us."

This had been brought up after I'd mentioned the lukewarm reception to some of the Alphas who had moved into the Sanctuary with their mates—many of the Omegas hadn't seemed all that receptive to their presence.

"It'll take longer to trust them and see them as *ours*," Kyra had continued. "But if an Omega like—oh, I don't know, an Omega like *Jas*, we'll say—were to bring home an Alpha, he'd be trusted faster because everyone already trusts Jas."

That train of thought had led Quinnlynn to mention Ander's courtship comments and the fact that a few Omegas had already disclosed an interest in meeting Alphas, so she and Kyra had taken the idea back to more members of the Sanctuary.

And here we were about to announce it to Blood Sector, several members from other V-Clan Sectors, and a handful of X-Clan wolves.

However, the X-Clan wolves in attendance weren't personally interested in the Eligible Omega Mates program. They all had mates already. But they might suggest that a few of their trusted Alphas apply for the program, which Kieran had approved.

Kyra ran her palms down my jacket, her green eyes holding mine. "Ready?" she asked.

I nodded, my hand still around her nape as I shadowed us to the ballroom in the heart of the Blood Sector palace. It was the same one I'd been in weeks ago for Kieran's coronation. Only this time, I didn't hide near a wall or stand by his side.

Instead, I went straight to the upper platform, just out of sight of the main doors.

Kieran and Quinnlynn were already there, awaiting our arrival. The former sported an all-black suit, just like mine. Meanwhile, Quinnlynn wore a deep maroon dress, one that revealed the slight bump in her abdomen—the future Blood Sector heir or heiress.

"Ah, it fits!" Quinnlynn said, her eyes on Kyra's dress.

Kyra pinched her lips to the side. "Unfortunately." She faced her best friend. "I'm only wearing this for you, you know."

"I know."

"Just like I'm only in Blood Sector for you as well," Kyra pressed. "Now *and* before, I mean." She glanced pointedly at Kieran.

"I know," Quinnlynn repeated.

"*And* I only mated him"—she gestured back at me with a thumb over her shoulder—"for you, too."

"I know," Quinnlynn said yet again, more exasperated this time.

"So don't ever claim I haven't done things for you. I have. A lot of things. Like wearing this dress."

Quinnlynn rolled her eyes. "Yes, your life is very hard."

"It is!" Kyra told her. "Do you know how much that damn Alpha likes to knot me? And how often? And how *hard* that is?"

Kyra, I murmured.

I'm not done. "It's really convenient, Quinn. Super fucking *convenient.*"

The Blood Sector Queen shook her head. "I don't even know what to do with you."

"Well, you could thank me," Kyra hedged.

"For which part?" Quinnlynn asked. "The dress? The mate you so clearly adore? Bringing me the mate that I love?"

Kyra considered it for a moment and nodded. "Yep, all of the above."

Quinnlynn gave her a look. "How about for giving you a brand-new sector and making you a princess?"

"Definitely that," Kyra said. "That's going to be a lot of work, you know."

"I do, actually," Quinnlynn replied. "Being a former princess myself. Now a Queen…"

Kyra nodded. "See? Exactly."

The two Omegas fell quiet for a moment, then Kyra giggled and pulled her best friend into a hug.

"Seriously, I love you," she whispered into Quinnlynn's ear. "You know that, too, right?"

"I do."

"Good. And I'm seriously fucking happy for you as well."

"Likewise," she replied softly, her gaze going from me to Kieran. "I love you, Kyra."

"I love you, too." Kyra hugged her tighter for just a second, then let her go. "All right. I suppose it's now or never."

"Definitely now," Kieran agreed, his arm sliding around Quinnlynn's lower back, his gaze going to the group of Omegas standing nearby. They would all be introduced tonight as Omegas looking for mates.

I glanced over them, my need to protect flaring to life.

These Omegas were part of *my* sector, thus making them my responsibility.

However, they would temporarily be residing in Blood Sector for the mating process. Therefore, I supposed they were currently under Kieran's care more than mine.

"Let's go," he said, his words for his mate. He would let Kyra and me know when he was ready for us.

Quinnlynn gave Kyra's shoulder a little squeeze, then moved with Kieran to step through the main doors and out onto the platform. They walked gracefully toward the railing that overlooked the room, their arms lifting to form a regal wave.

I glanced at Kyra, my palm going to her lower back. *Ready to take this mating of convenience to a new level?*

Her catlike gaze glimmered in the low candlelight-esque lighting of the room. *I am.*

Good, I replied, angling my head toward Kieran and Quinnlynn. *Because I'm about to make you my real mate.*

Didn't your knot already do that?

Amusement threatened to curl my lips. *Several times, mate. Several times.*

So what's different about now?

Now? I'm going to make sure every Alpha in that room knows you're mine. Because that dress is positively sinful.

What about the Omegas?

Oh, they already know, I promised. *My wolf's been smitten with you since the moment you turned around and bit me, all the while plotting my murder. No one else has ever stood a chance. A single look at my face when I'm gazing at you confirms it. My wolf doesn't hide. And neither do I.*

"Welcome!" Kieran greeted the room. "Queen Quinnlynn and I are very pleased you could join us tonight, as we have several announcements to make. The first of which is about the formation of a new V-Clan Sector."

We listened as Kieran explained the claiming of the new territory in the Arctic, my cousin carefully sidestepping the exact location or how it'd been founded. He simply stated its existence and the need to give me—his too-powerful cousin—a new sector to lead.

The art of creating new sectors or packs was common practice for when Alphas rivaled each other in strength. Rather than try to share the same wolf pack, they often diverged and created new packs.

Kieran's explanation left little room for questions and made it clear that challenging me was a very bad idea. Because he was essentially saying he didn't want to fight me for Blood Sector Alpha, thus he was helping me start a new sector instead.

Which wasn't exactly true since the Sanctuary had already existed, but only the Alpha Princes, some X-Clan Alphas, and the handful of Alphas who had been welcomed in as Protectors knew the island's secrets.

Hopefully, it would stay that way.

"Well, I suppose we'll get right to the point, then, shall

we?" Kieran said as he stepped to the side, Quinnlynn moving with him. "Lorcan, Kyra, will you join us, please?"

Now or never, I thought at Kyra as cheers sounded through the room.

Now, she said, her heels clicking as we moved together through the door and into view.

Her hand began to lift in a wave, but I wasn't ready to greet the room. Instead, I pressed my mouth to her pulse, my teeth nibbling her for all to see. Because this Omega was mine and I wanted the world to know it.

But that wasn't enough for Kyra.

Because of course it wasn't.

The little vixen grabbed my jacket and immediately went onto her toes to repeat the action against my own throat, her wolf very much in her gaze the whole time. *I don't hide either, Alpha,* she told me, playing on my earlier comment about not hiding my interest. *You're mine.*

And you're mine, I returned. *My very convenient mate.*

So convenient, she returned, her eyes sparkling with mirth. *My real mate.*

Yes, I agreed, leaning in to nuzzle my nose against hers. *My love.*

Love? she repeated, her eyes holding mine. *I think I like that.*

Me, too, I admitted. *Better than "Alpha killer"?*

Yes.

Better than "mate"?

Maybe the same as "mate," she replied.

How about... I love you, mate. I didn't voice it as a question, but as a statement. Because it wasn't a question. I knew how I felt. This female was mine. For better or for worse. For forever and eternity.

I really like that, she whispered. *I love you, too... mate.*

My lips curled then, the background and audience no longer mattering. I kissed her. Soundly. Intently. *Lovingly.*

I'd once thought I didn't want a mate.

I'd been wrong.

It had taken meeting and knowing Kyra to make me realize that.

She was the ideal mate. *My* mate. And I wouldn't have it any other way.

Kieran's chuckle barely pierced my thoughts, my focus entirely on my mate.

But then he announced, "May I present the new crowned Prince and Princess of Night Sector." His words echoed through the room, followed by a series of howls that underscored the importance of his statement.

Because he'd just announced my future. *Our* future.

As the Prince and Princess of Night Sector.

EPILOGUE

CILLIAN

I sipped my blood wine from the shadows, my lips threatening to curl.

Prince Lorcan, I mused, responding to Kieran's announcement regarding the new Prince and Princess of Night Sector. *Has a nice ring to it, doesn't it?*

It does, Kieran agreed. *As does Prince Cillian.*

I snorted in response. *No, it really doesn't.*

Hmm, Kieran hummed. *We'll see.*

We won't, I countered, my gaze scanning the room to take in everyone's reaction to the news of Lorcan's new territory.

Two wolves in particular earned my scrutiny more than the others—Myon and Fritz. I hadn't wanted to let them attend, but Quinnlynn had requested it. She said they couldn't be blamed for what Fare had done to them.

I disagreed.

Which was why I had them on a tight mental leash.

Their surface-level thoughts seemed pleasant enough. For now. But I wouldn't be far, my telepathic talent fully ingrained in their minds.

I didn't trust them.

Fuck, I didn't trust most of the wolves in this room.

But that was par for the course with being a mind reader. I could hear their desires. Their truths. Their jealousy. Their fears.

Everything.

It gave me a fucking headache.

Alas, it was my job to listen, and listen I did as Kieran announced the Eligible Omega Mates program to the room.

Alpha intrigue spiked about a thousand percent, some of their thoughts turning so vulgar that I had no choice but to grab another glass of wine. I downed half of it before the first two Omegas were introduced to the room.

Quinnlynn had prepared just a handful of statements for each Omega candidate, mostly focused on their names and their designations. The majority were V-Clan wolves, but there was also one vampire, a Z-Clan wolf, and a W-Clan wolf.

I plucked a third glass of wine off a tray as the last of the candidates was revealed.

Twelve Omegas.

All desiring Alpha mates.

It was going to be hell to supervise. But I understood why Kieran had volunteered to house it here. We had the best resources for it. And we couldn't exactly host it in Night Sector.

"Our thirteenth and final Omega candidate is a late addition," Quinnlynn said, causing my brow to furrow as I glanced up at the platform.

What? I spoke the word into Kieran's thoughts. *I wasn't told about a thirteenth addition.*

No, he agreed. *You weren't.*

I was about to ask why when Ivana stepped onto the platform, her white-blonde hair glittering in the low lighting.

"Ivana is a V-Clan Omega from Blood Sector. Her

interests are in analytics, advanced technology, and weaponry." Quinnlynn's words floated over the room, the introduction causing me to clench my fist around the wine glass.

What. The. Fuck? I demanded. *What the fuck, Kieran?*

What? he countered. *I told you we opened the option up to Omegas here in Blood Sector. Ivana expressed interest, so Quinnlynn added her to the program. Is that a problem?*

Yes, it's a fucking problem, I thought. But the words were for myself, not for Kieran.

Cillian? he prompted.

I finished my wine and set it down. *It's fine.*

It was absolutely *not* fine.

How the fuck was I supposed to help guard the program with Ivana as a candidate?

I waited for the ceremony to wrap up, the shadows around me as dark as my thoughts.

Ivana is a candidate. An Omega candidate. Seeking an Alpha mate.

It was... unexpected. And yet, entirely expected at the same time.

She was fucking stunning. So beautiful it *hurt* to look at her. Mostly because she hadn't made it a secret that she wanted me. And it had taken all of my physical and mental restraint to deny her.

She deserved better. An Alpha who could devote his life to her and her alone.

That Alpha wasn't me.

Kieran was my priority. Always.

Ivana needed an Alpha who could put her first.

Will she find that in the program? Is there even a male worthy of her?

She had such a quiet mind. Always pensive, but never loud about it. She was one of the few who seemed to be capable of masking her thoughts around me, too.

It made her easy to be around. And difficult at the same time.

I watched her move through the room, her long legs carrying her with an ease many others admired.

It's that damn dress, I thought, eyeing the slits up to midthigh. *Reveals so much and not enough.*

Her long white hair was piled up on her head as well, the curls a taunt that had my fingers itching to feel if those strands were as soft as they looked.

And her eyes.

Fuck me, her eyes.

Silvery blue. *Like ice.*

Gods, the woman was positively divine.

And apparently putting herself in a program for a mate.

What the hell? I thought again. *Why didn't she tell me?*

She always told me things, even when I didn't want her to. Yet she'd been… distant lately.

I frowned. Actually, she'd been distant since the coronation. Not coming around to chat or to poke fun at my various hiding places.

I hadn't realized it until now. But she hadn't once tried to engage me since that night, which was nearly a month ago now.

Why? I wondered, starting toward her.

The last time I'd seen her, she'd been a bit out of sorts, her shoulders oddly hunched.

They weren't hunched at the moment, though. They were straight and confident, as usual. So whatever had happened that night, she'd clearly gotten over it.

I'd tried to follow her, to find out what had occurred, but she'd disappeared before I could reach her. I wouldn't bring it up now.

No, instead I would ask her, "What the hell are you doing?"

Ivana's eyebrow crinkled as she turned toward me. "Excuse me?"

Okay, right. That... that wasn't what I'd meant to ask. "You enrolled in the Eligible Omega Mates program. Why?"

Her slender arms folded over her exquisite chest. "How else am I supposed to find someone *more in my league?*" she demanded, causing my own brow to furrow.

"What?"

"You know, an Alpha who might appreciate my... what was it? Oh, right. My *misplaced confidence* among my other *unsavory qualities.*"

I blinked at her. "I'm sorry, what?" I had no idea what she was talking about.

"Come on, you're the one who said I needed to start looking for a more appropriate mate, one who won't mind my..." She looked up, then snapped her fingers. "My penchant for telling Alphas what to do. Maybe I'll find that Alpha through the courtship program. Perhaps he'll like my *childish games*, too."

Okay, hold on... "Ivana—"

"It's fine, Cillian. I already told Quinnlynn that I'll happily relocate to Night Sector. Soon enough, you won't have to worry about my unsavory company at all." She patted me on the arm and shadowed off before I could say a word.

Not that I knew what to say.

Because *fuck*.

She'd heard everything I'd said to Lorcan at the coronation.

That damned woman was always lurking, her skill for disappearing into the shadows nearly rivaling mine. It was how she always found my favorite hiding spots.

I'd once told her eavesdropping would get her into trouble. But it seemed she wasn't the one in trouble at all. It was me and my inconsiderate mouth.

Shit.

A vision of her from the coronation flashed through my

mind, her shoulders crumpled over in a way that told me someone had hurt her.

I'd threatened to kill whoever had dared upset her or reject her.

And Lorcan had replied, *Technically, you rejected her. You reject her all the time. Are you going to punish yourself?*

My jaw clenched.

Damn it.

I had been the one who'd hurt her that night.

And now she was entering the courtship process to find a new Alpha.

Because she'd finally given up on me.

That'd been my goal for years—wanting her to find a more appropriate mate. But the reality of it... the realization that I was finally going to lose her for good...

It fucking sucked.

Ivana's white-blonde hair caught my attention on the other side of the room, her lips curled into a polite smile as Prince Cael bent to kiss the back of her hand. Her eyes lit up with an interest I knew *very* well. An interest that used to be reserved solely for me.

No, I thought. *Fuck. No.*

I'd pushed her away. I'd hurt her. I'd *rejected* her.

I didn't deserve her.

But that had never stopped my wolf from craving her.

He raged inside me now, demanding I stake my claim. *Bite her. Knot her. Take her.*

I swallowed, taming the urge.

Only it heightened with each passing second while I watched Prince Cael make her laugh. *Mine,* my inner animal seemed to snarl. *That female is mine.*

Except she wasn't mine at all.

She was an Eligible Omega Mate.

Part of a program I was supposed to supervise and guard.

You look ready to kill Prince Cael, Kieran murmured as he

shadowed to my side. *Has he done something I should be concerned about?*

My teeth ground together as I narrowed my gaze at Kieran. *He's flirting with Ivana.*

And?

And nothing, I snapped. *She's an eligible Omega, right?*

Right, he agreed. *Unless she's not...*

I said nothing.

Well, the next few weeks should be fun to observe, Kieran mused. *Let me know if you want to be added to the suitor list. You have until tomorrow to decide...*

Ivana and Cillian's story is next in *Eclipse Sector*...

Eclipse Sector

I loved an Alpha once.
An unattainable Elite.
A former V-Clan Prince.

I thought we had a connection.
A unique bond founded in our shared values and aspirations.
Then he broke my heart with a few choice words.

He doesn't want me? Fine. I'll find an Alpha who does. Which is how I end up on the stage being introduced as Candidate Thirteen of the Eligible Omega Mate program.

Except, there's just one tiny problem—the Alpha who broke my heart is in charge of supervising the mating activities. Which means he's privy to every interview. Every date. Every *kiss*.

How am I supposed to find an appropriate mate when he's watching me with those smoldering irises?
Purring possessive comments in my ear…
Growling at every male who looks my way…
Prowling around my nest…

It doesn't help that someone is attacking the Omegas in the program.
Now my Alpha is even more territorial, his feral nature that much more potent.
Because he's refusing to leave my side.
And he's promised to do whatever it takes to protect me.
Even if it means claiming me for himself.

Author's Note: This is a standalone dark shifter romance with Omegaverse vibes—A, B, O dynamics with kn*tting, nesting, and biting. Check the trigger warnings in the introduction for more details.

USA Today Bestselling Author Lexi C. Foss loves to play in dark worlds, especially the ones that bite. She lives in Chapel Hill, North Carolina with her husband and their furry children. When not writing, she's busy crossing items off her travel bucket list, or chasing eclipses around the globe. She's quirky, consumes way too much coffee, and loves to swim.

Want access to the most up-to-date information for all of Lexi's books? Sign-up for her newsletter here.

Lexi also likes to hang out with readers on Facebook in her exclusive readers group - Join Here.

Where To Find Lexi:
www.LexiCFoss.com

www.ingramcontent.com/pod-product-compliance
Lightning Source LLC
LaVergne TN
LVHW021017250326
834688LV00021B/185/J